THE PROSPECT OF MY ARRIVAL

a novel

Dwight Okita

Printed in the United States of America

ISBN-13: 978-1460959893
ISBN-10: 1460959892

Library of Congress Control Number: 2011903379
CreateSpace, North Charleston, South Carolina

This is a work of fiction. Names, characters, places, and incidents either are the product of the author's imagination or are used fictitiously. Any resemblance to actual persons, living or dead, business establishments, events, or locales is entirely coincidental.

The *Publishers Weekly* quotes refer to the full manuscript as reviewed as part of the 2008 & 2009 Amazon Breakthrough Novel Award contests.

First Edition was published in September 2011. Second Edition was published in April 2013. (Enhancements include the addition of discussion questions, book review quotes, and jacket copy. There is also now a preview of the author's forthcoming novel *The Hope Store*.)

"Takes the reader on an engrossing and moving journey into the meaning of life...keeps the pages turning until its satisfying and touching conclusion."

— *Publishers Weekly*

"Suppose you had the chance, before birth, to decide whether you wanted to be born? How might that work?...These are some of the intriguing questions raised in this elegant book by Dwight Okita...*The Prospect of My Arrival* is a book that is serious, poignant and engaging."

— *The Windy City Times*

"I loved this book. The premise is genius, and the beautiful writing totally delivered the goods....It's quirky and delicious. Like ice cream with bacon. But it's also profoundly uncomfortable in places. One moment two loving parents are tucking their child in under a magical lit up ferris wheel mural, the next moment something incredibly dark unfolds."

— Joni Rodgers
New York Times bestselling author
Bald in the Land of Big Hair

"...a deceptive simplicity, deepening excitement, addictive prose, and a sense of melancholy and wonder throughout. Okita is a name to be watched on the Indie front."

— Alison DeLuca
The Crown Phoenix Series

THE PROSPECT OF MY ARRIVAL
by Dwight Okita

A human embryo is allowed to preview the world before deciding whether to be born. The embryo, named Prospect, is given a starter kit of human knowledge, and his consciousness is inserted into a synthetic twenty-year-old body. To help him make up his mind, he will meet a range of people or Referrals. Among them, a greeting card writer who excels at sympathy cards, and Prospect's very own inscrutable parents.

Trish Mesmer is the scientist charged with counseling Prospect. Through her bio-experiment, she wonders if a world of humans who are here by choice might lead to a more peaceful, vibrant society. At the same time, one of the Referrals grows increasingly committed to derailing the bio-experiment all together.

THE PROSPECT OF MY ARRIVAL is a cautionary tale served up with equal helpings of whimsy and dread, with just a dash of hope.

I dedicate this book
to my late, great mother
Patsy Takeyo Okita

Once we were talking and I asked you if you thought life was magical.
It was the kind of thing we enjoyed talking about.
You paused for a moment and then said, as only you could say it:
"Is life magical? I think you have to make it magical."

CONTENTS

WELCOME, STRANGER

MONKEY BUSINESS

TUNNEL OF LOVE

ACKNOWLEDGMENTS

I'd like to thank the various good people who gave their input on The Prospect of My Arrival. My manager Nicholas Bogner of Affirmative Entertainment has been a champion of this book ever since he became aware of it. Writers Anne V. McGravie, Madhavi Konduri, and Rosie Cook have been close readers of the novel over the past few years. They are my north stars.

Kudos to my editorial and design teams at CreateSpace for their guidance, and to Harriet Baker for her editorial suggestions. Gratitude to Floyd Kemske, Diane Korhonen, Joni Rodgers, the League of Extraordinary Authors, Susan Namest, Smiling Authors, my brother Clyde Okita, my late father Fred Yoshio Okita, Josie Henley-Einion, and the countless writers I've met online. Thanks to illustrator Christian Northeast for giving me permission to use his "tunnel boy" image for the third section. Many hands have given this book a push in the right direction. You know who you are.

A thumbs-up to the Amazon Breakthrough Novel Awards (ABNA). In 2008, The Prospect of My Arrival was selected by Penguin editors as one of the top ten books out of five thousand. The popular vote got me to the top three. Thanks to the folks of the ABNA discussion boards for rooting for me. Many have asked when the book would be out. Here it is! My next novel-in-progress is called *The Hope Store* which is about the first store which claims to sell hope over the counter. See a preview of the new book at the end of this one. Also, I'm including discussion questions for *Prospect*. For interested book clubs or fiction classes reading my novel, I may be able to join your discussions via Skype. I can be contacted through my website: dwightland.homestead.com.

Much appreciation for my SGI Buddhist practice. If I rested on the eleventh day of a twelve-day journey, how could I admire the moon over the capital? This has been a journey. It is a journey that ends here for me as the writer, and begins here for you as the reader.

WELCOME, STRANGER

1. ABOUT MY NAME

"I was given the name Prospect because people have high hopes for me." Those were the first words out of Prospect's mouth when he met Trevor Grueling.

Prospect has high hopes for himself, too, but right now he's just staring out the windows of Trevor's penthouse suite, watching the steady sweep of headlights across Lake Shore Drive. He is thinking about how high it is up here on the fifty-sixth floor, but a high view and a high hope are two different things. Don't ask him how. Don't force him to compare and contrast. He can't do it right now. He's too worn out from a great night of dancing at Hallucination. Upstairs, Trevor and Kitty have jumped into the shower of the master bathroom, so Prospect jumps into the shower downstairs because he needs to remove the scent of smoke and alcohol that clings to his skin.

A chrome spiral staircase connects the main floor to the upper one. It reminds him of a big strand of DNA. Once he's out of the shower, he feels new. He opens a window. The gentle hush of traffic is surprisingly soothing. It is like putting a seashell to his ear, but instead of hearing an ocean, he hears a city and all its voices.

A door swings open. "Prospect, you rat bastard!" shouts a man's voice from the floor above. "Are you stealing stuff down there? I've got security cams everywhere." The man laughs.

"Why would I do that, Trevor? All I have to do is ask nicely and I'm sure you'll just give me things."

"Yeah, right," the man says.

Prospect sits on the endless leather sofa in Trevor's sunken living room. The sofa encircles half the room. From anywhere he sits, he can watch the three huge flatscreen TVs flicker with activity.

On the first screen, women on the Home Shopping Channel are modeling ugly dresses at attractive prices…and business is booming. 962 SOLD! The two women, identical twins, wear the same dress style but in two different colors: chocolate mousse and butterscotch.

On the second screen, a man in uniform shouts words in another language as he raises a large silver sword in the air. Below him, a blindfolded man kneels on the ground. The young man pleads in English, "I'm a father! I'm a husband! I'm human…like you!" He lists all the things he is as if the list will protect him, but it doesn't. The uniformed man swings the sword and slices off the man's head in one solid blow. The head falls to the ground like a ripe piece of fruit. The rest of the body falls a few moments later.

But it is the third screen that fascinates Prospect the most, for it is on this screen that he witnesses the delicate growth of a human fetus. And then the baby is born, and its body ripens into a healthy teenager with the hopeful beginnings of breasts. A cell phone floats down gently into her hand like a new appendage. Through the miracle of time-lapse photography, Prospect now sees her body wrinkling, her brunette hair going undeniably gray, her spine curling into a question mark. And then she is dead. A thousand rose petals rain down upon her. It is so sad, he has to turn off all the TVs just to stop thinking about it.

⚬⚬

He thinks back to what Trevor told him in the car as they drove away from the nightclub. He said how enraged he was the first time he heard about the Pre-born Project, the notion of scientists again playing God, allowing an embryo to decide its own destiny. That was sacrilege. Trevor was not a church-going man, but the thought of a Pre-born looking at the world for the first time with an infinite sense of wonder—this stirred in Trevor a curious mixture of jealousy and longing. "Prospect, I'd like you to seriously consider quitting the Pre-born Project," he said.

"Why?"

"For one thing, you lack the wisdom and maturity to make such a large decision. Tell them you refuse to decide," he said. "Besides, man does not have the right to control the destiny of future generations. Translation: Stop fucking with God's perfect plan."

"I'm not trying to—do anything to anyone's plan," Prospect told him. "I'm just trying to do the right thing."

Trevor laughed at him. "God has already *done* the right thing...by inviting you into this world. Who are you to turn down His invitation? Just tell Trish you want out of the project. That you want to be born the old-fashioned way, according to His divine plan."

"What would you do if I told you that I'd already made up my mind? That I plan to continue with the project?" Prospect studied his Referral's face, but it went blank.

Now Trevor smiled a smile that made him look both happy and not happy at the same time. "Then, my Pre-born friend...I'd have to kill you."

୭∿୨

But the real story begins earlier than this. A story must be told in sequence to cast its spell properly. And before there was a Trevor, there was a Trish.

2. TRISH MESMER

"I was troubled by the rise in cultural vulgarity: mean-spiritedness, violence, despair, really bad taste. Where is it all coming from, and when will it end? Why does the modern world keep churning out such miserable citizens? I wondered if a baby was born by her own choice rather than by chance…would such a baby grow up to be a happier adult? What would it be like to live on a planet filled with people who were here by their own choosing? I want to find out."

— Dr. Trish Mesmer, Scientist
Big Science Magazine

They gather in a blinding white room accented only by a single orange tulip that rises like a flame from its vase. A large pitcher of iced tea and a bowl of lemon wedges rest on a table. They are in a special area of Infinity Medical Center in Chicago but inside it's just the two of them: Prospect and this woman wearing a nice, white lab coat. And a smile. They sit down facing each other across a small round table. Prospect doesn't remember how he came to this room, or where he was before, but here he is.

"Hello, Prospect," whispers the woman in white. "I'm pleased to meet you. My name is Trish Mesmer. I'll be your Facilitator for this beautiful bio-experiment. I call it the Pre-born Project." She shakes his hand. "Welcome. This will be your room for the duration of the project." Trish has reddish blonde hair with girlish bangs. The hairstyle draws you into her kind blue eyes. She cradles her iPad tablet in one arm and types notes now and then. She could be a kindergarten teacher, and he could be her student.

Trish gently pours iced tea into two glasses. As the tea pours, almost in slow motion, the words pour from Trish. "My father was a science teacher. I adored him. The feeling was quite mutual. Ever since I saw him make a hard-boiled egg disappear into a Coke bottle, science experiments have consumed me." She laughs a high-pitched laugh like the ringing of a bell. "These days scientists are making amazing discoveries about the human body, mind, and soul, Prospect." Presently, her eyes fill with water; that's how much feeling she's feeling. "So I devised an experiment of my own. And you, Prospect, are a very important part of that." Again the bell-like laugh. "You'll be the first baby ever who'll be given the chance to *preview* the world—before choosing to be born or not. You will have three weeks to make up your mind. Welcome to Week One. At the end of the bio-experiment, a press conference has been scheduled where you will reveal your decision on live TV. Invitations have already gone out for the conference. Posters have been printed. The train has left the station, if you know what I mean."

Prospect is not totally sure if he does know what Trish means. He understands about every other sentence that she utters, though he likes the sound of her voice and laugh very much. He has no idea about the train station. Prospect drinks his iced tea as his Facilitator goes on. The tea is very good, though he has nothing to compare it to as he's never drunk anything before. It's sweet and cool. At least he thinks those are the right words to describe it. He likes the beverage very much. Trish says he will have the chance to meet a range of people from all walks of life...to help him make up his mind. These people (she calls them "Referrals") will help Prospect get a taste of the world. Trish hopes that the Referrals will form a kind of constellation which will light his way home... wherever home turns out to be.

But no one ever told him he was lost in the first place. That he wasn't home already. By the end of the experiment, Prospect can either choose to be born—or choose to be returned to the gene pool. No hard feelings.

"Trish, if I return to the gene pool...does that mean I'll never be born, that I've given up my chance forever?"

"That's a great question, Prospect." Now Trish types something into her computer. He tries to read what she's written, but she holds the tablet at an angle away from him. "To be honest, science isn't sure on that one. We think it means you go back into the pool of possibilities. One of those possibilities is that you can be born at another time. But this is still uncharted territory."

"What is a Pre-born exactly?"

"Ah," she says, shaking her head. "I never explained that, did I? A Pre-born is simply someone who has yet to be born, an embryo like yourself. You exist in a state prior to birth."

Trish's face looks calm, so it makes Prospect feel calm. She has answered all his questions for the moment. He looks at the door. He senses that once this conversation ends, his day in the world will begin. He will walk out that door, and his adventure will begin. She types again on her computer. "I've prepared a basic starter kit in this messenger bag to help you as you leave the hospital and begin meeting your Referrals: a wallet, ID, cell phone, credit card, a spiral notebook, several pens, a computer tablet, some snacks." She places the bag on the floor beside him.

"Oh, another thing," she adds, "the physical body you are temporarily occupying was manufactured by Big Farm Technologies to my specifications. They're the sponsors of this experiment. It's a twenty-year-old body, and it should serve you just fine. Now since it's temporary, we decided there was no need to give the body fingerprints, or any unique identifying DNA. So if you were to commit a crime—not that you would—there'd be no way to trace the crime back to you." She laughs. "I just offer that up to you for you, FYI. A fun fact to impress guests with at a cocktail party." Prospect files this information away in the back of his mind.

"If I haven't been born yet, how is it that I can walk and talk? How is it that I can think these thoughts and feel these feelings?" His comments start Trish on a flurry of typing. Her hands cannot move fast enough to capture whatever it is she is trying to capture. She seems delighted.

"Again, excellent questions," she says. "I'll make you a deal. You can ask whatever questions you want to…but I'll only answer the ones I think will be useful to you. How is that?"

"Do I have a choice?" He smiles at her.

"Absolutely not." She laughs. He laughs too because it looks like something fun to do. It is.

"Now to answer your question, and I don't want to overwhelm you with information, but…there's a reason you can speak so well and do all those different things. We've inserted a powerful microchip in you called a *CyberSavant*. While you were in your mother's womb, it empowered you with the gift of language. It downloaded basic starter information into your brain: played little movies in your head, showing you the highlights of human history, basic customs, where to get a really good cup of coffee. But it's not the same as experiencing things firsthand. It's the reason that people will think you're both innocent and well informed. There are gaps in your knowledge. Watch out for those gaps. They can get you in trouble…" *Something something, whatever whatever.* And after a while, he can't really absorb any more information. He tells Trish that he needs to take a nap and closes his eyes.

The ringing of a phone wakes Prospect from his sleep. He answers it. "Hello?"

The voice on the phone whispers, "What you're doing is an abomination."

"Excuse me?" Prospect says.

"Only God can choose when a baby is to be born," the voice whispers. "Leave the Pre-born Project at once or suffer the consequences." And then the connection ends. He doesn't know what to make of it.

Prospect now notices a note has been placed under his door. It's from Trish. When he awakens, he is to come to her office.

Trish's office is full of interesting things to look at. There is a clear plastic model of a pregnant woman that lets you see the little baby growing inside her. In one corner of the room stands a flip chart sketched in with his Referral schedule, the start dates and end dates marked in fluorescent colors. A few laptops shimmer with text and colorful pie charts on a coffee table.

"Hope you had a good rest," she says.

"Yes, thank you." She pours him a cup of hot coffee with cream and sugar.

"Have some coffee." He takes a sip. It's delicious.

"Now just because a computer chip was implanted in you—that doesn't really make you a genius," says his Facilitator. "At the end of the day, Prospect—you're basically booksmart and experience-stupid. You know a little bit about a lot of things…and not a whole lot about anything." Her blue eyes are kind, but they are also very serious. She wants him to pay attention.

"Can you give me an example?"

"That cup of coffee in your hand," she starts. "It's good isn't it? But you didn't know until a few moments ago that you'd like it. Until you experienced it yourself. Do you follow me?"

"Yes. You've made me thirsty for more coffee!"

"No," Trish frowns. "The point is, Prospect, you must go out and get some experience under your belt. Then come back, and we'll have something to talk about. Find something—or someone—you can love. Something that will love you back. Because without it, you will starve in this world. You will shrivel up and die faster than if a bullet had struck you down. Having something to love will help distract you."

"Distract me from what?" he asks.

"From the occasional pain and disappointment of being alive." And with that Trish vanishes into the hospital hallway without even looking back. Not even a tiny glance. Her whole body moves with purpose toward the next important moment ahead of her, like a magnet is pulling her.

Prospect jots a note to himself on a piece of paper: FIND SOMETHING I CAN LOVE. He folds the paper again and again till it is small and hard like a stone. He puts it deep into his pocket where it falls past a granola bar and some coins. But he can't waste another minute wondering what those five words mean. He has to be on his way…for now something is pulling him too.

Prospect is going outside. He has never been outside before. He turns the doorknob and the door opens to a white, white hallway. As Prospect steps out, he is almost run over by a speeding gurney. He's not hurt—just shaken up. The gurney doesn't stop; it just keeps on rolling toward its destination. Prospect rides the elevator down to the main floor. It feels like he is falling. Like his stomach is still two floors above him. The doors open at the first floor. He checks for speeding gurneys. No gurneys.

∽

Shortly after Prospect has left his room, Trish is summoned for a meeting. Karl Bangor, head of new product development at Big Farm Technologies, wants to see her. Big Farm is one of the larger biotech companies in the Midwest. Their logo shows a red barn surrounded by happy animals and vibrant acres of crops, but everyone knows that Big Farm is really short for "big-ass pharmaceutical company." The logo designer wanted to create an old-fashioned, down-home feeling. It's a valiant attempt, though not necessarily successful.

Karl Bangor likes to wear pinstripe vests because he thinks they make him look dapper. In fact they only make him look heavy. Heavier. Inside his vest pocket is a pocket watch. Yet another affectation that makes him seem more like an escapee from the Royal London Wax Museum than from the pages of GQ. The nicest thing you can say about Karl's demeanor is that it's a fashion statement. Let's leave it at that. He is one of those people in corporate America who moves up the ladder not because of his talent or tailored suits but because of a winning mixture of ambition and amorality.

He doesn't just see the gray area...he is the gray area.

In spite of her dealings with him, Trish still sees the Pre-born Project as a true experiment. Bless her heart. Karl sees it as something else. An annoyance. A necessary evil. He clearly wants only one outcome: for Prospect to choose to be born. Anything else is to be discouraged. If he chooses not to be born, if he can't make up his mind – this results in a delay. A delay of data translates to a delay of profit. He doesn't see this bias and potential interference in the Pre-born Project as a manipulation of the bio-experiment. He sees it as giving progress a little push in the very right direction.

"How is our little experiment going, Trish? Has the little fellow made up his mind yet?"

"Karl, he's barely left the hospital," she says. "I think it will be most fruitful if he meets his Referrals first. Don't you?"

"This is what I think, Trish, and you don't have to be a mind reader to know this. I think the sooner the little bugger decides that he wants to be born—the sooner we both get paid. That's what I think."

Trish smiles nervously.

"I'm sorry, was that crass of me?" he says. "What can I tell you? I was born this way."

Trish is afraid of Karl Bangor—not just because he is a powerful person at Big Farm who could cut off her funding on a whim—but because he is a force to be reckoned with. She's afraid that at any given moment he might reach over his desk and choke her with one hairy hand. It's an irrational fear, but she feels it anyway. She has never seen Karl actually choke anyone. But then why is it so easy for her to picture it?

☙

Wandering around the first floor, Prospect sees many people waiting in the waiting area. But it is the gift shop that pulls him toward it with its bright lights and rich aromas. Inside, there are so many sweet-smelling hand soaps and flowers and "Get Well" balloons to choose from. But the thing he likes most is a paperweight in the shape of Infinity Medical Center. It is silver and shiny. Prospect likes how the paperweight feels in his hand. Solid. If he ever gets lost, he can show it to the bus driver, and the driver will know how to bring him home. He buys the paperweight, and the lady puts it in a nice plastic bag. The bag is clear so everyone can see what he has purchased and want to buy one for themselves. And though he likes the paperweight an awful lot—is it something he truly loves? The kind of thing Trish said he should try to find? He doesn't think so. But then, he's still new here.

Moving through the hallway, he turns and sees a twenty-year-old man looking back at him. The man is none other than himself. His reflection in a mirror. Prospect can see he is a mixture of races, though he can't begin to say which ones. He is more brown than white. His eyes are almond-shaped, rather than round. A stylish goatee on his chin only adds to his cool look. And on his head there is a navy blue baseball cap which bears the single word "EVOLVE."

"Hello," Prospect says to the fellow in the mirror. And the man in the mirror says "Hello" back to him.

At the main entrance, people are coming and going. They move at different speeds. Some are in a hurry; some are taking their sweet time. Some men have ties around their necks; some ladies have gym shoes on their feet. A young woman pushes on the metal handle of the door as she walks through it. He pushes too, and out he goes.

It's very bright outside. Perhaps the gift shop could have sold him sunglasses for a day like this. Had he known it would be so bright outside, he would've bought himself a pair. As Prospect makes his way down the street, he tries to look like everyone else. Like he has been walking down sunny streets all his life.

The bus stop is right at the corner where Trish said it would be. As he waits at the bus stop, he pulls out the letter she has written to him.

Dear Prospect,

Your first Referral is none other than your mother, Rebecca Boulanget (pronounced boo lan JAY). Like many Americans these days, she is multiracial—of Japanese and African ancestry. There are still uniracial people in this country, but ironically they now have become the new minority. They are a dying breed. It was once predicted that inter-marriage might have a profoundly neutralizing effect on violence in America. That sadly has not been the case. People never seem to run out of things to fight over.

I should share with you that you are not the first child in the Boulanget family. They had a daughter once named Joyce who ran away from home and was never seen again. If she's still alive today, she hasn't made any attempt to contact your parents. She was a difficult child. The last time they saw their daughter, she was thirteen. An unlucky number, any way you slice it.

Dr. Trish Mesmer

"I have a sister?" he wonders to himself.

Big news for such a short note. He reads the note over and over. Finally he fishes his cell phone out of his pocket and dials. "Trish," he says into the phone. "I just read your note. What is this about me having a sister?"

3. THE FAMILY TREE

Just as Prospect's bus arrives, his cell rings. He climbs onboard and takes a seat near a window. It takes him a while to remember how to answer his phone. He pushes this button and that button. Finally he figures it out.

"Hello, Prospect," says the voice on the phone. It's his Facilitator. "How is everything going?"

"The bus is very large and blue inside. I like it."

"You wanted to know more about Joyce Boulanget. Maybe when your first Referral is complete, we can talk about her. Would that be all right?" Trish asks.

"I just want to know why she ran away. I want to know if she's alive."

She sighs. "We'd all like to know the answers to those questions, but this is a bigger subject than we can cover by phone. We'll talk afterwards. I hope you enjoy your first Referral." And she hangs up. Just like that. Their conversation is over before it's started. So he might have a sister. If she's dead, how did she die? And if she's alive, why hasn't she contacted their parents?

Little by little, Prospect is learning about his family. Memories come back to him also from his days inside his mother's body. He remembers the woman in bed placing one hand over her belly, rubbing it gently. For a moment the room went dark. Then he saw a hand, a woman's hand. Huge. A wedding ring adorned by a small diamond sparkling in the summer sunlight. She rubbed her stomach tenderly through the cotton hospital gown…as if to make sure that he was still there.

His mother.

The truth is—it's easy to love a baby who hasn't been born; it hasn't made any big mistakes yet. Give the kid some time. "It's a nice feeling to have a mother, a family," he thinks to himself. "To come from something. A family tree to climb. To have people who are looking forward to your arrival. But as important as it is to come from a good place—it's equally important to have a nice destination." He knows that just beyond his mother's loving touch, just outside Infinity Medical Center…is a world. Prospect has seen it through his Cyber-Savant while in his mother's belly. Something about what he's seen—it makes him shiver. He tries to shut it off, but he can't. It's always there. It won't go away.

The world.

Prospect is on his way to meet his first Referral. But he suddenly realizes he has not been paying attention to where he is going. He doesn't know where he is. He's scared. He calls Trish. "I'm lost, Trish. Can you help me?"

"Prospect, please don't take this the wrong way, but your phone is only to be used for emergencies. If you keep calling me, you won't be in the present moment. The truth is: I *can* help you. But it's better if I *don't*," she says. "Being lost is a natural part of life. Did you know that the average adult spends one third of his or her life being lost?" She lets out a laugh. She is deeply tickled. "If I told you where you were, I'd be denying you the pleasure of finding your way." Again with the laugh. "Now the last thing I want to do, Prospect, is to deny you pleasure. Or to stand in the way of the many discoveries you are about to make over the next few weeks."

Though they are talking on the phone, he pictures Trish's mouth moving, her red lips opening and closing. Like little red gates. When he glances out the bus window, all the houses and streets blur together. It makes him dizzy. "Delaware is next," the driver announces over the speakers. "Transfer here for the purple line." Decisions, decisions. But Delaware is not the street he wants. This world is not the world he wants. Trish's father was a scientist who made eggs disappear into bottles. But who is *Prospect's* father? *Prospect's* mother? Who is he? How is he? Why is he?

Prospect doesn't like being lost. It's…uncomfortable. Maybe this being born idea isn't such a hot idea after all. Trish speaks again. "Now if you continue to call on your cell phone—I'm going to have to screen you and let your calls go to voice mail. You may not understand now, but hopefully you will later." Her voice sounds a million miles away. "Now go out and have a great day!" He hears her cell phone disconnect. Like a door closing. Like an egg disappearing into a bottle.

∽

The bus is very interesting. When you walk onto a bus, it's like you're walking into a party to which you haven't been invited, but to which you are instantly welcome. And you can talk to the other guests until it's time to leave. There are little signs overhead with advertisements for pain relievers and runaway children and food products.

Prospect asks the bus driver for help in finding his way, and to his surprise, he gets it. The driver drops him off very close to the home of his Referral. He walks up to his parents' house and presses the doorbell. A hand pushes back the curtains on the door. "Roberto, he's here!" says a voice in the house.

The door opens, and a pretty woman stands there with a heart-shaped face. She looks smart. He can see that in her eyes, in the way she stands in the doorway. She wears a simple dress with polka dots of many colors. Her eyes are somewhat almond-shaped. As if she was going to be Asian but changed her mind at the last minute. "Oh, hello, Prospect. Come in, come in. I'm your mother, and I'm so happy to meet you." She gives him a hug. She hugs him for a long while. The man next to her looks on patiently. The woman smells like pears, like the delicious soap he smelled in the gift shop of Infinity Medical Center.

The handsome man with caramel-colored skin standing next to her must be Prospect's father. His black hair is wavy like a small black ocean. He looks like a man you can trust, a man that you'd vote for if he was running for president of a very large country. "Hey, Mr. Man," he says. They shake hands quite officially. "We've been expecting you." He smiles.

"Yes, I'm sure you have," Prospect says. He must've made a little joke because his father laughs. They laugh together. Why did they laugh? Ah, because one word meant two things at the same time.

"Did you have any trouble finding the place?" he asks. "We would've been happy to pick you up, but Trish said you wanted to try public transportation."

"I had no trouble finding you. And I'm glad to meet both of you. No matter what happens at the end of my three weeks—I am still glad to meet you." There is a funny pause, and his mother purses her lips together.

"I'll let the two of you get to know each other better and do your Referral business," says his father. "Your mother's your main Referral here. I'm what the scientists call...a peripheral Referral. But once you get to know me, I think you'll see there is nothing *peripheral* about me." He winks. Then he turns to Prospect's mother. "Becca, did you see my palm pilot? It seems to have sprouted wings again." He is a nice man. Prospect likes the way he says things.

"I just saw it in the kitchen."

"Ah, of course," he says. Then off he walks.

Prospect and his mother sit down on the sofa. She leans close to him. "Prospect, we would love love love for you to be born, but please keep in mind that you *aren't* part of the family yet. Do you understand?" Prospect nods.

The woman who would be his mother smiles at him. She isn't being rude; she is only being clear. "Do you think I'm a mean person? You can be honest." Before he can answer, she speaks again. "Because I'm not. I'm just nervous…that I'll get to know you too well, and get too *attached* to you." There is something in her eye, and she wipes it away quickly.

Again he nods. "You're in a very…complicated position. I can see that now."

"Let me show you to your room and let you get settled," she says. "I'll bring up a snack for you. How does that sound?"

"Great," Prospect says. Because that's exactly the way it sounds. Great.

If coming into this world happens all at once, then actually living in this world happens little by little. For example, when you first start out in the world, the human race is a mystery. But then one day, you're introduced to your first Referral. And that person is everything you know about the human race. Then you meet a second person, and now the first person is only half of what you know, because now you know two people. And so on. This is how Prospect will learn. Little by little. One Referral at a time.

4. SHE'S NOBODY NOW

Prospect and his mother walk up the stairs of his parents' house. The walls are filled with pictures of his mother and father at various times in their lives. Some are from before they met, his mother explains. Many are after they met. Their wedding day. There are pictures of them with other people too. Prospect notices faded pictures of what looks like Rebecca and Roberto as babies themselves. Pictures of various trips they've taken around the world. One particular picture strikes him. It's not a photo, but a small painting. His mother, his father, and a girl. "Who is that girl?" Prospect asks.

"Oh!" His mother seems surprised. "I thought your father took that picture down. She was just a girl. A girl in the neighborhood." Mother lifts the picture from the wall and places it in a corner of the room. "She's nobody now."

"I see," he says, but he really doesn't see. By the time they come to his room, he feels like his parents' whole lives have flashed before him.

"This is your room here," says his mother. "Make yourself at home. Okay?"

"Okay." She leaves him at the door and goes back down the stairs. And what a room it is. The walls are wallpapered with a scene of an amusement park dominated by a huge Ferris wheel. A baby crib stands next to the wall, its mattress still wrapped in clear plastic. Along another wall is a blue futon with big fluffy pillows shaped like clouds. A small mountain of toys sits on a table. Prospect opens the dresser drawer and finds brand new packages of baby clothes—things he couldn't possibly fit into in his present size. He picks up a package of knitted booties and opens it carefully. He places one bootie on his thumb. Rebecca walks in carrying a plate of brownies and a glass of milk.

"We bought all those things for you," she says. "For the baby you will become. If you choose to be born, that is." Prospect is embarrassed and carefully puts the bootie back into its package.

"Let me ask you another question. Not a scientific one," he says.

She perks up. "Please."

"And I hope you don't get mad at my question."

"Feel free to ask me anything. That's why you're here."

He tries to choose his words carefully. "Did you have a choice whether or not to be a part of this project?"

It's an interesting question, she thinks to herself. "Well… they asked if I would…participate." She walks to a window and watches the cars pass in the street. "I was chosen randomly out of all the pregnant mothers in Chicago. They told me that if I chose not to participate—I would be standing in the way of human history. I wouldn't want to do that! They also said that there could be...*repercussions.*"

"What are those?"

"They're little...punishments for not doing what your government asks you to do." Now his mother calls out loudly to his father to fetch some sheets from the hall closet. It must be nap time. Prospect lies down on the futon. He rests his head on a passing cloud. His parents lay a white sheet on top of him. They are tucking him in. He loves how the sheet floats down on top of him. His parents stand beside the Ferris wheel painted on the wall, Prospect notices they are taller than the tallest roller coaster. They are giants.

"Rest well," says his father.

His mother chimes in, "If you need anything: food, water, air—"

Then his father takes over, "If you want to talk to us, if you want to be left alone—"

"If you want to watch TV, if you're too cold—" says his mother.

"If you're not cold enough—" says his father.

"Anything at all. We're right downstairs in the living room," his mother says. She pulls down the window shade.

When she flips off the light switch in his room, something magical happens. The ceiling light goes off, but at the same time the huge Ferris wheel that covers the wall lights up. Little lights carefully imbedded into the wall form a hoop of white light, a halo. And when Prospect lies on the futon and tilts his head just so—he can almost picture himself in one of the cars on the Ferris wheel...rising, rising. Through his bedroom door, Prospect can hear his parents chatting in the living room. A program is on TV in the background.

Prospect is standing on the edge of an enchanted forest. Trees tower over him. They whisper secrets to each other. It is night. A car moves along a road, its headlights searching, shimmering, in the dark. "She was only thirteen," says a voice from somewhere deep in the forest. Prospect walks into the woods toward where the voice is coming from. "An unlucky number. Any way you slice it," the voice continues. Finally he comes to a clearing and sees a bed. His parents lie in bed talking. Dead leaves fall over them. He's confused. What is their bed doing in the forest?

"We weren't in our right minds," says his father to his mother.

"She was just a teenager, Roberto," she says. "She had barely arrived in this world."

"Where do you think she is now?"

"Maybe she's back."

"Back where?"

"To wherever she came from."

"She came from us, Rebecca."

"No, you know what I mean," she says. "Maybe she returned to the elements. Everybody recycles these days. Donates their bodies and souls to science." From the road, Prospect hears a car turn off its motor. The bed in which his parents had been lying has suddenly disappeared. There are just leaves scattered on the ground.

And now the car with the shimmering headlights rolls to a stop at the edge of the forest. A car door swings open, and out steps his mother! "Get out of the car, Joyce," she says sternly to a shadowy figure in the back seat, but no one emerges.

"Make me," says a tough girl's voice. Then the girl's head peeks out of the car. She spits in her mother's face. The mother reaches into the back seat and yanks the girl out. The girl is dressed for the summer, with a skimpy halter top.

Prospect's mother looks at her with sadness, or something very much like it, in her face. "This is as far as we go together as a family. I'm sorry it didn't work out."

"We were never a real family. We were a faux family. We were majorly fucked up."

And now Prospect's father emerges from the car. "We gave it our best shot, Joyce," he says. "I'm sorry you can't see that. You're too old to abort, too young to join the marines."

"This is child endangerment. I saw it on Nightline. When I find my way back, I'm going straight to the police." She is a clenched fist of a girl. If there is a tender heart inside her, she keeps it well hidden.

"No you're not," says his mother with confidence.

"What makes you think I'm not going tell the world how you abused me?"

"Give me your cell phone, Joyce."

Prospect's father holds her down as his mother empties the girl's pockets. Her cell phone, her wallet, her Hello Kitty back-pack. And out the girl walks off into the dark, starless night wearing yellow flip-flops on her feet. Everything fades slowly to black.

"Aren't you forgetting something?" says a voice in the forest. Prospect recognizes it as his father's voice. He is in bed again under a blanket of leaves. His parents lie side by side, staring up at the starless sky.

"You mean the part about how we drugged her and suffocated her?" asks Prospect's mother.

"Yes, that part."

"We aren't monsters, are we, Roberto?"

"We aren't social workers either."

"That child, that anti-child—it did not come from us, Roberto. I would not have killed something that came from us." And now a breeze shakes the branches of the trees above them, giving Prospect's parents a proper burial.

When Prospect opens his eyes, he sees he is lying in bed. The Ferris wheel on the wall glows in the dark. Prospect sneaks downstairs toward the living room. His parents are watching TV there, deep in conversation.

But when he enters the living room—his parents stop talking, and he hasn't started talking, so there is this funny silence. And so the TV talks for them. The TV fills in the blanks that they can't fill in for themselves. And for a moment, everything in the house seems almost normal.

Almost, but not quite.

5. TUNNEL OF LOVE

It is morning at the Boulanget household. Prospect has slept much longer than he expected. He walks downstairs, past the photographs on the wall. There is an empty space on the wall where the small painting had been of the girl. In the kitchen, Prospect hears someone moving, the sound of plates being set out on a table.

"There you are!" she says. "Are you hungry?"

He nods. "Yes, I am. But I'm not sleepy anymore." His mother pulls out a chair for him, and he takes a seat.

They sit at the kitchen table eating tuna salad sandwiches. "I've included all the basic food groups in your sandwich," she says. "The pineapple chunks are from the fruits and vegetables group. The oatmeal bread—that gives you your grains. The tuna gives you your essential protein. And the vanilla yogurt, which I use instead of mayonnaise, hails from the dairy group." Prospect eats slowly, chewing each bite. His mother sips her coffee.

"You are a very good cook," Prospect says.

And for a few moments, they are silent. There is just the sound of traffic from an open window, the sound of kids playing in the distance. A silence has fallen over the table, and neither of them tries to fill it. He wonders what she's thinking about. He wonders if she wonders what he is thinking about—or is he alone in his wondering? Finally he speaks.

"Who's Joyce?" Prospect says.

"Where did you hear that name?"

"It was in your Referral folder."

"Then you know who she is." She smiles a tight smile. Mother takes her coffee to the sink and dumps it down the drain. "Prospect, I know you want to know about everything. After all, you're here to learn. But it makes me sad to talk about…what you want me to talk about. You don't want your mother to be sad, do you?"

"No."

"Maybe we could talk about her some other day."

"Okay."

For a while Prospect just studies his mother's belly. She's pregnant with him, and yet he is also sitting in the kitchen with her as well. So he is in two places at once. His physical self is inside his mother, just a tadpole of a person. But his spirit is inhabiting this borrowed body. How strange.

Prospect pretends he has X-ray vision and stares at his mother's belly. "What do you think is going on in there?" he asks pointing at her stomach.

"I was hoping you could tell me." She places her hands gently on the sides of her little belly.

"Well, there's a lot of down time. I can tell you that," he says. "Life in the womb is not all fun and games. You sleep a lot...you dream some...you extract nutrients...you divide your cells over and over. But to be honest, sometimes it's kinda boring." Now it's his turn to have a light bulb moment. "Ah! Please tell me more about this love thing. How will I know it when I see it? Can anyone be loved or just some people? And if someone can't find love, what does he or she do *instead*? You see, I need to find something to love before I starve to death and someone shoots me with a gun."

His mother laughs nervously. "What on earth are you talking about, Prospect?" But he doesn't really know how to explain it any better than that. His mother gathers up their dirty dishes and takes them to the sink. "You are one unusual child," she says, and Prospect thinks she means that in a good way, but he can't be sure. "So many questions... Your father and I want to take you out to an amusement park called Great Millennium this afternoon. Then we'll go to a nice restaurant for dinner. How about we talk about all this later over a nice meal?"

"Does the park have a Ferris wheel?"

"It has a terrific Ferris wheel," says his mother. He remembers learning about Ferris wheels from his CyberSavant, and he is very interested in experiencing one.

"Like the one painted on my bedroom wall?"

"Just like the one painted on your bedroom wall, but a lot bigger," she says. Now he is really excited.

When all the dishes are washed and his father has finished doing his wire transfers for the bank he works for, the three of them climb into the car and off they go. On the way, his mother explains that Great Millennium has modern rides like the Virtual Roller Coaster and the Inner Tilt-a-Whirl that are quite modern. All the motion occurs in your mind rather than your body. But the park also has old classics like the Octopus, the Tunnel of Love, and the merry-go-round. Those are the ones that interest him most.

"What happens in the Tunnel of Love?" Prospect has to ask.

"It's just a sweet little ride that takes you into a dark place. After a while you get so turned around, you forget what's happening in the world around you. But eventually you come out into the bright light again. The cars are shaped like big swans."

"What do you *see* in the Tunnel of Love?"

His mother thinks. "It's been a while since I've been in there, but I think it has little scenes that light up of romantic things: the Eiffel Tower, a picnic, maybe a small wedding in progress with a bride and groom."

"What do you *find* in the Tunnel of Love? Do you find love there?"

She smiles a bittersweet smile at Prospect. "It's just a ride, sweetie."

"Oh." And now he feels a little foolish. He knew that it was just a ride. Why did he think it would be more?

Somewhere in the back of his brain, he thinks how the birth canal is also a kind of tunnel. A tunnel of love. He thinks this to himself, but tells no one. Because who else would really understand such a comparison?

Prospect's phone rings. "Prospect, can you talk now?" says Trish.

"I think so."

"Are you having a good time?" she asks. "With your first Referral, I mean."

"Yes. I'd have to say I am, Dr. Mesmer. My mother is an excellent hostess. But some things make her sad, so I can't talk about them. Is that normal?"

"Yes. People are very complex. More complex than the fanciest microchip. And they're unpredictable too."

There is a pause. For a moment they just listen to each other breathing. And beyond the breathing, they are listening to each other listening. Then Trish breaks the silence. "So have you figured it out yet, Prospect?"

"What?" he says.

"What you're doing here? What *we're* all doing here? The grand scheme of things?" Prospect tells her that he hasn't figured it all out, but that he will add it to his list of things to do. It is a list that grows longer each day.

6. THE AMUSING PARK

Prospect is very much looking forward to their trip to the amusement park. When he mispronounces it as "the amusing park," everybody laughs. He's not sure why they laugh, but it's fun when that happens. Everybody smiles all at once. "Well, let's hope it *is* amusing," says his mother and his father snickers. After a long ride, the family car finally rolls into the huge parking lot of Great Millennium. Even before Prospect gets out of the car, he marvels at how the real-life Ferris wheel in the distance fills the windshield. It is so much taller than he expected. His father buys rolls of tickets for the rides, and he lets Prospect hold some.

The Pre-born's mother reaches to hold his hand through the crowd. But his father thinks it looks funny for her to hold his hand. "Prospect, you are in the body of a twenty-year-old," his father explains. "Your mother is in her thirties. So if you two hold hands, it looks...*funny.* Like you're on a date. That's just wrong for a lot of reasons," his father says. Prospect looks at him, waiting to hear more. "We don't really have the time to go into all the reasons just now. You're just gonna have to trust me on this one." His father gives a squeeze to Prospect's shoulder.

There are so many people at the park. Prospect has never been around so many people. First, they stop at a food stand, and his father buys him a pink puff of cotton candy. The cotton candy is a cloud of sweetness. It melts in his mouth. As they walk, Prospect is not sure where to look next: at the interesting people, at the whirling rides, at the curious booths. Everything is fighting for his attention.

Suddenly Prospect stops when he see a man fall into a tank of water with a big splash. Everyone laughs, even the falling man. He climbs back up to his perch and waits for whatever is to happen next. When Prospect looks up again, his parents have disappeared! They have vanished into the crowd. It is there—in a sea of people and pinwheels and pink cotton candy—that he gets lost. At first, he runs toward where he saw them last. And just about ten feet ahead of him—he sees them. The crowd is so thick, it's hard to move. He knows his parents by their clothing. But when Prospect runs up to them and says hello, he sees it isn't his parents at all. The woman pulls her purse close to her body like she thinks he has come to steal something.

From behind him, there is a tap on his shoulder. Finally, he has been found! He's wrong again. It's a man on stilts, and his face is painted white. He is peering down at Prospect like he's a bug. Like *he's* the funny-looking one.

"Where are my parents? Did I lose them?" he asks the very tall man. But the man shows no concern for his questions.

He throws back his head and laughs in slow motion without making a sound…he holds his stomach with one hand. That's when Prospect remembers his cell phone. He reaches into his pocket and dials the only number he knows.

"Hello, Trish?" he says into the tiny phone. But just then he remembers that she has told him to use his cell phone only for emergencies.

"Hi, Prospect. I'm working on an important paper right now. What is it?"

Several rowdy children are chasing each other, running circles around their parents.

"Nothing," he says. "I just wanted to say hi and to tell you I'm having a good time with my parents."

She laughs her birdlike laugh. "I'm happy for you, Prospect. I can't wait for our debriefing period later." And then the voice stops speaking, and that's how he knows Trish is gone.

For a moment, Prospect just stands still as the crowd moves around him. The sky darkens, and he wonders if he will die here. He wonders if anyone will ever find him, or if he will always be a missing person. It starts to rain, and his cotton candy melts away to nothing…to a sticky, sticky mess. People are running in all directions. Prospect is inches away from crying. Out of the corner of his eye, he sees an opening in a tent. The cloth flaps open in the wind…like it is winking at him. He peeks inside and just sees darkness. But he wants to be where it is dry and safe. So Prospect goes inside this tent where anything can happen.

Slowly his eyes adjust to the light—or the lack of it. "Look what the thunderstorm blew in," says a voice in the dark.

7. THE STORM

"You looked a little lost out there," says the hooded teenage boy. The boy has a Spanish accent. His CyberSavant showed video clips of different cultures and some of those people had an accent like this. Prospect can't really see his face because the hood of his black jacket covers most of it. He is sopping wet and cold from the rain.

"I *felt* a little lost out there," Prospect says, laughing nervously.

The rained-upon young man reminds the boy of someone he used to know, though he can't remember whom. Someone he hasn't seen in a long time and misses.

Inside the tent, the ground is covered with a red and white checkered cloth. The teenager invites Prospect to sit beside him on the cloth. Nearby are two dummies reclining, posed like they are drinking wine. A wooden basket filled with goodies sits beside them. Their paper plates are filled with cheese and grapes and cookies.

"I just met my parents, and now I've lost them," Prospect says.

The boy looks at him. "At least you met yours. I'm still waiting to meet mine," the boy says.

Now Prospect looks back at him. He studies the teenager's face. He is Latino, a little firecracker. His attention is scattered. One moment he is studying Prospect like a bug under a microscope, the next minute he is poking the woman dummy with a stick, the next he is hopping around on one foot like he's playing hopscotch on an imaginary playground.

The teenage boy said he was waiting to meet his parents, and it makes Prospect wonder. "Oh! Are you a—"

"Yes, I am," the teenager says. "And I'm not ashamed to say so."

It has never occurred to Prospect there might be other Pre-borns out there, other bio-experiments happening at the same time as his. He is suddenly excited to have made the boy's acquaintance.

The teenager pull outs a huge salted pretzel from a paper bag and bites into it. "I'm still trying to make that big decision, you know," he says.

"I know what you mean," says Prospect. "Who's your Facilitator?"

He thinks. "My what?" As his eyes adjust to the dark, Prospect notices there are large pink hearts painted on the walls. There are wooden train tracks that wind their way through a tunnel of some kind.

"Mine is Trish Mesmer. She's pretty cool."

He thinks for a moment. "Oh, that's cool," the boy says, though he doesn't really know what Prospect is talking about. "So how many foster homes have you lived in?"

This confuses Prospect "What do you mean?"

"You said you just met your parents for the first time. You're an orphan, right?"

"I'm a Pre-born. I thought you said you were a Pre-born too." Prospect feels the ease of their conversation disappear. There is a gentle roar in the distance that gradually gets louder. A train car of some kind is approaching.

"I don't even know what a *Pre-born* is." He says the word "Pre-born" like it means nothing, like it's a joke of a word.

But but but. Prospect needs to get to the bottom of this. "But you said you were trying to make *that big decision—*"

"The decision that all orphans have to make when they turn eighteen: Should I try to track down my biological parents, or just get on with my life? I thought that's what we were talking about."

And suddenly Prospect feels alone again. The teenager feels alone too. Prospect realizes the teen is not a Pre-born; the teen realizes Prospect is not an orphan. Suddenly they are strangers again. And it is storming outside again. They sit in the dark across from two plastic dummies at a fake picnic.

But then a huge pink swan car floats past them and everything changes for the better. Several swan cars roll by on the tracks filled with passengers. And now Prospect knows where he is. And if he knows where he is—he can't be totally lost. He's in the Tunnel of Love.

"Next month I turn eighteen, and I can just walk out the front door…a free man. I'm waiting for that day," says the teen, poking into the dirt with his stick.

"So you don't know who your parents are?"

"Nope. And I probably never will."

Prospect thinks his new friend is brave to walk out into the world alone, and he's glad he'll be a free man. But he worries for him too because that means he's looking for something to love also. In the distance, more swan cars are approaching. The swans grind to a halt in front of the picnic scene.

"Do you want to hop on?" says Prospect's new friend. "The cars stop for about two minutes in front of each display. There's usually room in the back."

"Okay," he says because he doesn't see what harm can come of it. And it will be his first amusement park ride of the day. When Prospect hops on the car, his foot slips, and he falls to the ground. The swan car starts moving. The teenager quickly leaps out and helps him into the car. Prospect has skinned his knee a little, but he will live.

They pass different scenes that light up in the dark tunnel. And just like his mother said…there's a wedding in progress with the robot bride tossing a bouquet into the air. The hard plastic bouquet hits Prospect right in the face. "Ouch! Love hurts," he thinks to himself. So now he has two souvenirs of this ride: a skinned knee and a scratch on his face. "I will tell Trish this is how I got wounded in the Tunnel of Love," he thinks to himself.

When the two young men finally come out of the dark tunnel, they see the rainstorm has stopped. The sun is shining brightly again like it had never rained at all. And even better than that: Prospect sees his mother jumping up and down, waving at him.

"Prospect! It's Mommy. We've been looking everywhere for you!" He is so happy to see his parents. Inside the Tunnel of Love, it was so dark he didn't know what was happening in the outside world.

"We were worried about you, Mr. Man," says Prospect's father who helps him out of the swan car. His mother inspects his knee, his face: She wants to know how he got hurt. "Love." That's all he can say.

Then Prospect remembers his new friend. He turns around to introduce him—but he is no longer in the car with him. He is nowhere to be seen. "I made a new friend in the tunnel. He's an orphan. He was here just a minute ago." But Prospect's parents hug him and refuse to let him go back into the tunnel to look for his friend.

"We thought you might be here," Prospect's father says. Prospect keeps looking back into the tunnel for his friend to appear. But it's time to go to the restaurant for dinner, and so they all climb into the car. As they pull away from the amusement park, Prospect wonders if he'll ever see the boy from the tunnel again. And as he watches the park shrink through the car's back window, he sees the halo of light that is the Ferris wheel. "I didn't get to ride it," he says softly…more to himself than to anyone else.

"What, honey?" says his mother. "What did you say?" But Prospect just points to the halo in the sky. His mother and father whisper. Suddenly the car screeches to a halt in the parking lot. They are turning around, driving back toward the park!

Prospect starts to wonder if he imagined his new friend or if he was real.

Now the three of them are waiting in line to go on the Ferris wheel. When it is his turn, Prospect hands his ticket to the young man because that is what everyone else does. The young man stands next to a big lever. Prospect is so excited he doesn't know what to do with himself. His mother gets into the Ferris wheel car first. When she steps in, the car rocks back and forth a bit. Next his parents help Prospect up into the car, and it rocks back and forth more. It is fun, this rocking motion. Finally his father climbs in, and the boy lowers a metal bar across them that snaps into place. And the whole car flies forward twenty feet, rising slightly. All the Ferris wheel cars are rocking like they are cradles filled with little babies.

"Are you okay, Prospect?" asks his father. He nods.

"Don't be afraid. We're here right beside you," says his mother. "When all the people are loaded into their cars, the ride will start. First we'll go up, up into the air...and then we'll fall gently down to earth. But we will never be in danger. And if you get scared—why you just reach out and hold your father's hand. That would be all right, wouldn't it, Roberto?" She gives him a look. He smiles.

"There's nothing to be afraid of," he says. "It's just a ride, Mr. Man."

Finally the last car is loaded. Their car is at the very top of the wheel and their feet and arms dangle freely. Prospect feels like he is floating. That rocking he liked so much when they were at the bottom of the wheel now feels dangerous, but the view from the top is really beautiful. Beautiful and scary at the same time. When he looks down, he sees the other rides: the roller-coaster zooming up and down the bumpy tracks, the merry-go-round spinning slowly like a top. The people are tiny. When the Ferris wheel truly starts to turn, to go in a smooth circular motion, no CyberSavant could ever convey what he is feeling now. He is flying. And that is when Prospect realizes his father is holding his hand. When did that happen? He can't recall. But it is a nice feeling to be held.

This time when he swoops down, Prospect sees the teen from the tunnel! He is just standing there in the crowd with his jacket hood up over his head. The teenager waves at Prospect, laughing.

"Hello! What's your name?" Prospect shouts as they swoop down to the bottom. "That's my friend. Did you see him?" His parents look at the crowd, but there are so many people.

Prospect reaches into his pocket for a piece of paper and scribbles his phone number onto it. When Prospect's car is halfway down in the wheel's revolution, he throws the sheet of paper toward the teen. But it floats so slowly…and it falls so far from where he wanted it to fall. The boy from the tunnel has to climb over a gate and sneak past the ticket taker to get it. The ticket taker yells at him. When the Ferris wheel car swoops down, it comes so close Prospect is afraid it will hit him. Finally as they ascend once more into the sky, he looks back at the ground.

His new friend is gone again.

8. HE IS A CAMERA

The body that Prospect occupies has a nifty built-in safety feature. The body was designed and manufactured by Big Farm to serve the needs of the project. There is a tiny camera built into the right hemisphere of Prospect's brain that allows Trish and others to monitor where he goes, whom he meets, how he spends his time. Everything that Prospect sees they will see also. This will come in handy should the Pre-born run into any real danger in his journeys. Prospect has not been told of this feature as it would only interfere with his spontaneous interactions.

The idea for a tracking camera, not surprisingly, was Big Farm's. They insisted on having a way to keep close watch on their expensive investment. Trish resisted, but Big Farm insisted. And not surprisingly Big Farm won. But they arrived at a compromise that the camera would only be used to observe and protect the Pre-born. That it wouldn't be used to interfere with the natural flow of his Referrals unless he was in danger. That's what Big Farm agreed to, verbally anyway.

They nicknamed it the "Preb-Cam," short for Pre-born camera (pronounced to rhyme with web-cam). Trish walks into her office and locks the door behind her. She has brought her lunch with her from the cafeteria. Tilapia in a lime coconut sauce is her main course, with a mint-flavored Italian soda. Trish is excited, for now it is time for Prospect TV, and she can hardly wait. She powers up her laptop, which is hooked up to a widescreen monitor against the far wall of her office. A title screen comes up first with the countrified logo (that big red barn, happy animals dancing in the crops like a goddam musical) of the pharmaceutical sponsor. The screen reads:

WELCOME TO THE PREB-CAM
Created by Big Farm Technologies for
The Pre-born Project

A scientific inquiry into the impact of birth choice on
the happiness of children who choose

Facilitated by Dr. Trish Mesmer

There are times when just seeing this title screen is enough to send Trish over the edge. Her name up in lights. A major bio-tech sponsor. Her very own brainchild. She has dreamed of times like this, when her wild ideas would be given validity by a major institution. And now here she is on the edge of a dream come true. Her colleagues are either thrilled for her or jealous of her. Some would love to see her fail, but she has no intention of doing so. Trish now turns her attention to the screen, where she will literally see the world through Prospect's eyes. At first on the screen, all she can see is a blur. Then she starts to make things out. Prospect is high in the air overlooking a park. He is on a Ferris wheel.

Then she watches as Prospect approaches his mother to ask about her daughter Joyce. Prospect wants to know exactly what happened to her. The whole fiasco of Joyce Boulanget is well-known to Trish.

Joyce Boulanget was no ordinary child. She was the very first Pre-born. And she made the decision to be born.

Back then the project had a different name. It was called "Choice over Chance." Joyce met her Referrals and decided that, though earth did suck majorly, there were enough potential perks down the road for her to want to give it a whirl. So Joyce the Pre-born was returned to her mother's womb, and when the time came, she was born. Trish tracked Joyce from the moment of birth to the moment she learned to walk and talk to her gradual emergence as a young person. The trouble was that this child-by-choice was forever moody and ill behaved. Her living example actually contradicted Trish's thesis that children-by-choice would grow up to be happier humans. So Big Farm paid a severance fee to make Joyce... disappear. She could never talk to the press or sell her story to the movies. She couldn't have any contact whatsoever with her birth family. She would just have to transplant herself to another city and forget everything of her past. If Joyce ever reached out to her family or to the media—she would be forced to pay back the hundred-thousand-dollar severance fee she was given. As hush money.

Trish defended her bio-experiment's thesis passionately, artfully, to Big Farm (BF). She started by reminding Big Farm how huge of a market there was for products that would guarantee happy children to mothers. That there were already collateral products BF could profit from that resulted from the Pre-born Project. The CyberSavant would surely become a hot seller for parents who wanted to give their precious children an advantage. She had developed the device herself with BF. And the Preb-Cam could have numerous applications. Some focus groups expressed interest in using them to track Alzheimer patients, small children, and pets...all of whom had a habit of getting lost.

Trish said that she was close to figuring out the proper algorithm to the Choice vs. Chance conundrum. In truth, Trish was not close, but she was determined. And on this particular day in contemporary history—science won out over business. She was greenlighted once again to proceed with her bio-experiment under the new name "The Pre-born Project." Big Farm signed papers with Trish cutting a sweet deal that allowed both parties to share profits, though BF of course took the bigger piece of the pie. Big Farm insisted that Karl Bangor of new product development provide close oversight to the experiment to ensure that things did not go awry again. Trish resisted; Big Farm persisted. Guess who won?

9. CLATTER OF
SILVERWARE

After the amusement park, Prospect's family heads over to New Tokyo for Japanese food and conversation. After that, they go home. Prospect's mother tucks him into bed for the night. He thinks about the excitement of the day. But he hears his parents fighting in the kitchen downstairs. Through the closed door, he can hear them raise their voices, and Prospect wonders if they are mad at him. So he creeps down the stairs quietly and listens in. At first it is hard to hear them because a radio is singing songs in the background. And because they are washing dishes together at the sink. Then he starts to make out some of the conversation.

"How is it my fault?" his father says.

"Roberto, I told you I should hold his hand so he didn't get lost in the crowd, and you objected. And so he got lost in the crowd. What if Trish found out we lost our baby? What then?" A large dish clanks against another.

"Rebecca, are you serious? What you should really be worried about is what would happen if Prospect found out what happened to his sister!" There is the clatter of silverware in the kitchen, and Prospect pictures forks, knives, and spoons tumbling into the sink.

"Shh," says his mother. Prospect waits on the other side of the door with great interest to hear more about his sister. But the floor creaks where he steps. His parents stop talking. They look at each other in alarm.

Prospect knocks on the kitchen door. He slowly pushes the door open. "Excuse me. I just wanted to get some water." His parents smile at him.

"We didn't wake you, did we, sweetie?" asks his mother.

"No. I was just thirsty." They stand in the kitchen, their aprons covered in soapsuds and splashes of water. His mother's eyes are a little red. She wipes at the corner of her eye. She tries to primp a little, fussing with her hair. But she is already beautiful.

His father speaks seriously in his low radio-announcer voice, "Prospect, about today…"

"Oh, I'm sorry. I forgot to thank you for a great time."

"No, we're sorry that we lost you," says his mother filling a glass with water. "We really plan to get better and better at this parent thing." His father opens the freezer and grabs some ice cubes and plops them into his son's glass.

"But if I didn't get lost, I'd never have met my new friend, and I'd never have wandered into the Tunnel of Love and seen all its inner workings. If I never got lost…I'd never know how nice it is to be found."

His father hands him a glass of water. "Really?"

"Really. Father, could you excuse us for a moment? I really need to talk to Mother alone for a moment."

"Of course."

"It's Referral stuff, you know."

"Of course. Suddenly, I'm feeling very peripheral." His father laughs at his own joke, as does the rest of the family. "I think I'll watch a little TV before heading for bed. Don't stay up too late, you two." And the head of the household is gone.

"Mother, I think it's time for that talk about Joyce."

She opens a cupboard and pulls down a bag from the shelf. She puts some cookies on a plate. Gently she guides her son to the table where they both sit down.

"What happened the last night you saw her? I need to know."

"Prospect, I know you're curious about everything. But it's also important to respect people's *boundaries*. Do you know what boundaries are?"

"Is Joyce alive?"

"I was thinking you might like to meet some of your relatives tomorrow on your last day with us. You could go hang out together at the mall with your cousins, or shop online if you prefer—"

"Because if she's not alive, there's nothing to talk about," he says.

"Or we could go to the zoo and look at the animals. When I was little…" She picks up one of the cookies and bites into it.

"Mother, I don't want to go to the zoo. I don't want to shop online. I'm not going to stop asking till I know what happened to Joyce. If you won't tell me, I'll ask Father."

"No. Don't ask your father. Your father and I have a very different view of what happened. The best way I can explain it is that Joyce was part of our family for thirteen years. She was the perfect child for most of that time. But when she entered her teens, she changed. We hardly recognized her. She was reckless, a danger to herself and others. And then she did something I couldn't forgive her for. Don't ask me what it was, because I won't tell you. So...we had to...let her go."

"Would you do that to me?" Prospect wants to know.

"What?"

"If I did something that you didn't like, would you let me go too?"

"Of course not, Prospect. We're different people now."

Prospect scratches his head for a moment. "What do you mean exactly when you say you *let her go?*"

"For godsake, Prospect, what do you want me to say? That I killed my only daughter? Okay: I killed my only daughter. End of discussion." She picks up the plate of cookies and shoves it deep into the refrigerator.

"But if you killed her, why didn't the police arrest you? Murder is illegal, isn't it?"

"Excuse me, but I'm going to shop online...because *someone* should. There are all those cute dresses that need to be bought, and I'm just the woman for the job. But just remember: *this* conversation never happened. Joyce never existed. You are our first and only child, and we do so hope you choose to join our family. Good night!" His mother leaves. He walks into the living room to find his father.

He is napping on the couch. Prospect touches his arm to wake him. "Are you and your mother done with your Referral business?" he asks.

"Father," the Pre-born says, "could you tell me in your own words what happened to Joyce? Mother won't tell me what happened to her, and I need to know."

"I'd love to talk to you about it, Prospect. Really I would. But I signed a non-disclosure agreement with your mother years ago. Whatever your mother told you…that will have to be enough."

"So Mother and you have a secret that only the two of you know."

"Something like that."

"Thank you, Father."

"For what?"

"It's all right that you have a secret. I don't have to know everything."

"That's very mature of you, Mr. Man."

Prospect climbs back up the stairs and lies down on the futon. He can hear his parents turning in for the night, getting ready for bed. Doors opening and closing. Lamps snapping off. And then it is night in the world.

10. HER SPECIAL PLACE

The next morning when Prospect wakes, he sees his mother's face peek around the door. "How would you like to go for a drive, Prospect? I'll take you to my special place." He tries to imagine all the places in downtown Chicago that his mother might consider special. They grab a quick bite of cereal and fruit and then jump in the car.

"Well, my mission," says his mother, "was to do three things on our Referral. I wanted to do something fun and relaxing together, so we went to the 'amusing' park. I wanted you to meet your father, which you did. The last thing I'd like to do is show you something that I love."

"Ah! So you found something to love," he says partly excited and partly envious. "Did it take you a long time?"

"Did what take me a long time, sweetie?"

"Never mind."

His mother looks concerned. "Please go on."

"There are some things I must discover on my own. Isn't that right, Mother?"

"I suppose so. Well, the place I want to take you is beautiful."

"I like beautiful things, Mother."

"I know you do. You take after me."

Prospect rubs his chin. The hairs of his goatee are soft to the touch.

The drive is quick and scenic with a view of a lake. They park in the lot and walk toward a large odd-shaped building along the lake. Once inside, they are surrounded by glass windows filled with things swimming past them.

"This is the Shedd Aquarium. This is what I wanted to show you. There's something so beautiful about swimming things, to be surrounded by them. I like to come here to think when I have something I can't figure out," says his mother. She says she herself hardly ever swims anymore, but some of her happiest memories as a young child are of swimming in water. Just being at the aquarium makes her happy.

"The saddest time in my life was when I realized that my only child, Joyce Boulanget, could no longer be part of our family. And that's when I started coming by the Aquarium after work, on weekends. Your father thought I was having an affair!" And here amidst Japanese blow fish and sting rays that move like dark flags through the water—and schools of angelfish too—Prospect's mother tells him what happened to Joyce. They sit on a granite bench facing a sea of swimming things. Prospect notices an angelfish hovering near the glass; it is listening carefully to their conversation. He taps the window and it moves toward him.

"It's true: I killed my child. It was my deepest wish to remove her from our family…and that's what I did. I'm not proud of it."

"The first day I came to your house to meet you and Father, I had a dream that you took her to a forest…"

"No, not a forest. It was a coffeehouse. But it was called the Enchanted Forest Cafe! How could you know that?"

A family walks up to peer in through the glass. Two parents and one child. The little boy just stares at the Pre-born. The boy senses there is something different about Prospect but doesn't know what it is.

"Your father and I are so excited to have you staying with us. You have no idea. When you first appeared at our door, I was thrilled," says his mother. "At the same time, I have to say it made me think of Joyce."

The little boy crosses his eyes, and Prospect is amused, but he doesn't laugh because he and his mother are having a deep conversation.

"In the dream, Mother, there were leaves falling. They covered you."

"I don't know what that means," say his mother.

"*How* did you do it, Mother? How did you kill Joyce?"

"Why does it matter? She's gone." His mother looks around to make sure no one is listening.

"I need to know. It may be important some day."

She is looking at the sea creatures. They all seem to be listening in. "Then I might as well tell you the whole truth. But you have to promise not to tell anyone. Do you promise?"

"I promise, Mother. Once you tell me your secret, I will try my best to forget it."

She looks up and down the halls of the Aquarium. Then she looks deep into his eyes. "Joyce was not only our first child. She was also *the first Pre-born.*"

Prospect can't believe his ears. He looks into his mother's eyes. "I don't understand, Mother."

"I'm not going to go into the whole sad story. I'm not even supposed to be telling this much. But it's only fair that you know," says his mother. "Joyce was actually the first Pre-born. She met her Referrals like you're doing now, and she decided to be born. But instead of being a happier child, she was the opposite. As she grew up, she was wild, foul-mouthed, a danger to the neighborhood. Trish couldn't control her. Big Farm paid a very large fee to make Joyce…disappear. And that is the end of my story. And no, you may not ask a question. Now please forget this conversation ever happened. And please, don't hate me." His mother reaches for a tissue.

"So you didn't kill her for real?" he asks.

And now his mother shakes her head. "No, Prospect, I didn't kill her *physically.* I killed her *mentally.* Which is much worse." She uses the tissue and wipes the corners of her eyes. "That day at Enchanted Forest, I murdered the *idea* of Joyce as my daughter. I stopped seeing her physically, stopped hoping things for her, stopped trying to *save* her. I told myself I never had a daughter. That's why the police never came to arrest me. The crime I committed was an invisible one."

Prospect puts his arms around his mother. Because he has made her cry, and a son should never make his mother cry. Meanwhile, the family meandering nearby with the cross-eyed boy moves on to peer into other windows, other families.

"I told Joyce that she should find a way to be happy without us."

Prospect wants to ask his mother one more hard question. He tries to be gentle. "Would you ever kill the idea of *me*?"

"Oh, Prospect. No," she says.

"But how do you know for sure?"

"I'm a different person today. I'd never…"

"It's okay, Mother. I was just asking. Can we go now?"

He and his mother now stand before the Aquarium windows. As they leave this place, jellyfish descend in slow motion like parachutes onto the bright coral reefs below them. Prospect thinks of the parachutes that people cling to as they drop from the sky. How a good parachute can save your life…and how a bad one is like having no parachute at all. And in that moment, Prospect makes up his mind. He decides that he must somehow find his sister. He makes that his mission. He needs to talk to another Pre-born like himself. So that he can make up his mind. He does not tell his mother of his plans for surely it would only upset her.

❧

For their last meal together, the Pre-born decides to take his family out to Bakers Square. They put several types of pie on a lazy Susan, and everyone gets to try a little of everything. "Well, before I head back to the hospital, I did want to hear your closing arguments on whether I should be born or not."

His mother begins. "I think you should be born… because there's so much you'll experience…"

For a moment, nothing is said.

"Words fail us," says his father.

"It's inexpressible really. Still…we try. Because what else can we do?"

"So much."

"Your first kiss," says his mother.

"Your first case of mono," says his father. They laugh.

"Slumber parties. Line dances. The internet."

"But there are bad things too," says Father. "Slumber parties. Line dances. The internet."

There is a brief pause. Then his mother speaks. "You," she says. "There's so much more of you you'll experience…if you stick around." And finally his parents are done. Prospect puts the meal on his credit card. They take the last slice of the pecan pie to go.

෨

Back at his parents' house, the Pre-born gathers up his things. His folks offer to drive him back to the hospital, but he insists on taking the bus. In fact, he is looking forward to it. "You're welcome here any time," says his mother, hugging him. She practically squeezes all the air out of him.

"In case I don't see you again…" his father starts to say. He embraces the man who would be his son. "What am I talking about? I'll see you again." And as Prospect walks away, the image he see is this: his parents waving good-bye, framed like a picture by the storm door they are holding open.

෨

On the bus, Prospect watches the houses fly past him as he wonders who he really is to these people. A winning lottery ticket? Another hungry mouth to feed ? A disposable boy? Or is he something more? A new green leaf on the family tree? A giant scissors-step into the future?

And who are these people to him? A mother who kills her own child with her mind? A father who loses him in public places? A sister who may or may not be alive, who walked deeper and deeper into the forest until she disappeared? But they are other people too. A mother who puts pineapple chunks in her boy's tuna sandwiches and a father who speaks in the reassuring deep tones of a radio announcer. A sister who may one day reappear from the dark forest that swallowed her.

The Pre-born turns on his tiny computer, admiring the pretty blinking lights and the Big Farm logo. There is the sound effect of a rooster crowing and cows mooing in the yard. Prospect's search for his sister begins in the most logical place he can think of: the internet. Though Prospect is not an expert when it comes to Google, he knows it is a great tool for gathering knowledge. He is used to his CyberSavant answering his every question. But he's not in the womb anymore. He clicks open Google and types the two words: "Joyce Boulanget." He presses enter and waits to see what he can see.

11. THE SHOUTING MAN

It is Tuesday morning on the Brown Line. There are only four people on the train. It's quiet. People are reading newspapers or books or just looking out the window at the passing buildings. Then from out of nowhere, this man's voice booms forth, *"I'm calling about my wife!"*

It startles Prospect because the man speaks so loudly and suddenly, like he was upset at someone. Prospect is not positive if the man said he was calling about his *wife* or his *lights*. Whichever it is, he knows by the sound of the man's voice that the subject is very important to him.

The Shouting Man continues, *"I'm her husband, Gunther Trudeau. Gunther. G-u-n-t-h-e-r. I spoke to a caseworker yesterday. We're going through a divorce. My wife, Kitty...she's bipolar. She's engaging in self-destructive behavior. Some days, I barely recognize her."* He is definitely not calling about his lights. It seems strange that he is telling a train car of perfect strangers—that his marriage is failing. Prospect feels sorry for

59

the man. He's had a bad day, and it isn't even lunchtime. Prospect can't bring himself to turn around and look at the man, though he's dying to.

"No, thank you—I'm fine," he shouts. "But I'm concerned about my wife. I don't know…how to make her happy anymore. She's in room three twenty-two. Could someone check on her?" He is a nice man. Prospect decides he likes him…even though he doesn't know him. Is it possible to like someone you've never met?

When his train stop comes and Prospect gets off, he steals a glance. The man is a Caucasian in his thirties, with a neatly trimmed beard and a kind face. Prospect thought he would be a businessman in a suit and tie with a face made up of sharp angles from all that shouting—but he isn't. The man walks off cradling his cell phone, and Prospect tries to picture him and his wife cradling each other on their wedding day— so happy and hopeful under a flurry of white rice. How did it end up like this? He hopes the Shouting Man's afternoon goes better than his morning. He hopes the man does not wind up having a rainy life.

Prospect walks the last few blocks to Infinity Medical Center, whose windows glisten in the distance. It is only his first return to Infinity and already it is starting to look like home to him. After meeting his mother, Prospect feels different than when he was just an embryo adrift in his amniotic sac. He now understands that comes from the DNA of his parents, that he may be the next branch on the family tree.

Before returning to the hospital, Prospect stops off at a funky coffeehouse called the Kopi Cafe. Indeed, there is so much funkiness inside, so much world traveler hipness – it's surprising it can all be contained within four walls. As Prospect steps inside, the first thing that catches his eyes are the Indonesian flying goddesses that descend from the coffeehouse ceiling on invisible strings. One wooden goddess flies through the air with a hand mirror in one hand and a brush in the other. Another goddess, apparently more contemporary, is texting on her cellphone.

He ponders the goddesses which turn in the air from time to time, propelled as they are by the occasional breezes from the front door or the philosophical conversations that are commonplace at the Kopi Café. Finally he makes his way to a table. It's four in the afternoon. Too late for lunch and too soon for dinner.

An elderly waitress spies him and ambles to his table carrying a menu in hand. She has to be at least in her eighties. Little glass chandelier earrings hang from her ear lobes. They rattle when she moves. She puts a menu down on the table and Prospect looks through it. "What's your pleasure today, Bob?"

He thinks, "Bob? My name is not Bob." He wonders if he looks like someone whose name really is Bob. It's possible. The world is a big place. "I'd just like a plain bagel, toasted, with some cream cheese, please."

"That's all you're having?" she asks. He nods. "Boy, we're losing money on you today," she says, then lets out a large laugh. She slowly gathers the menu and ambles away, her earrings rattling as she leaves. Prospect has only talked with the woman for a minute, but he is sure he'll never forget her.

In just three days, the Pre-born has experienced so much: cotton candy, a rainstorm, the help of a stranger, the joys of public transportation. He has tried six different kinds of pie. A robot bride has hit him in the face with her flowers. He has met his mother and father. As the light of day starts to fade, he calls Trish and tells her he is here. He will meet her in her office shortly.

Lately Prospect has gotten homesick for the womb. He mostly misses the peace and quiet. And sometimes too he misses his old CyberSavant. But it occurs to him that this device, as smart as it is, can only take you so far. It can take you to the very edge of a cliff—but it can't leap off that cliff for you. And each person who leaps off a cliff may experience that particular cliff differently. How you experience something— that's your fingerprint. It's what makes you unique from every other leaping person on the planet.

His favorite waitress brings him his snack. In the beginning, the CyberSavant acted as Prospect's only link to the outside world. But now information flows into him through so many portals. There is the internet, television, there are his Referrals, and there is the very world itself around him and its millions of messages bombarding him.

His waitress leaves his check on the table and gives him a flirty wink. "See ya, Bob," she says and off she walks. All that is left of her is the rattle of her chandelier earrings. In his mind, Prospect says to her, "See ya, Sally." Because the waitress should have a name too. And if Prospect can be a Bob, surely she can be a Sally.

And somewhere the Shouting Man's train rolls on down the tracks. Through tunnels, up hills, under rivers. His train rolls and rolls. Where it stops—nobody knows. Maybe his train will fly off the track and fall into an ocean, and the

Shouting Man will never be heard from again. His sick wife will wonder why her husband never visits her anymore. Why has he forsaken her? She will imagine that he has met an exotic dancer named Delilah and moved to Tazmania. She will finally stop waiting for him to come visit her. She will eat her orange Jell-o with little mandarin slices floating in it. She will not know how much her husband cared about her…even from the bottom of a very large ocean.

12. HOMEWORK

Prospect sits for a moment at his table. It is so peaceful here at the Kopi Cafe. Suddenly his cell rings.

"Hello?"

"Hi, I met you yesterday at Great Millennium," says a voice with a Spanish accent. "In the Tunnel?"

"I'm so glad you called. But before I forget—please tell me your name."

"My name? Oh…well…my name is Fulton," he says. He rides his skateboard as he gabs on his cell. He dodges pedestrians. A typical teenager.

"Fulton. That's a funny name." He turns his coffee cup right side up as this is the universal sign that one is in need of caffeine. His waitress promptly fills it with aromatic, piping hot coffee.

"What's yours?"

"My name is Prospect."

"And you think *I* have a funny name?" Fulton laughs. Prospect joins in.

"You must have gotten the piece of paper I threw down from the Ferris wheel," he says.

"I did. On one side it had your phone number…but on the other side it had a big message for me."

"A message? What did it say?"

"It said, FIND SOMETHING YOU CAN LOVE." The teen jumps into the air but misses his skateboard coming down. He lands on the ground in a heap.

Suddenly Prospect is embarrassed. It was a note he'd written for himself. "That wasn't for you."

The teen picks himself up and is on his way, walking with his skateboard now. "But, Prospect, it made perfect sense to me. You were telling me it doesn't matter what has happened in the past, being an orphan and all," he says. "You were trying to help me. Weren't you?"

Does it matter that he gave Fulton the note by accident…as long as it helps him? "That's right, Fulton," Prospect says. "I was trying to help you." Out of the corner of his eye, he sees a customer is purchasing the flying goddess holding the handmirror. That was the one that he wanted!

"You're the man, Prospect. Hey, my foster folks finally came back from vacation. I gotta dash. They're calling me to dinner." Fulton gives Prospect the phone number to the home where he is staying.

"Okay. Have a good dinner," And they hang up.

To his growing list of questions in his notebook, he adds one more: "Is there such a thing as an accident?" Buddhists believe there are no accidents in the universe, that everything

happens for a reason. That you can live a life that is enlight-
ened. Prospect hopes so. But for now his time at the Kopi Cafe
is over.

He is late for Trish. And according to the CyberSavant,
he recalls that Trish hates to be kept waiting.

∾

Prospect sits in his Facilitator's office as she makes a fresh
pot of coffee. Hovering above Trish's desk is a beautiful hologram in the shape of a million tiny white sperm cells swimming toward a single egg. (A hologram is a picture that is
not really there: just a lot of light beams bumping up against
each other, pretending to be something they aren't.) Trish sets
down two steaming mugs of coffee on the smallish wooden
table.

"Shall we get started?" she asks gently and—without
waiting for his answer—turns on a tape recorder on the table
between them. He just stares at it for a while, watching a small
red light wink at him.

"Trish, could I ask a question?"

"Certainly."

"I know that there is a Facilitator's Oath…because you
showed it to me. Is there also a *Referral's* Oath?" he asks. He
takes a sip of the coffee. He loves this feeling of warmth flow-
ing into his mouth.

Trish smiles and types into her iPad. "That is a superb
question," she says. A bell-like laugh floats out of Trish's
mouth. It is a sound that Prospect didn't realize he missed

until he just heard it again. She pulls out a sheet of paper from her file cabinet and hands it to him:

REFERRAL'S OATH

1. I will allow the Pre-born to experience the world as completely as possible—the good parts as well as the bad. I will hold nothing back.

2. I will do everything I can do to help the Pre-born make up his mind about his birth decision. I know he is counting on me, as someone who has lived on this earth longer.

3. I understand there are no limitations on what a Referral and a Pre-born can be to each other: friends, enemies, colleagues, co-conspirators, extended family. I am limited only by my imagination.

"Why do you ask?" she wants to know.

"Because now I can see what an excellent Referral my mother is. She..." But he has started the sentence before he has figured out how to complete it.

"Yes?"

"She told me about the good parts and the bad parts as well. She held nothing back."

"Are you're saying that as a Referral, your experience with her was a positive one?"

"Yes."

"Would you say that meeting your first Referral, in some ways, made you want to be born?"

Prospect thinks for a moment. He sips his coffee. "I would say this: Meeting my mother...made me curious. About what it's like."

"About what *what* is like?" Trish asks.

"This," he says, and he makes a big swirling gesture with his hands to indicate the room around him. But he also means to suggest what is outside of this room as well, what is outside this moment. Prospect means to suggest something that is bigger than the both of them.

But he's not sure if he's successful.

13. TRISH'S JOURNAL

"There has been much energy and politics devoted to the rights of mothers to choose or not. But talking about birth in such reductive, binary terms—pro-choice or pro-life—completely leaves out the right of the baby to choose. What's exciting about the Pre-born Project is that it dares to bring the baby's wishes into the equation, which is surely a voice to be considered."

— Dr. Trish Mesmer, Scientist
Big Science Magazine

As is the case with any experiment or adventure that Trish embarks upon, she keeps a journal on her iPad. It is a little more informal and personal than the notes that she keeps throughout an experiment for future publication purposes.

These notes are more for her eyes only. The notes she jots today are as follows:

Something tells me this just may be my favorite bio- experiment of all...for reasons I won't go into right now. I am at the start of something big. I can feel it. It combines three of my favorite variables: the innocence and honesty of children, free will as a species, and the chance to speed up the evolutionary process.

Prospect is full of questions. He asked where his borrowed body comes from. But I will only tell him what he needs to know. No need to confuse him. Prospect has bonded with his mother, his first Referral. That's great. The bottom line is that his first Referral experience has made him even more eager for his next one. I've recommended to Prospect that he start writing a blog to capture his thoughts about the people he meets, his new experiences. He is very excited about this idea.

INITIAL PHASE—THE FIRST THREE WEEKS

What is the tipping point? How does the Pre-born arrive at his decision to be born or not? What factors are most compelling to him? Least compelling? How welcoming and viable do earth and its inhabitants appear to the Pre-born? Is the range of Referrals offered to him a balanced and representative one? How much will the Pre-born's final decision be influenced by non-externals—such as his own inherited personality traits? Is he safety-seeking or risk-seeking by nature?

INTERMEDIATE PHASE—BIRTH DECISION OUT-COME

Will the Pre-born choose to be born or not? Can either of these outcomes be considered a success from a scientific POV? From the experiment's POV? From the funders' POV? Or will only an affirmative decision be useful in moving the thesis of the Pre-born Project forward? Memories accumulated in this initial period will be erased once the Pre-born makes his or her decision.

What preparations should take place in anticipation of the Pre-born's birth? Once we are sure the birth is healthy and successful, we will want to launch multiple and simultaneous Pre-borns on their way in this process (selecting birth parents, introducing Referrals, etc.). To have the most compelling data, we will want at least ten to fifteen Pre-borns who have chosen to advance toward birth, so that we can study and monitor their life development.

FINAL PHASE—THE FIRST FIVE YEARS OF THE PRE-BORN'S LIFE

What outcomes will we be looking for, once he has chosen to be born? What criteria should be measured and tracked on an ongoing basis? More joy, more goal-oriented behaviour, heightened self-esteem? It's not yet clear. I'm hoping the outcomes will be obvious, will announce themselves to me. If there is no measurable difference in the Pre-born's chosen life—does this mean that the project has failed? What other meanings can be derived? Will enhanced, evolved behavior in the Pre-born be evident in the first five years of life? The first ten years of life? How will we know when this bio-experiment is complete? What will qualify as a success? A failure?

On a more personal note, I'm curious how much Prospect will keep in touch with his Referrals as he meets them. Will he move episodically through them or cumulatively? Will he favor some Referrals over other ones? Will the deciding factor for Prospect be the experiences shared by his Referrals—or will his own experience be most persuasive?

Just off the record, I'm a little concerned about how much KB might want to become involved in this project. He seems very hands-on. I'm not used to that, and it unnerves me a bit. I understand the pressure on him to turn out a marketable service or product at the end of all this. And I know Big Farm didn't become big just by being philanthropic. They are a for-profit after all. I've never partnered with a pharmaceutical this large. It presents wondrous opportunities and horrid challenges.

To me, it's all about the data and the purity of the experiment. We do an experiment because we don't know what the outcome will be. If KB wants to influence that outcome, it is no longer an experiment; it's new product development. That is all fine and good, but then what do they need me for? I don't develop products; I make scientific inquiries. If my inquiries lead to a breakthrough and to the development of a vital new product, that's icing on the cake to me. But I'm always gonna be more interested in the cake itself!

14. STRANGE BEDFELLOWS

As much as Trish might like to imagine she is the queen in the kingdom of her bio-experiment and that she rules, she knows better. With Big Farm dollars behind her, she will always have an angel on her shoulder. Karl Bangor is her dedicated angel. He will ensure that the costs of the experiment are within reason, that the project wraps up by its deadline or sooner, that the products and services emerging from the Pre-born Project are as profitable as possible. And that Karl Bangor gets his due credit for shepherding the project to its fruitful conclusion.

She submits her report via email to Karl on Prospect's first meeting with his first Referral, Rebecca Boulanget, his mother. She waits anxiously for Karl's response. This will tell her a lot about how closely they will or will not be working. She keeps hitting the refresh button to see if he has replied yet. And finally his email appears in her in-box. There is no body to the message. Only a subject line: "PLEASE ARRANGE A

MEETING WITH ALL REFERRALS ASAP." The shouting capital letters tell Trish that Karl Bangor may be a bit of a control freak. When she gently emails back to him to clarify the focus of the meeting, he simply writes that the purpose of the meeting will be discussed at that time. End of discussion. So be it.

She contacts the Referrals and books a conference room for a meeting tomorrow afternoon.

༄

The Referrals sit around a smoked glass table that is oval-shaped. They have only met twice before, at the orientation meetings a month ago. Lito likes this table because he can look through the glass and see his sneakers below him, watch himself tap his toe if he feels like it.

"Does anybody know what this meeting is about?" asks Victor Pastel, breaking the silence. "I have a very busy day today."

"I read your bio," says Trevor. You're the painter, right?"

"Trying to be."

"I used to be quite fond of painting. My mentor told me that I could've been a contender. But that was before I had my…procedure."

Irene watches Lito peer through the glass table top, as his feet dance. "The table is quite lovely, isn't it, Lito?"

"I like it! I can see my *shoes,*" he says.

Rebecca leans forward with her elbows on the table. "Trish was kind of mysterious about the purpose of this meeting in her email. Prospect has met the two of us so far: Lito and me. I hope there isn't a problem with the Referrals."

"Maybe you did or said something…inappropriate," Trevor says. "Not that I'm all that appropriate myself."

"I said a lot of inappropriate things," says Lito. "I don't remember any rule about that. We're supposed to be ourselves, aren't we? I gotta be me. Know what I mean, jellybean?"

The other Referrals nod in agreement. Just then Trish enters the room, followed by Karl Bangor dressed in his usual pinstripe vest and pocket watch. "Good morning, everyone. Thanks for coming today," she says. The Referrals mutter their hellos back. "I wanted to introduce you to a colleague of mine. He works with new product development at Big Farm. This is Karl Bangor."

"Hello, everyone. I'm thrilled to finally meet you all. I recognize you from the photos we have of you on file." He does a visual scan around the room, making sure to establish eye contact with each one of them. "We won't keep you long today. And you will be compensated, along with your main Referral fee, which you'll receive after you've completed your tasks. Big Farm thanks you for your interest in the future. I just wanted to make sure we are all on the same page. In terms of what you Referrals are to accomplish."

Now there is a silence. The Referrals are not sure if Karl is going to tell them what he expects of them or if he is opening up the discussion for people to put in their two cents. Trish searches the face of Karl for a clue and decides to jump in. "Would you like people to just share what they envision a Referral to be?"

"We could do that but that would take extra time, and then we'd have to pay them!" Karl says. His laugh is like a machine gun: fast, loud, a sudden burst of sound. It makes Irene flinch. "Why don't I just cut to the chase? Trish has kept me posted on the progress with the first two Referrals. They sound excellent. They do. But we'd just like to be more time efficient. If you have up to three days to spend with the Pre-born, why not wrap up in a day or two if you can?"

Irene nods her head. Trevor has a puzzled look on his face. Lito is now looking at everyone's shoes through the glass table "There are currently four more Referrals slated to meet Prospect. But if he meets with just one more of you and arrives at a birth decision—that's even better! The sooner the experiment wraps, the sooner we can all go home. So I just encourage you to be focused in your presentations, and then send the little bugger on his merry way.

"And I don't want to influence you or the outcome of this project," Karl says, "but having Prospect choose to be born…that's probably a more useful outcome than his choosing *not* to be born. It just is. But forget I said that. The point is, the human race is suffering and depending on the Pre-born Project. We can't keep progress waiting, now can we?" Karl pulls out his gold pocket watch and notes the time. "Now that's what I call efficiency. Have an efficient day, everyone. We'll be checking in with you all periodically." Karl Bangor is out the door.

Trish gets up and closes the door. "Does anyone have any questions?" she asks.

Irene raises her hand, as if she is in class. "Is it my imagi-nation or did that man just tell us that he'd rather that Prospect choose to be born? Sounds like he's tainting the outcome a bit."

Trish is nodding. "Well, his approach to bio-experiments is different from mine. I don't think he's dictating what you can say to Prospect. He's just giving the more corporate perspective. In the end, you have to do and say what your heart tells you to."

"I'll have no trouble with that," says Trevor. "No one has ever accused me of being subtle. Lord knows I don't beat around many bushes."

"I don't trust him," Lito interjects. "Did anyone else notice he has no eyebrows? How can you trust a man with no eyebrows?" The other Referrals laugh. "I look at the dude and can't hear a word he's saying cuz I'm wondering what happened to his face."

Trish smiles. "Well, I think he has eyebrows, Lito. I just think they are…on the thin side."

"I'd like to say something if I may," Irene says.

"Please," says Trish.

"And Trish, please don't take this the wrong way…"

"I always get nervous when someone says that."

"Well, I know this is your project, your baby, Trish, but I also know that Big Farm is investing a lot of time and money in this," Irene says. "I guess I'm wondering who's advocating for the integrity of the experiment? Who's looking out for Prospect's best interests? If Mr. Bangor insists that we try to influence Prospect in a way that's beneficial to Big Farm—would you intervene? Could you intervene?"

"That's a good point," Trevor says. "The Pre-born Project is my idea. I'd certainly be the best advocate. Whether my voice has any weight, well, time will tell."

"With the money that Karl Bangor makes at Big Farm, I think we should demand he buy a decent pair of eyebrows, because he's creeping me out with the naked brow look," says Lito. Trish smiles at this.

"I appreciate everyone's input, and I am going to do everything in my power so that your engagement retains its authenticity. I can't promise anything about Karl's eyebrows though."

"I'm sorry but I really do have some time considerations today," says Victor, standing up. "Are we done here?"

"We're almost done here, Victor. I promise."

Rebecca Boulanget waves her index finger in the air as if motioning for a small cab. "This all probably doesn't relate to me, does it? Since I finished my Referral already," she says.

"Well, there's always a chance Prospect may try to keep in contact with some of his Referrals after the fact." Rebecca nods. "Does anyone have any more questions? I think the takeaway from Karl's comments is: Be persuasive. Don't dillydally. And the sooner you can complete your Referral, the better. So, again, thank you all for coming and being part of this important project."

As people file out, Trish turns to Lito. "Lito, you're Prospect's next Referral, and you're also our youngest Referral. Would you allow me the honor of treating you to lunch?"

"Well, I've never been one to turn down a free meal." She is so taken with Lito that she hasn't even noticed that all the Referrals have left the conference room. Trish grabs her purse, and off they go. She drives them to Hamburger Mary's.

What Lito doesn't know, and what Trish can't tell him, is that their relationship extends beyond mere Facilitator and

Referral. Almost two decades ago, Trish gave birth to a son, but for a variety of reasons, she could not raise him. Lito Sanchez was that child. Lito does not know this fact. Trish cannot forget this fact. It is no random event that he is part of Trish's bio-experiment. It is very likely a serious conflict of interests. But Trish Mesmer doesn't care. What she cares about is that after seventeen years she and her son are about to have lunch together for the first time in their lives.

∽

They enter the restaurant to the pumping sound of disco music. "Shame" by Evelyn Champagne King plays on the speakers, as if the disco era had never died. A drag queen seats them at a large comfy booth. "I hope you like hamburgers," says Trish.

"I do."

The waitress places large tumblers of ice water in front of them. They place their orders. Their huge burgers come served with a steak knife stabbed into the heart of the sandwich for dramatic effect. The restaurant checks come tucked into a woman's high-heel shoe and placed on your table. It's a gay-friendly joint with creamy milkshakes and unlimited french fries. Trish figures Lito will find it to his liking.

"So please tell me about yourself, Lito. I know you've been living in foster homes. Do you know anything about your birth parents?" The music now changes to a disco version of Gordon Lightfoot's ballad "If You Could Read My Mind."

He laughs. "Only that they dumped me like a hot enchilada. They've never once tried to find me. Not a single stinking letter or birthday gift. I've got my own great personal website that would make it easy for anyone to find me, but nothing. I feel like Jodie Foster in the movie *Contact* with this huge contraption aimed into outer space. And every day she points the contraption toward the heavens and listens for a sign of life. And hears nothing, just the grinding of stars."

"Oh, but I'm sure it wasn't an easy decision for your parents to give you up," she says. "In fact, before we chose you as a Referral, I did some research. Your mother was deeply conflicted. She desperately wanted to keep you—"

"You talked to her?"

"Very briefly, in the very early stages of the project," she says.

"She put me out with the trash. If she wanted me, she would've kept me."

"There was an abusive husband involved," Trish explains. "She was concerned for your safety. She felt as long as you were with her, you would always be in danger of being abducted."

Lito takes several gulps of ice water.

"What if I want to talk to her?"

Trish takes in a deep breath, then exhales. "I'm afraid she passed away this year." This news fills Lito with several feelings at once, not any of them good. Trish wonders if she should have told such a painful lie. She had decided it would be best."

"That's not very long ago. Did you ever get to meet her...in person?"

"I did meet her just once. She was a lovely woman. Very sensitive. You look a lot like her. I told her about the Pre-born Project. She knew that you'd had a rough time growing up in foster homes. She hoped that this project might help you in some way. In terms of the money. And that it might spark your interest in science."

Lito finds himself getting emotional. He is moved by hearing of his mother's wishes, but furious that she wouldn't have tried to meet him face to face. Especially if she knew she was dying. And he's angered by hearing of her recent death. It's like losing her twice. And he has no interest in meeting his abusive birth father.

"She did tell me that if I ever got the chance to talk to you personally, that I should tell you she never stopped loving you. That if she had it to do over again, she would keep you." Trish looks at this perfect young life in front of her. She sees his tears. "Letting you go was the biggest mistake of my life." Trish suddenly realizes what she has said. "*Her* life. She said it was the biggest mistake of *her* life."

Lito's face is unreadable. It's too much information for his ADD-addled, teenage mind to process. "No offense, Trish, but I really don't want to talk about this right now if it's okay with you." The waitress brings their hamburgers with a knife stabbed into each one.

"I understand."

"In fact, do you think you could drive me home? I'm not feeling very hungry right now."

"Oh, are you sure? We can talk about something else if you like."

"I've kinda lost my appetite."

"Well, at least take your bleu burger and fries with you. And they can put the chocolate shake in a to-go cup. Excuse me, waitress?" Trish makes sure everything is packaged up nicely and easy to carry for Lito. She feels like she's packing a lunch for him for school. Pangs of regret shoot through her. As she drives Lito home, they don't speak. When she arrives at his house, it is the middle of the afternoon. Trish gives him a clumsy hug because she knows she may never get this chance again. Then she watches him disappear into the house. Through the sheer drapes of the living room, she watches Lito turn on a lamp. For a moment, he becomes a silhouette. A cardboard cut-out:

Boy In A House With Only His Sorrow For Company

15. SOLAMENTE, ALONE

Prospect's next Referral is none other than Lito Sanchez. Lito has gotten back home with enough time to watch a few mindless episodes of television. His appetite has returned to him full force and he is devouring the amazing bleu burger. He sits eating, glad he has some time to think of nothing, time to clear his head of the big information that Trish has just laid at his feet.

Prospect decides he wants to take his time getting to know his next Referral. He wants to discover him slowly... like a flower opening in the sun. He must remember to ask Lito how you say "flower" in Spanish. Prospect buys a box of "turtles" at the House of Chocolates. Actually the candy does not contain real turtles at all! But they are shaped like turtles. This will be his gift to his host. Outside the chocolate shop, he pauses to read the next letter from Trish:

Dear Prospect,

Here is some biographical background on your second Referral Lito Sanchez. Though Lito is only seventeen, he is world-weary before his time. He is biracial —of Mexican and Scottish descent—and he has no parents to speak of. He is what is known as an orphan. That means, for whatever reason, he was given up by his parents at an early age. Probably because his mother felt she could not properly care for him. It certainly doesn't mean he was rejected or that the mother was a terrible person. In fact most mothers who give up a child to adoption continue to yearn for their child for years. "Orphan" is such an ugly, old-fashioned word. I prefer to think of such a child as "family free."

Another thing you should know is that Lito suffers from Attention Deficit Disorder (ADD). His attention span is very short, and it wanders quite a bit. You, Prospect, come from a very specific family. Lito is interesting as an example of someone who does not. Any kind of family that Lito finds in his wanderings in this world will be of his choosing.

Dr. Trish Mesmer

P.S. Enclosed you will find directions to the home where Lito is staying. I look forward to hearing of your adventure upon your return. By the way, you had specifically asked to meet three types of people. One who is truly happy, one who is difficult to get

*along with, and one who wishes he was never born. Sadly, Lito is
your representative of this last category.*

Prospect steps onto the Halsted bus. He is headed for
the colorful neighborhood of Pilsen…home to many artists,
and apparently at least one orphan in search of a good home.
When he gets to 18th Street, he looks for Lito's address. There
is a Latino boy sitting in a chair on the front porch, playing
with a yo-yo. His hair is buzzed shorter than a bald eagle and
he wears earrings in both ears like a little pirate, but it is his
face that is a wonder to behold. Across his face flicker dozens
of fleeting emotions, thoughts, and complaints like a sign in
Times Square…demanding attention, though unwilling to
give much attention in return.

Prospect reaches out to shake Lito's hand, but Lito
reaches instead for the box of chocolates in his other hand.
"Are these for me?" he asks, ripping off the gold ribbon and
yanking open the lid.

"Yeah, I don't know if you like—" But before the Pre-
born can finish his statement, Lito Sanchez has scooped three
chocolate turtles into his mouth and is hard at work chewing
them into something manageable. "Glad you like 'em," Prospect says.

"Are you friggin' kidding me? Who could turn their back
on a turtle? That perfect combination of chocolate, caramel,
and pecan morsels. This is rich-folks food. I'm sorry. Let me
start over. Did I mention I'm Lito Sanchez. And you must
be…"

"Prospect," They shake hands.

"Nice to meet you, Prospect."

Lito helps him with his travel bag, wheeling it into the house. In some ways this house is not all that different from the one his parents live in. There is a living room with a sofa and TV. A kitchen with many cups and plates. But he also notices that the plants on the windowsill are drooping a little. There is a box of opened cereal lying on the floor and what looks like dried up spaghetti in a bowl next to it. Instead of pictures of the family hung on the wall like at his parents' house, there are pictures of places. They are pictures torn from magazines and taped to the wall. Prospect can't tell if they are places they have traveled or maybe places they'd like to go.

"Could I meet your foster family?" Prospect asks.

"You could if they were here, but you just missed them. The Valderamas just left for sunny Palm Beach for two weeks. So I guess I'm in charge." Lito carries Prospect's bag up the stairs to his room. "I'm the chief cook and bottle washer. The senior grass mower, mail sorter, and message-taker. And some-times...just sometimes...I'm even their foster kid."

"So do you know where your birth family lives?" Prospect asks.

"Well, I found out that my dad was a wife beater, so I have no interest in him. And I found out my mom passed away about a year ago. Though she sent her love before she croaked. So that kinda ends that story," Lito says.

Prospect likes Lito. The way he says things. His direct-ness. In some ways Lito's everything he's not. Lito's a loud talker; Prospect talks softly. Lito laughs at jokes even if they're only slightly funny; Prospect laughs mostly when he's embar-rassed. Lito's carefree where he is careful. "You're a nice fellow. Why haven't you been adopted in all these years?"

Lito just shrugs his shoulders and sets the bag on the bed. Prospect starts to unpack.

"This is quite a coincidence," the Pre-born says. "I met another boy who was an orphan just the other day."

"Yeah, we're everywhere."

Prospect opens up his notebook. "Lito, could you tell me how to say *flower* in Spanish?"

"*Flor.* If there are more than one *flor*—and I should hope to hell there are—you call them *flores. Las flores.*"

He listens carefully and then repeats. "*Las flores.* The flowers." These are the first words he ever says in another language. He likes the way they sound…like he's telling himself a secret.

"Did Trish tell you I'm practically a poster child for ADD?" Lito asks, digging through the little brown paper cups in the box for the remaining turtles. Prospect nods. Lito leaves a trail of wrappers on the floor. "Boy, these turtles are awesome. Are you gonna eat the rest of these chocolates, cuz if you're not, I thought I'd save some for my foster brothers."

"They're for you. Do with them what you wish." Prospect smiles as he watches him put the lid back on his treasure.

"That's why I keep jumping from thing to—Oh shit, man, I'm late for swimming. Wanna come?"

"Well…"

"Follow me. I think you'll fit into Mr. Valderama's trunks. Don't you worry. The Lito's got you covered."

"I can't swim," he says.

Lito shoots a look at him. "You never know what you can do…until you're in the water. That's what I always say."

And off they go, Prospect's new friend Lito Sanchez and he, in search of a pool.

As they make their way to the YMCA down the block, Lito says, "I have a confession to make. I've met you before."

It's the strangest thing anyone has said to Prospect so far. It seems so unlikely, considering how new he is to the world. "I haven't been...*around* that long. Are you sure?"

Lito holds up his index finger, asking for patience. He takes a black hoodie out of his bag and puts it on...pulls up the hood so that Prospect can't see his face. Then he speaks in a funny voice, "Look what the thunderstorm blew in." And now of course there's no mistaking it: It's his friend from the Tunnel of Love! He uncovers his face.

But but but. How? Why? And what brought him to the park that day in the first place? Was it another coincidence? And Prospect thought Lito told him his name was Fulton. There are so many things he wants to know all at once.

Lito says that he didn't really lie about his name: Fulton is his middle name; Lito is his first name. When he knew he was chosen to be Prospect's second Referral, he asked Trish if there was a way that he could secretly observe him? Trish liked this idea. A kind of "cross-pollination of Referrals." And she liked how resourceful Lito was. She said he might make an excellent scientist one day. She emailed him pictures of Prospect and his mother and father. Told him what time they were expected at Great Millennium and that Prospect's mother would bring him to the Tunnel of Love at noon. And so his host reveals himself to be quite the clever young man. He opens himself to Prospect slowly...like a flower.

"But then I got lost, and the storm began," he says. "You couldn't have known that would happen. And it wasn't noon when I met you."

"I didn't know that you'd get lost or when the storm would hit. But I figured you'd show up at the Tunnel of Love sooner or later. And you did."

So. Sometimes what looks like an accident is really part of a plan…and sometimes a plan is just a string of accidents. "I'm very happy to meet you, Lito Fulton Sanchez," Prospect says. *"Again."*

Prospect asks Lito what conclusions he came to after observing him. He says he discovered that Prospect trusts people too easily. That at the rate he's going, the world will chew him up and spit him out like old chewing gum.

Lito spends the better part of an hour teaching his new friend how to float on his back. How to float higher in the water by filling his lungs up with air. Most of what Lito knows about swimming he's learned from his swimming coach, Coach Dinwiddie. When Prospect floats on his back, he can't hear anything because his ears are underwater, so he just looks up at the sky, and it is so peaceful—it makes him feel calm and happy. He floats and loses track of time until a big kid comes along and does a cannonball dive off the board, sending a tidal wave in Prospect's direction, making him sink into the blue water.

ᦂ

The next morning, Lito and Prospect go back to the Y so the Pre-born can meet Coach Dinwiddie to ask him more questions about swimming. But that's not completely true. Prospect wants to ask about Lito's life, his foster family.

"I like swimming, Coach Dinwiddie," Prospect says, "but that's not really the reason I wanted to talk with you." The coach is a tall, thin African American man. He has a pair of swimming goggles around his neck.

"So what's on your mind, young man?" the coach says, rubbing his chin.

"I'm kinda worried about Lito," he says. "I'm staying with him for a short time, and he seems depressed that he's never been adopted."

Dinwiddie lets out a deep, rich laugh. "Is that what he told you? He's only the most popular foster kid I've worked with at the YMCA, and I've worked with a lot. That boy is a *parent magnet,* know what I mean?" Dinwiddie says, drumming a pencil on his desk. "Tell you what. You seem like a sincere person. It's against my policy to talk about a student's personal problems, but I suppose we could talk about him as long as we never refer to him by name."

"It's a deal," Prospect says.

"Well this Certain Somebody has attention deficit disorder. The boy's attention keeps wandering. Sooner or later, the foster parents give up. They get tired of fanning out through the neighborhood after dark with flashlights in hand, trying to find him. And find him they do: fast asleep on a swing in someone's backyard, or on a bus stop bench curled up like a little homeless person. Sooner or later, the prospective parents return a Certain Somebody to the foster care system. It isn't because they don't care about him; it's that they feel…unable to guide him properly." Coach Dinwiddie says that this young man never seems to remember that so many people want him. Only that he was rejected. "I can't break through to him," sighs the swim coach. "I just hope someone does...before it's too late."

"What do you mean 'before it's too late'?" Prospect says.

"Before he gives up. Calls it a day. Checks out of the Hotel of Life forever. Know what I mean, jellybean? Lito needs a purpose. A passion. A goal he can work toward. It might help focus him." And Prospect knows what he means. So he nods and smiles, and Dinwiddie smiles too, and that's how he knows it's time to leave.

16. STARFISH

Prospect heads back to the pool where he finds his new friend Lito doing backward somersaults underwater. Lito holds his nose to keep the water out. Gradually he stops twirling and comes to a halt. Prospect smiles at a job well done.

A girl sits down along the ledge of the pool, dangling her feet in the water. She looks at them as they drift on their noodles. When Prospect looks at her, it looks like she's about to say something. But then she stops herself and looks away. He thinks about asking her to join them in the pool, but he feels shy. Maybe he will ask her the next time he sees her.

"I'm planning to escape this summer," says Lito.

"Why?"

"After I turn eighteen, I'll be free. I'll leave the foster funhouse forever! Get my own place, get a decent job. Doesn't even have to be a great job. I'll be free." Little kids are doing cannon balls in the deep end of the pool, making little watery explosions. The two fellows float on their backs with their noodles under their arms.

"Lito, I need your help with something. It's kind of an important project. Do you think you could lend me a hand?"

"Maybe. What's the project?"

"Are you good with computer searches? Are you good at finding things that are lost?"

"I'm fucking extraordinary with computer searches."

"I need to try to find someone. She's missing."

"Cool. Who is it?"

Prospect stands up in the pool to face Lito. "She's…my sister. I found out she was the first Pre-born. But you can't tell anyone about this. Swear?" Lito stands up in the pool also.

"Holy crap. For real?"

"I need to hear you swear."

"I swear."

"I want to find her. For one thing, she's my sister, and I should meet her. For another thing, I think she's the only other Pre-born in the world. I'll pay you for your time. But you only have a week to find her. And when I say find her, I mean you have to figure out a way for me to meet her in person. Deal?"

"Deal. Sounds like an awesome project," Lito says.

"I've got access to some funds," the Pre-born says. "I could pay you a thousand dollars total if you bring me face-to-face with my sister within the week."

"Damn! You ain't playin'."

"Tell you what. I'll pay you five hundred now and five hundred when you bring her in. That money includes expenses, so if you need to travel and eat, use that money, ok? I'll give you more if you need it. I'll pay you back at the house."

"I won't let you down, man. In fact right after I get out of the pool—I'm gonna head for home so I can start googling. Just give me her name and as much information as you have on her." Prospect is encouraged to see Lito taking this project seriously. Plus, he's dying to meeting Joyce. They'll have lots to talk about.

Lito gets out of the pool and says he'll start the search right now. Prospect decides to stay in the pool. It reminds him of something. What does it remind him of? Gradually, it's gotten very busy at the pool. There must be about fifty kids in and around the water: some floating in inner tubes and some swimming like tadpoles, some guys standing in the shallow end talking trash with their pals, some pretty girls in sunglasses tanning themselves in lawn chairs like they're movie stars.

He searches the ledges for the shy girl who dangled her legs in the water earlier today, but he doesn't see her. His eyes scan below the surface of the water. The good swimmers are doing laps, kicking off when they come to the end of the pool. That's when he sees something, something at the bottom of the pool. It's a teenager's body, resting on the bottom like it's sleeping. Why is he the only one who sees this?

The body does not stir. "Shit shit shit," Prospect mutters to himself. "I'm going in!" he announces, even though he doesn't know how to swim. He pretends he is one of the good swimmers. He twirls his arms like a propeller and kicks his legs the way they do. And suddenly, miraculously, he is swimming. When Prospect touches the body, there is no reaction. He carefully pulls the body toward the surface. That's when he sees it is a pretty young girl with very short hair like a boy's.

It is the girl who looked like she was about to say something.

As Prospect pulls her to the edge of the pool, the real lifeguard finally appears. He pushes him away like he has done something wrong, as if he has harmed her instead of helping her. "Whatever," he says to himself…because that's what young kids say in situations like this. The lifeguard begins his life-saving techniques. All the kids crowd around clutching their inner tubes to see what all the excitement is about. But despite all efforts, the lifeguard is unable to bring the girl back to life. She has already left for parts unknown. Prospect suddenly wishes his new friend Lito was here. But there is no one here for him to talk with, to share the terrible news with. Finally the ambulance comes to cart the girl away, and the crowd goes back to whatever it was doing…floating on floatation devices, laughing with friends.

Prospect wades over to a tall athletic boy in the pool. "Did you know her, the drowned girl?" he asks. No, he's never seen her before.

Finally a girl comes up to Prospect and says, "That was Luz. Luz Ramirez. She was fourteen, I think. Her name means *light* in Spanish, but in English I think it means *to lose*…as in the opposite of winning." It is only a small piece of information she has given him, but it is more than he had before, back when Luz was just a girl without a story. He is full of questions. "Was she happy?" "What were her best subjects in school?" "Who were her friends?"

But the girl doesn't even try to answer his questions. "She's dead. Get over it. Let the poor girl rest in peace." She walks away, vanishing into the crowd of teens whispering secrets in one another's ears.

Prospect goes back to the house, but Lito is not home. He lies down for a moment just to close his eyes and catch his breath. When he opens his eyes again, he is surprised to find himself underwater.

He's lying on a bed of seaweed at the bottom of the ocean. High above him he can see bits of sunlight sparkling on the ocean's surface. He knows it's the ocean because there are starfish moving in his hands. From time to time, they reach out with their star points, tickling his palms. A trio of boys backstroke their way lazily through the water about ten feet above him, blotting out the sunlight. And then a pretty girl's face floats up next to his. She has short, punky hair like a boy's. She reminds Prospect of someone, but he doesn't know who. When the girl and he speak, they hear each other, even though they are underwater in the middle of an ocean.

"It's you, isn't it?" Prospect says.

"Me?" she asks. He feels a starfish begin to move in his hand.

"The girl who drowned. The girl who was about to say something."

She smiles shyly. "I suppose I am. I had hoped I would be remembered for greater things."

"I'm sorry I didn't know you better," is the only thing Prospect can think of to say. The starfish carefully climbs out of his hand and falls in slow motion to the ocean floor making no sound when it hits bottom. It then slowly climbs up Luz's leg, then to her

stomach, pausing for a moment on her bellybutton. He wonders if it tickles.

"Are you my next Referral?" Prospect asks.

"I don't know what that means," she says. "But I thought you should know that my drowning wasn't an accident. It was a choice. But your trying to save me was probably the sweetest thing anyone ever did for me in my whole life."

The starfish now comes to rest in the middle of Luz's face, veiling both her eyes. He can only see her lips. She leans over Prospect and kisses him on the cheek. He has never been kissed by another person before. It feels good, like a blessing. As the starfish stirs once more and climbs down from her face—Prospect sees it is not Luz any longer, but Lito. They are standing so close. Lito is kissing him, and Prospect is letting him. A seventeen-year-old man kissing an embryo in the body of a twenty-year-old man. Who is taking advantage of whom? This is complicated. This is a gray area. Prospect doesn't know what he's doing, but the kiss feels so wonderful it can't be wrong.

When the Pre-born opens his eyes this time—*really* opens them—he's back in his room, and it really is Lito leaning over and kissing him on the cheek. What does it mean? Prospect is afraid to say anything for fear it might break the spell. Finally Lito says, "You were sleeping. I was trying to wake you. Like they do in fairy tales. With a kiss on the cheek."

"Lito, something terrible happened at the pool," he says. And now they both know what they have do: turn on a lamp, sit up, and pretend nothing has happened when in fact something has happened. Was it a fairy tale kiss like Lito said? Or something else?

"A girl drowned in the pool," Prospect says and turns on the light. "Her name was Luz Ramirez. Did you know—"

"Oh shit! Luz!" he says. "Very short hair, right?"

"Like a boy's," Prospect says, nodding.

MONKEY BUSINESS

17. THE WONDERS OF THE PREB-CAM

Karl Bangor and Trish Mesmer watch Prospect's Referral with Lito via Preb-Cam with great interest. They are in Trish's office at Infinity and they are mesmerized. When the screen first came up, they found themselves in the middle of Prospect's underwater dream of the drowning girl, which was confusing as heck. Then when Prospect woke up, things were a little easier to follow—though Trish and Karl were both surprised by the kiss from Lito. And then they realized that Prospect had witnessed the drowning of a young girl at the pool.

"Wow," says Karl Bangor. "A lot is happening in this Referral, and not one moment of it is dull, but I'm not sure enough of the right things are happening. Apparently my pep talk about getting to the point of the Referral had no effect whatsoever on Lito. Two days have gone by and the subject of Prospect's birth decision has not even come up!"

Trish powers down the Preb-Cam and chooses her words carefully. "Karl, they may not have spoken directly about the birth decision, but Lito has clearly shared his experience of the world with Prospect. I think that's just as valid. He's shared his love of swimming, his disappointment with the various families he's been a part of…"

"If this was a reality TV show, that would be wonderful. But this is a bio-experiment. Do I have to remind you that several clocks are ticking, Trish? We have a major press conference coming up, and frankly at this rate—I'm not sure we're going to have anything newsworthy to report. What do you think?"

"I'll call Lito and Prospect right now, and remind them to discuss the birth decision ASAP. That they must stay focused for the sake of the experiment," Trish says.

"Fine," says Karl. "Because if you aren't able to provide the proper oversight to this project, I'm sure there's someone at Big Farm who's just dying to step in and take over for you."

Trish picks up her cell. "That won't be necessary, Karl. But I appreciate your candor."

She calls it candor, but really that's just a code word. When she says "I appreciate your candor" what she really is saying is "Fuck you, you micro-managing son of a bitch." But if she said that, she'd lose her job. And she does not want to lose her job.

18. THE HOUSE IS TOO
BIG TONIGHT

Prospect's cell rings. "Hi, Trish." Karl watches the conversation by Preb-Cam. She proceeds to talk to him about the goal of each Referral. The need for focus. Then she asks to speak to Lito.

"Trish, that blue cheeseburger was awesome, by the way. Thanks again." And she basically tells Lito the same thing. That he's being paid to act as a Referral. To influence Prospect in his birth decision based on his own experience. Lito tells her not to worry. That they will talk about that shortly. They hang up.

For dinner, Lito sends out for pizza with every possible topping. It's their last supper. A six-pack of root beer. Cheezy Bread. It's a feast really, but Prospect isn't very hungry. He'd like more time, but he knows Trish is looking for less time, not more. "Here's my question for you," he says to Lito. "If you knew back then what you know now…would you have chosen to be born?"

"Hell no! Listen, Prospect, there are only two things I'm sure of in this world: One, my folks didn't want me, and two, I didn't want my parents. And I clearly didn't want to be born. They had to pull me out of the womb."

"What? What do you mean?"

"With forceps!"

"You're kidding! I didn't know they used—"

"I know someone who knows someone who manages the database for the hospital where I was born," says Lito. "It started out, he was trying to help me find out who my birth parents were. Then he came across my mother's medical records. I shoulda asked him what my mother's name was but I didn't think of it at the time and I didn't want to get him in trouble. What he did find out was that they had to pry me out of my mother with forceps! It was fucked up! I mean, if a kid doesn't want to be born that badly, they should honor his wishes or some shit like that. Know what I mean?"

"I didn't know they used forceps…" is all Prospect can say. "I'm sorry that happened to you, Lito."

ᔆᔆ

Meanwhile at Big Farm, Karl Bangor and Trish Mesmer watch the Referral in progress with great interest. "At least they're talking about birth decisions. Prospect takes direction well," Karl says. "Now if you can just fix Prospect up with some folks who aren't clinically depressed, we'll be in business."

"Prospect's mother was pretty happy," she volunteers.

"Yeah, if you don't count the way she killed her daughter with her mind." He pulls out his pocket watch from his vest pocket. He can either draft a report to Corporate on how the Pre-born Project is progressing—or go grab some salmon roe at Sushi Central. Or both.

"Oh. Well, his other Referrals include a very upbeat greeting card writer, a successful businessman, and a gifted painter." Trish turns the Preb-Cam off. The two colleagues prepare to leave Infinity for the night.

"You know I'm going to be watching Prospect's adventures very closely, as are the various decision-makers at Big Farm," Karl says. "If I start to feel that things are starting to go south on this project, I will jump into the experiment myself and take my turn as a Referral. Don't think I won't. I've done shows in community theater. If I can't convince the little bastard to be born—nobody can."

"I assure you that won't be necessary," she says. "But thanks for the offer of support, Karl." Of course she is being sarcastic as hell, but Karl doesn't think she's capable of sarcasm, so he just thinks she's sucking up. But she's not sucking up. She's searching for the proverbial chink in his armor that might lead to his downfall.

"You've done some good work tonight, Trish. Don't let me down. Don't let yourself down." As they depart, she flicks the light switch and locks her office door. Karl walks off down the hall. Trish suddenly has a taste for angel hair pasta smothered in pesto sauce at Leona's. Comfort food.

❧

Back at the Last Supper of Lito and Prospect, they are still talking about forceps and birth choices.

"I mean, did anyone ask me what I wanted?" Lito says. "Did they send me a formal invitation to come into this world? No!" He is almost yelling now. "They just assumed. Who wouldn't want to be born into this Technicolor world of ours…with its built-in laugh track and IKEA placemats? Me. That's who." When Lito closes his eyes, he appears to be crying. Prospect can't blame him. He has upset him, and that was the last thing he wanted to do.

Prospect reaches out awkwardly and gently rubs his back. "It's okay, Lito. I'm glad you were born anyway." And that's when Prospect does it: returns kindness with kindness. He leans over and kisses Lito on the cheek. It is smooth as a peach.

And now Lito returns the kiss. But this time he kisses Prospect on the lips.

And it feels right. Prospect is filled with so many feelings he doesn't know what to do. It's as if in this moment the world makes sense. With this one magic kiss so much happens. They are protecting each other, they are loving each other, they are choosing each other. The kiss feels hot, forbidden, permitted, perfect. Prospect doesn't want it ever to end. When it finally does end, the two fellows look at each other. They look each other in the eye without an ounce of shyness or shame.

In the morning the fellows do not talk about the kiss, but they do not forget about it either. It is the last day of their Referral. "Hey, how's the search for my sister going, Lito?"

"Damn, I knew there was something I was forgetting about. I'm gonna work on that this week."

Prospect is disappointed. "Because you know today is the last day of our Referral."

"No problem, P-man. I am on the case."

"I just want to make sure you're making progress, ya know? Cuz time is of the essence," Prospect says.

"Absolutely. Plus I won't get the other five hundred dollars if I don't come through."

Prospect starts to wonder where Lito's foster parents are. Why haven't they called to check in with him by now? Maybe he's been abandoned again. That would be unforgivable: to give a kid the gift of a house—but not a home. Finally Lito brings out a carton of Chunky Monkey ice cream. He fills their bowls with mountains of banana ice cream topped with chunks of chocolate and walnuts. Once more Prospect confirms that Lito still has his cell phone number, that he'll keep it in a safe place. Prospect asks him to call to keep him posted on his search for Joyce. Lito promises to stay on the case.

Just then a news show comes on. To their surprise, they see Trish Mesmer seated at a table across from a reporter. She has a tiny microphone pinned to her dress. "That's my Facilitator! I know her!" Prospect shouts.

"I've met her too," Lito says. "She took me out for cheeseburgers." They huddle around the TV.

Reporter Robin Thomas looks straight into the camera. "Now here's something that sounds more like a science fiction movie than a bio-experiment," she says. "If you could *preview* the world before choosing to be born—would you? And if you did choose to be born...how might your life be different knowing that you are here by your own choosing? That's the fascinating question behind the Pre-born Project. The results won't be in for years, but that won't keep us from talking about it now on the Discovery Channel. We're here today with Dr. Trish Mesmer, the scientist behind the Pre-born Project. Trish, welcome."

The camera cuts to Trish. "Thank you, Robin. I am thrilled to be here. This project is all made possible by generous support from Big Farm Technologies."

"The premise of your experiment…it's bold. It's sexy." Onscreen behind the women, there is an animation of a cartoon baby crawling through a flowchart, one square at a time.

"That baby must be me!" Prospect says.

The reporter says, "This points the way to a whole new generation of children, doesn't it? A whole new species?"

"Well, we'll still be homo sapiens. But you could say it points the way to a new generation of *possibilities*—"

"Here's what I mean," says the newscaster. "And I'm sorry for cutting you off. One by one, these new children appear. Hopefully some of them will *choose* to be born. Now suddenly, I'm feeling a little old school. Why wasn't I given the chance to choose?" Robin is pouting now in a childlike way that tells us her question is only half-serious.

"I see your point. But that's really the nature of evolution, isn't it? The latest iteration of a species *should* have the best options and capabilities." Onscreen behind her, the cartoon baby has now crossed a finish line, and the cartoon crowd goes wild, jumping up and down. The baby grins from ear to ear.

"You're right, Trish. But what will you do if the Pre-borns choose *not* to be born? Let's face it: the world has got its upsides, but Utopia it ain't. We still have wars that solve nothing, that we learn nothing from. We finally cured a horrible disease like AIDS last year, and that's great—but three new baffling diseases have popped up in its place. Plus as a species, I don't know if we're *evolving*. Sometimes I think we go one step forward, two steps back."

"Robin, you bring up an excellent point. I've talked to the good people at Big Farm about this. And we are prepared for whatever the outcome of the Pre-born Project will be. Perhaps we'll learn less about the Pre-born and more about ourselves. It may turn out to be a report card for planet earth. How viable, how attractive, are we as a destination point to the casual visitor? Whatever we learn, it will be valuable for humanity. I have no doubt of that."

"Well, you certainly have thought about all the angles here. Thanks for stopping by today." Now Robin looks straight into the camera again. "When we come back—personality pills. Which ones really work, and which ones could be fatal?"

Prospect turns the TV off. "I'm famous. They were talking about me! Okay, so they didn't mention me by name or show my picture, but they talked about the Pre-born Project."

"I didn't know there was a celebrity in the house," says Lito. "But why didn't they show a picture of you? That was lame."

"They're trying to keep my identity a secret, I think. For my own safety."

"Gotcha."

There being nothing more to say, the two fellows turn in for the night, each headed to their separate, lonely rooms.

The Pre-born tosses and turns. It is the last night of the Referral. He can't seem to find a comfortable position to rest in. He gets out of bed and pushes open the curtains so he can see the real stars, not the ones painted on the ceiling with luminous green paint. His mind wanders.

And now out loud, he says these words as he writes them into his notebook. "Once you get over the miracle that you are born at all, you have to get over the next miracle: that you're still here. That you have survived all this time without being hit by a car…or being killed in a war…or being crushed to pieces by everyday sadness."

Suddenly there is a knock on his door. "You up, Superstar?" asks Lito.

19. FALLING STARS

"Come on in," says Prospect. Lito is wearing a T-shirt from Disneyland and gym shorts. The air conditioning throughout the house makes it very chilly. "How you doing, Lito?"

"I can't sleep."

"Me either. Want some Pringles?" Prospect says, grabbing the can from the nightstand. He crunches into an artificially formed potato chip.

"Prospect, my man, I wanted to ask you a favor. Could you take me with you when you leave here?" He doesn't know what to say. "I'm no trouble." Prospect just looks at him and raises an eyebrow or two. "Okay, so I'm a little trouble."

"Lito, I don't even know where I'm going yet myself. Know what I mean?" Lito bites into another chip without looking at him. "Tell you what. I won't say yes, I won't say no. Let me look into it. I'll call you."

"You'll call me. That's what everyone says," he complains. Lito seems restless. He can't sit still. Finally he says, "Can I sleep in your room? The house is too big tonight."

It's hard for Prospect to say no to Lito. So many people have said no to him already.

So he lets him stay in this bedroom whose ceiling is painted with fake, glow-in-the-dark stars. But he decides that once Lito is asleep, he'll take a pillow and sleep on the floor. And before long, Lito is snoring. But before Prospect can make his getaway, one of Lito's arms lands gently around his shoulder. As if it just fell from the sky like a falling star. Like the arm had a will of its own. And that's how the two men sleep through the night...Lito's arm cradled over Prospect's shoulder. Prospect has to admit he likes this feeling an awful lot. He feels safe. No, more than just safe. *Needed.* It's a feeling that's new to the Pre-born. This is a moment he must remember. Frame it behind glass and hang it on a wall for all the world to see.

When Prospect awakens the next morning, Lito is nowhere to be found. There is no note, no nothing. He scans the house for a souvenir, some memento that says their time together was real, was not a dream. All he finds is Lito's black hooded jacket. It is enough. Prospect stuffs it into his bag. Lito will have to come find him to get the jacket back.

He gathers the rest of his things and locks the door behind him, leaving the key under the door mat. Prospect says good-bye to this too-big house. He wonders if Lito is watching him from some secret place...hiding in a sycamore tree, or sitting in a friend's car peering at him from behind dark glasses. Prospect heads for the train that will take him back to Infinity Medical Center.

He waves good-bye to anyone who might be watching.

❦

Back at Infinity, Trish is eager to debrief. She has filled the table in the conference room with a tempting array of Danishes, donuts, and bagels. The cream cheese flavors range from salmon to spicy pumpkin. And of course there is plenty of coffee to keep him wired and talking. Prospect is aware that she didn't put out this kind of spread for his first Referral debriefing. When Trish walks in—he jumps up to greet her. "I saw you!"

"Good morning, Prospect."

"On TV, I mean. I saw you on TV last night."

She seems embarrassed. "Oh, that! It's part of my job description to do those media appearances. To get people excited about the project. I would have told you about it—"

"You should have. Because it was about me too, Trish! That cartoon baby on the screen was me, wasn't it?"

"Yes, I suppose it was." Trish grabs some coffee for herself and a blueberry Danish. "What I'm excited about is that you've now met two of your Referrals. How is it going so far?"

"Before we get into that, what's the occasion?" he says gesturing at the array of sweets on the table.

"No occasion. Humans don't need a reason to treat themselves well."

The Pre-born is far too hungry to argue with her. He grabs a raisin bagel and spreads pumpkin cream cheese over it. It is a combination that can only be further enhanced by coffee. Meanwhile Trish has flipped open her laptop and switched it on. "So? How did it go with Lito Sanchez? I want to know everything—your impressions, your activities, your conversations."

"Lito…well, he's something. In some ways, he's fearless, and in other ways, he's like…I don't know…glass. Like he could break apart into a million pieces."

"Ah. So there is more to Lito Sanchez than meets the eye. Why does it not surprise me that you'd see that?"

He proceeds to share Lito's regret that he was ever born, the forceps story, his hope that Prospect will choose *not* to be born. But of course she has heard all this through the Preb-Cam. Still she types up notes in her iPad. "Did he have any impressions of me, as Facilitator? I mean, I hope he felt comfortable with me. I want all project participants to feel…*valued*."

"Uh, well…he didn't really say anything particular about you…"

"That's good," she says. She is disappointed of course.

"Oh wait, he did say…he said that he thought you were a very good hostess. And charming," he offers.

"He said I was charming?" Trish appears to be blushing. Giddy almost.

"He did." Prospect wonders why Trish even cares what a Referral thinks of her. Isn't it more important what Prospect thinks of the Referral?

"So tell me, how would you say your encounter with Lito Sanchez has swayed you in your birth decision versus your encounter with your mother? What pros and cons came up for you?"

"I'm not sure if I've really thought about those things yet," he says.

Trish's hands hover over her computer. She purses her lips. "Let's try a non-linear approach. If Lito and Rebecca were pieces of silverware, what kind of silverware would they be?"

This question catches Prospect off-guard, but he tries to answer as best he can. "Well, if my Referrals were kitchen utensils—and I don't exactly know why they would be—I guess my mother would be a spatula. And Lito...he'd be a fork."

"Why would Lito be a fork?"

Prospect smiles at Trish. "Don't you want to know why my mother would be a spatula?"

To his way of thinking, it's much more intriguing to describe someone as a spatula than as a fork. She looks at Prospect; Prospect looks at her. It's as if he has caught her doing something wrong. This extra special interest in all things Lito. She takes a sip of coffee; he takes a sip of coffee. It is a moment that has become larger than it should have been.

Finally she says, "Of course, Prospect. I'm interested in *all* your Referrals." Prospect bites into his raisin bagel; Trish bites into her blueberry Danish. And for a moment everything almost seems normal again. Almost, but not quite.

He explains how Lito is like a fork because he's little and direct and goes straight for what he wants. The way a fork does. But his mother is different. She is a server, a gatherer. Just as a spatula is. But Trish doesn't seem to be listening. She is somewhere else. Her eyes look blankly out the conference room window. Prospect doesn't ask her what she's thinking. If she wanted him to know, she would tell him. People are entitled to have their secrets. Even scientists.

20. PROSPECT'S BLOG

I was hit by a CTA bus today. The Broadway 36. I didn't feel any pain. But in that instant, my soul flew out of my body and into the small body of a passing pigeon. This is how I learned I am afraid of heights, because birds are always flying so high above the earth. The view made me very dizzy. I don't know which is worse: getting hit by a bus, or being a bird that is afraid of heights.

This is the start of my brand-new blog. Do you like it? I hope so.

Trish said it would be a good idea if I wrote down my thoughts. To tell the story of my time here, so that I might learn from my experiences. She told me that any good story has to grab the reader's attention…and never let it go. And that is why I started off my blog today by talking about getting hit by a bus. (I wasn't really hit by a bus, but I've ridden on buses, and I know they are big, so I imagined what it might be like to be hit by one.)

And then the part about the bird—I just made up. I hope it's okay to make stuff up. If it's not okay, I'm sure Trish will tell me.

Lito. Lito. Lito. I keep thinking of him. Why?

I think something is happening between us. I think we are becoming friends. My first friend. But what did it mean when he put his arm around me in his sleep? What did it mean when he kissed me on the cheek during my starfish dream? It was as if he was trying to break a spell. Or trying to cast one.

21. BOYS AND THEIR TOYS

Prospect and his new Referral talk on the phone; his Referral tells him he will be driving a shiny blue car. It is getting dark, so Prospect is happy that he will be getting a ride.

Dear Prospect,

For your next Referral, you will meet Trevor Grueling (pronounced GROO-ling). By trade, he is an account exec specializing in mergers & acquisitions. At forty-two years of age, Trevor is your first Referral who openly and vehemently opposes the Pre-born Project. He said he wanted to represent a divergent view of the experiment. I trust you two will have plenty to talk about. Oh yes, Trevor is a representative of the second type of person you had wished to meet: someone who is difficult to get along with.

Class is a big deal in America. Wealth. Lifestyle. The Haves and the Have-Nots. What can money buy? What can it not buy? Trevor has a comfortable life. I hope you enjoy your time with him. By the way, your Referral after this one is with Irene Iwanski. Irene is a representative of the last type of person you wanted to meet: someone who is truly happy. In some ways, she is Trevor's polar opposite. She's quite easy to get along with and quite happy with her modest life. A retired greeting card writer, she believes there is a card for every occasion in life. And if there is no card for your unique situation in life—she will make one for you while you wait.

Dr. Trish Mesmer

Now a sapphire blue sports car pulls up to the curb. "Get in," he says, "it won't bite you." He pushes a button, and the door swings open to welcome him. Prospect peers down at the driver's face and sees a man wearing sunglasses, though it isn't sunny at all. When he gets in the car, the car *does* bite him: his shirt tail gets caught in the automatic car door. "Sorry," the man says, setting his shirt free with the push of a button. "What's your name again?"

"I was given the name Prospect because people have high hopes for me."

"Right," says the man.

"I assume you're Trevor Grueling."

There is a pause. He looks Prospect in the eye and says, "Trevor who? Can't say I've had the pleasure." What's going on? Prospect wonders.

"I thought you were my Referral, Trevor Grueling..."

He reaches over and grabs the Pre-born's hand very hard and whispers, "I'm *sick*." He is creeping Prospect out. Is he in danger? There is a hovering moment of silence between them. Prospect looks out the window and tries to gauge how fast the car is moving. Can he leap to safety? Suddenly, the man bursts out laughing, hysterically. "Boy, you shoulda seen the look on your face! I had you going there."

And in that single moment, whoever this man turns out to be, Prospect does not like him. This man he has known for all of three minutes who is indeed Trevor Grueling. But then, he got what he asked for: someone who is difficult. Trevor's eyes are focused on the road ahead. "You must forgive me. I can't resist practical jokes. It's genetic," he says, still laughing. "It runs in the family. Pranksters, every last one of us. So how do you like the world so far, Prospect? Have the scientists removed any interesting vital organs yet?"

"So far, so—" and before he can finish the sentence, off they speed onto Lakeshore Drive, leaving a plume of white smoke behind them. They can't really have a normal conversation; they may have broken the sound barrier a couple times. Before Prospect knows it, they are home. Trevor angles his car into the garage and tosses his keys to a kid on duty with a pierced eyebrow.

As an account executive specializing in mergers & acquisitions—Trevor can't say which he likes more. *Mergers* are great because he gets to bring together two companies with different cultures and merge them into a single entity, whether they like it or not. It's a process that Trevor finds both traumatic and cost-effective. *Acquisitions* are great because he gets to arrange the outright purchase of a smaller company to be absorbed seamlessly into a larger one. This process is known as "corporate osmosis" or the diffusion of two corporate entities through membranes or porous partitions.

Trevor's talents in this arena are not limited to the board-room. His personal mergers as he calls them (i.e., his indulgence in meaningless sex) are only matched by his personal acquisitions (i.e., the stunning array of toys he's acquired as a member of the well-to-do). These toys manifest in the form of various cars, homes, leisure options, and assorted gadgets. "Ain't mergers and acquisitions grand?" he says.

"Hmm," is all Prospect says.

Trevor tilts his head for a moment and looks at the Pre-born, but he is doing his best Sphinx impersonation. Trevor inserts his key into the door and says, "By the way, I should tell you up front: I don't like bio-experiments, and I trust Trish Mesmer as far as I can throw her." This is the first time Prospect has heard anyone speak badly of Trish, and it surprises him. But the Sphinx remains silent.

When Trevor opens the door to his home, the first thing the Pre-born's eye is drawn to is the sunken living room. It is in the shape of a perfect circle. Lighted recessed steps lead you down into the area. One half of the circle is devoted to a large black leather sofa that fits like a crescent against the wall. The other half of the circle is devoted to three large flat screen TVs. Each monitor is tuned to a different station. On one screen is a music video; on another is a news broadcast; on the last is a movie. Trevor explains that there are matching headphones so that if three people want to watch three different shows they may do so without ever leaving one another's side. He explains that this creates a sense of community.

"Hmm," Prospect says again.

There are little fountains around the place…water spilling out onto different shapes of rock, glass, marble. They make a relaxing sound. The walls of his home are filled with old movie posters: *The Graduate, Jules & Jim, Annie Hall.* He says it shows women he has a sensitive side. "Your place is kinda cool," Prospect says.

"I'm thinking of moving at the end of the year. I'm bored with it already," Trevor says. They step down into the sunken living room. Trevor leans close to one of the screens and breathes on it; he rubs the glass with a handkerchief.

"So please tell me more about your concerns with bio-experiments in general and the Pre-born Project in particular," Prospect says.

"Ah…before we talk business, let me try to be a good host and offer you a drink."

"Oh. A cola would be great if you have it."

"You're kidding." Trevor pauses. "You're not kidding. One cola coming up." His Referral rescues a can of soda from the fridge. "Hey, do you know any single Pre-born girls you could introduce me to?"

"No, Trevor, I don't," he says. "And if I did, I wouldn't."

Prospect watches as the carbonation bubbles bubble in his glass. Trevor fixes himself a martini. "I guess I just keep looking for love in all the wrong places. But it's hard to know what the *right* places are. Know what I mean?" Prospect just smiles, and he enjoys the nice leather sofa. Then he reaches for the TV remote and starts clicking buttons, watching the images change. Suddenly Prospect feels sentimental, for it reminds him of his days in the womb with his CyberSavant.

"So you were telling me your feelings about the Pre-born Project..." Prospect begins.

"You got a girlfriend, Prospect?"

"I haven't been born yet, remember?"

"But you have a body. You have needs. You ever have sex before?"

For some reason, this conversation makes Prospect very uncomfortable. With remote in hand, he turns off the TV screens, one by one. Then he turns to face his host. "Look, Trevor, do you mind if we focus a little more on why I'm here? The Pre-born Project?"

Trevor is in the middle of downing his whole martini in one long gulp. He holds up an index finger to request patience. "Let's talk some shop then, shall we? I have nothing against Pre-borns, per se, kiddo. But this project is all wrong."

He looks around Trevor's place to see if there are any signs of caffeine in the kitchen, as he suspects it's going to be a long night. "You don't have any coffee, do you?"

"I do, as a matter of fact," he says. They move to the kitchen area. The Pre-born sits at the table as his Referral scoops some aromatic coffee into the coffeemaker.

"Here's the way I look at it," Prospect begins. He thinks back to Trish's own explanation. "Science is about moving forward—not staying where you are. Is it fair that in the last century thousands, maybe millions of people suffering from depression either killed themselves or were forced to live horrible, sad lives, while people of our time can find relief as close as the corner drugstore? You see, it isn't really about fairness.

It's about choice. Each generation *should* have more choices than the one that went before it." Wow. Prospect can't believe he just said all that. It sounded like he was channeling Trish Mesmer.

Trevor pours a steaming mug of coffee for his guest. "Call me a conservative because I certainly do, but I don't think science belongs in the delivery room. Whatever happened to mother nature? Doesn't she have a say in these things anymore? Test tube babies, personality pills, memory transplants, Pre-borns—all that stuff gives me the creeps," he says. The Pre-born watches the cream swirl as he stirs his coffee. "No offense. Science is your religion, Prospect. That's understandable. It's where you came from. It isn't where I came from."

"And where *did* you come from, Trevor? Weren't you born in a modern hospital powered by electricity?" He takes a deep sip. The coffee hits the spot perfectly. "Weren't you turned into a three-dimensional image with the help of an ultrasound? Weren't you surrounded by all the finest breakthroughs of science, all the bells and whistles, that big money could buy?"

Trevor doesn't miss a beat. "I didn't come from CyberSavants and petri dishes."

"And what about penicillin, Prozac, and contact lenses? Do you disapprove of those things too?" For the first time, he doesn't have a snappy comeback. There is only a lovely silence filled by the calming trickle of water fountains. "I'm sorry you didn't get to choose to be born," Prospect says. "But if you knew back then what you know now, what would you have chosen?"

Trevor takes a deep drink of his coffee and thinks for a moment. Then he just looks at Prospect and says, "We'll never know, will we?" He stirs the sugar at the bottom of his mug. It is a musical sound. "Prospect, I have something to tell you, and I hope it doesn't change anything. On second thought, I hope it changes *everything*...for the better. It's a little secret I've been keeping from you. From Trish too."

"What is it?" Prospect studies Trevor's face for clues.

He just smiles. "Once I was the subject of a bio-experiment myself."

22. HALFWAY HOME

"One key to the success of the Pre-born Project is in the selection of Referrals for the Pre-born to meet. For that reason, we have selected a very diverse group of individuals. Some you'd love to have brunch with, some you'd be afraid to meet down a dark alley at night. The Preb-Cam device allows us to view everything the Pre-born sees for safety purposes. Intervention would only occur if the Pre-born was in harm's way. We don't anticipate that such an occasion will arise."

— Dr. Trish Mesmer, Scientist
Big Science Magazine

Trish adjusts the focus on the Preb-Cam. She's been watching Prospect's Referral with Trevor, and it makes for a prickly viewing. "I trust Trish Mesmer as far as I can throw her," is one choice quote from the Referral that she will not forget anytime soon. And Trevor's confession that he was the subject of a botched bio-experiment certainly will give Prospect pause as he considers his next step. This is no accident. Trish wanted to introduce doubt into the Pre-born's 360-degree view of the world and the dilemma facing him, but now she's starting to wonder if she was too successful.

Three Referrals almost complete, and two to go. Trish is eager to assess how the experiment is going. She needs to prepare a mid-point report for Karl.

*** REBECCA BOULANGET ***

This Referral was fairly life-affirming. Prospect got a chance to spend some days with his potential future family. To go to the amusement park and have meals together. Rebecca and her husband presented themselves as capable, if nervous, future parents. **Best Quote:** "There's so much more of you you'll experience…if you decide to stick around. To be born, that is."

Downside: It was all going positively until Prospect started to inquire about his missing sister Joyce. It is not yet certain what impact she will have on his birth decision.

*** LITO SANCHEZ ***

This Referral was probably most successful in that Prospect developed a true friendship with Lito. Since Lito is a teenager and the youngest Referral, it makes sense he would feel a stronger affinity with the Pre-born. These two definitely bonded. There is reason to believe that there was some romantic/physical attraction between these two as well. **Best Quote:**

"Prospect, I know you're leaving soon. I was wondering if you could take me with you."

Downside: Lito's wish-I-was-never-born worldview made the Referral ending a bit of a downer. And his attention deficit issues introduce the notion of mental illness and how it colors perception. Time will tell whether these two will stay in touch. It will be interesting to see which is a bigger deciding factor on Prospect's birth choice: the powerful bond that friendship can be, or Lito's perception that life is an endless parade of disappointments.

*** TREVOR GRUELING ***

The jury's still out on this Referral-in-progress as they are just meeting, but Trevor is definitely a loose cannon, a wild card. He is the Referral most likely to introduce the world of sex and politics to Prospect. The fact that Trevor was also the subject of another bio-experiment will surely intrigue the Pre-born. **Best Quote:** "Science is your religion, Prospect. That's understandable. It's where you came from."

Downside: Trevor's distrust of bio-experiments in general and the Pre-born Project in particular will likely have some influence on Prospect. Trevor's anti-science stance seems to stack the cards against Prospect's choosing to be born at this point. But it's good to represent diverse opinions.

Is Karl Bangor correct in wanting to skew the Referrals toward the birth-positive side? She thinks of the final Referrals: Irene Iwanski and Victor Pastelle. Trish starts to seriously consider the advantages of letting Karl step in as a last-minute Referral. This would allow Karl to give the big push toward being born. And if the project doesn't yield an outcome that Big Farm is happy with, at least Karl can't say Trish didn't involve him at a substantial level, and the blame will not fall so squarely on her small shoulders.

She resents that there is Corporate pressure for Prospect to choose to be born. It flies in the face of her scientific training to prefer one outcome over the other. Science and business are not always the most comfortable bedfellows. Maybe she can turn a blind eye for the sake of the greater good. Who knows what other advances would never have happened if scientists dug in their heels and insisted on taking the high road? Maybe Prozac, HIV cocktails, artificial hearts, deep brain stimulation, and face transplants would never have seen the light of day. It's hard to say. But choices are rarely black and white. Right or wrong. They are a million shades of gray.

23. THE WONDER OF IT ALL

Prospect is shocked to hear that Trevor has been part of a bio-experiment. "That first day that you arrived at Infinity, you got a phone call in your room," Trevor says. "A man told you the Pre-born Project was an abomination...that only God could help you."

"That was *you*?"

He nods. He tells Prospect that six years ago he was placed front and center in a bio-experiment called The Persona Project. Each subject was given a chance to donate one of his or her personality traits to science. The trait would be removed permanently so that scientists could study it and find a way to transplant personality traits into personality-challenged recipients one day. In return, the donors would be given significant shares of stock in this cutting-edge research company. Along with a possible place in bio-history.

Trevor found the bio-experiment fascinating. He had just such a personality trait that he'd be willing to give up to science. And an investment in bio-research companies had become the hottest thing on the market and sounded lucrative. The trait that Trevor was willing to part with (he had considered many) was his sense of wonder. The women he dated initially found this trait endearing. He could, for instance, watch the way rain fell across a window pane for hours on end, or listen to a song twenty times and still not be satisfied. But they soon found this behavior childish, spacey, and worse, unmasculine. It was a deal-breaker, romantically.

So Trevor asked the technicians to remove his sense of wonder. After all, he was a businessman, not a poet. What did he really need a sense of wonder for? He signed a contract with the research company and was prepped for surgery which was a simple outpatient procedure. Later with his sense of wonder gone, he found that his interest in romance also was gone. For to be able to love, one needed to be able to imagine. While the procedures were local, the effects were global. The Persona Project had many casualties like Trevor, and so the bio-experiment was a failure.

Trevor moved into this high-rise playhouse and started sleeping under an enormous glass dome each night. He was looking for a chance to be surprised. It's why even now he keeps all three of his TVs on night and day. He doesn't want to miss anything. A breakthrough. A moment of beauty. It's a desperate attempt to rediscover his sense of wonder. He even underwent an operation to reinstall a sense of wonder into his brain. He had to go to Amsterdam for the procedure, as it had yet to be approved in the States. But alas, his body rejected the trait. His wonder-less body had grown accustomed to a state of lowered expectations. (Trevor Grueling is turning out to be a much more complex person than Prospect imagined him to be.)

"I am less a man now than I was before I started the bio-experiment," says his Referral. "I am a walking cautionary tale."

Prospect listens carefully. "But isn't risk part of everything in life, Trevor? Whether it's making a big leap of faith or just…crossing with the light. If there was no risk, wouldn't it be something *other* than life?" Again, there is a silence. A silence filled only by the trickle of water fountains in the penthouse. But he and Trevor are done talking. They have gone as far as words can take them—and they have taken them a good distance.

∽

Trevor Grueling announces that he'd like to take Prospect to a meeting of his support group. It's called Conservatives in an Increasingly Liberal World or CILW. (Members pronounce it "SIL wah.") For in these days of the new millennium as the culture wars rage on – those that embrace the most extreme conservative values find their numbers dwindling. But what they lack in membership – they more than make up for in shrillness and vitriol. Common sense is often kicked to the curb. "Give states the right to secede from the union!" "Let's put an end to minimum wage so we can put more of the unemployed back to work!" These lost souls find refuge in this unique support group.

At the meeting, there are nice little snacks on silver trays. And coffee. Always there is coffee…wherever Prospect goes. One woman walks up to the snack table. She wears black eyeglasses that make her look like the comic-book character Cat Woman. He had once seen this character while surfing through his CyberSavant on pop culture. She wears a tiny black dress that looks like it could fly away in a breeze. The woman scoops up some red punch into her cup and says, "Have you been following this whole Pre-born Project comedy-of-errors in the news?"

"I am aware of the project," he says with a poker face. He doesn't even bother to ask what she thinks of it. No one in this group is likely to approve.

"It's so obvious what they're doing...they're taking the right to choose to a whole new ridiculous level. They're saying abortion is cool as long as it's the baby's own idea. Since when is an embryo capable of making an informed, life-or-death decision?"

Prospect just blinks his big eyes at the woman.

She blinks her cat eyes back at him. "The Pre-born Project gives the embryo the option to abort itself. Doesn't the fact that an embryo has a will of its own prove that it is a living thing—not just an unformed ball of flesh?"

"I guess I see your point," he says.

Trevor appears with an electric blue drink in hand. "I see you've met Kitty." Prospect smiles upon hearing her name.

"Yes. She has some very interesting opinions."

And though Kitty proceeds to ask what brings him to town and how does he know Trevor—Prospect does not mention his true identity as the famed Pre-born. And Trevor fills in the blanks very skillfully. They agreed before the meeting that it's best that he not reveal himself. At least to a tough crowd like this one.

The support group itself turns out to be lively. The opinions expressed are clearly conservative, but not unreasonable. It's not a touchy-feely group, though Prospect suspects that everyone—regardless of their politics—wants to be touched and felt in one way or another.

"Hi, I'm Joan, and I'm a conservative in an increasingly liberal world."

"Hi, Joan," says everyone in the room.

"Tonight I have a terrible confession to make: I'm falling in love with a Democrat." There are audible gasps in the room. Many shake their heads but remain sympathetic. "It's nothing I planned. It's nothing I'd wish on any of my conservative sisters and brothers. But it happened, so there. I don't want to be judged, but I am asking the group for its clear-eyed vision on this matter."

"What do you even talk with him about over dinner?" asks a young man with a smirk in his voice. Several people chuckle at that, much to Joan's discomfort.

"We talk about how our days were, what books we're reading—fiction mostly, what movies we want to see on the weekend..." says Joan.

One woman takes a stab, "I'm trying to be supportive here, Joan. I really am. But don't you spend a lot of energy *avoiding* talking about the things that matter most to you? Have you tried to enlighten him as to the beauty of conservatism?" The whole group is nodding at this remark.

Before she can answer, Trevor jumps in. "Mixed marriages never work. Period. I don't care if the relationship is mixed politically, racially, philosophically, economically, or spiritually." Suffice to say, the discussion goes downhill from here.

At one point, Joan has had enough. "I think maybe I don't belong here anymore, maybe I never did. I think the truth is I'm a conservative in an increasingly *lonely* world." She looks around the room. "I think *that's* what CILW really stands for!" It is so still in the room, you can hear the hum of fluorescent lights overhead.

"Have a blessed day, Joan. Have a blessed life," says an older woman who acts like she might've had her sense of compassion removed. And Joan is out the door.

Trevor moves to the snack table to get some carrot sticks. "The only thing worse than a bleeding-heart liberal is a bleeding-heart conservative. Yikes." Kitty just smiles back at him. The Pre-born is on pins and needles throughout the rest of the meeting, terrified that Kitty will bring up the Pre-born Project. Thankfully, she doesn't. Still that doesn't spare him from a few hours of nervous sweating. And though Prospect can't see his face, his face feels warm…like he may be blushing. Like he's the reddest thing in the room.

After the meeting, the three of them leave CILW Central. "Kitty," Prospect says, "I want to tell you something, but you have to promise to keep it a secret. Okay?"

"Shoot."

"You see, I'm the Pre-born."

Kitty's eyes widen. She shakes her head slowly. She stands up. "You are a devil-child!" she shouts. She holds up two fingers in a sign of the cross.

"No, I'm still the same person I was. I'm just not born yet." Kitty is thinking, thinking.

"I'm going to tell everyone I know who you are! I'm gonna put this on the CILW listserv!"

"Please, Kitty," he says. "You can't tell anyone!"

She stares at him for a long while. Then she lets out a wild cackle. "I'm just jerking your chain, Prospect! Trevor told me before the meeting. Oh, that was fun!"

"You knew?"

"I knew." She is laughing so hard, she is almost crying.

24. ARE WE HAVING
FUN YET?

By the end of the night, Trevor has already hatched a plan for Kitty to join the two of them on an excursion to a nightclub called Hallucination. They ease into Trevor's car. This time Prospect makes sure the automatic door does not take a bite out of his shirttail. Trevor and Kitty sit up front, while Prospect relaxes in the back seat. For a moment, he feels like they are his parents in a parallel world, and he is their child. And they are going on a trip somewhere. Like they have replaced his own sweet parents. Not that he'd want to replace his parents. Still, it's a nice feeling to ride in the back seat and know that someone else is in the front seat watching the road for you. He wonders to himself if Kitty and Trevor are dating.

"So tell me about yourself, Kitty," Prospect says. "What do you *do?*"

She looks at Trevor through her cat-eye glasses. "I don't know. What do I do, Trevor? How would you explain my purpose on earth?" He just keeps his eyes on the road. "I'm a homemaker, Prospect, in a home whose foundation is tragically falling apart."

"Oh. Is it a structural problem?"

Kitty laughs and turns to Trevor. "Yeah, that's a good way to put it. But seriously, Prospect, what's happening is this: my husband is divorcing me."

"I'm sorry to hear that," he says. "Would you like me to send you a card?"

"A card?"

"Yes, I hear that my Referral Irene Iwanski has lots of them. She says there's a greeting card for every occasion in life, especially the sad ones."

For a moment, Kitty just looks at him unsure of what to say next. He has thrown her off balance without meaning to. "Your Pre-born pal seems quite innocent at first. But I do think I detect a note of sarcasm. I didn't see that one coming!" She and Trevor let out a wild laugh. Now Trevor is honking at the cab ahead. Maybe he knows the cab driver.

"Kitty is unfortunately married to a man," explains Trevor, "who doesn't understand her, doesn't appreciate her, and doesn't fuck her properly."

"To be fair, it's not all his fault. I'm manic. I had a major episode recently and had to be hospitalized. Got my first jolt of electric shock therapy. Boy, that was different," she laughs. She lights up a cigarette and blows a puff of smoke out the window. "What makes it worse is my husband is just so intense about everything. Frankly, he exhausts me."

"What do you mean?"

"He's a shouter."

And that's when a light bulb goes off in Prospect's head. "Kitty, does your husband by chance take public transportation to work?"

"Yeah. He refuses to pay the downtown parking rates. Why?"

"His name wouldn't be Gunther by any chance, would it?"

Kitty looks at Trevor. Trevor steals a glance back at Kitty. "Do you know him?"

He nods. "Sort of." So the Shouting Man is married to Cat Woman. What a small world.

She throws her cigarette out the window. Prospect starts to tell her about how he first met the Shouting Man. How the man wanted to make sure she was all right. How he confessed to a group of strangers on a train that he no longer knew how to make her happy. By the time Prospect is done, Kitty is weeping into a handkerchief.

"That bastard," she says. "It'd be easier if he stopped caring about me. He's never approved of my...*wild side.*"

"Do you love him?" he asks.

"I'll tell you, Prospect, I don't even know what that means anymore. When I hear the word *love*, I just hear *blah blah blah.*" She lets out a laugh. Sad and happy. Two poles at once. Bipolar.

Trevor turns up the radio and some exuberant dance music is playing. He starts dancing from behind the wheel, bopping his head, shaking his shoulders. "Now I want you two to stop all this serious talk. We are going clubbing, and for a few hours we are going to leave all our troubles at the door. Understood?"

"Deal," Prospect says. He starts tapping his fingers to the beat.

When they get to the nightclub, Prospect can barely tell it's a nightclub. It looks more like an abandoned warehouse. There is no sign announcing the name of the club, though Kitty assures him they are at the threshold to Hallucination. There's just a doorman checking IDs with a flashlight and a long line of patrons waiting to get in. As they walk inside, the music is so loud that even when Trevor cups his hand to the Pre-born's ear to talk to him, he can barely hear him. He is saying something about the floor show, and a big surprise… but Prospect can't make out the details. With each thumping beat, martini glasses filled with brightly colored liquors jump a little along the chrome ledge of the bar. They sit on barstools that glow in bright luminous colors. Now the most amazing thing happens: two gigantic figures rise up before them on the dance floor. They must be at least two stories tall! One is a man and one is a woman. Both are completely naked, very sensual and beautiful—all muscle and sweat, all twist and shout they are.

Trevor explains that though they look like holograms, they are something more. They are something new called "hyper-holograms." They are touchable and have substance. The crowd eagerly reaches up to caress them. One young woman climbs up the hairy hyper-hologram leg of the giant man like an expert rock climber. Using the erect member of the male giant as a diving board, she leaps from the impressive appendage into the arms of the waiting crowd below. Next a lean young man scales the voluptuous mountains that are the Amazon woman's breasts. He nuzzles his face against a breast.

Then, losing his grip, the man dangles from a nipple the size of an eggplant. He drops into the roaring crowd.

"Would you like to climb the giants?" Kitty asks.

Prospect shakes his head no, though actually he would like to. But he is feeling shy with so many people watching. "But I would, however, love to try to dance," he says. "I've never danced before." His two club companions point him to the dance floor, and he carefully makes his way into the center of the crowd. Over the sound system, a woman is wailing, the percussion is exploding, the hyper-hologram giants are swaying above them. Prospect closes his eyes for a moment to recall all the motion clips his CyberSavant has shown him of dancing: from tango to tribal African to gay country line dancing. He lets the music find him, and it does. Prospect can't point to the exact moment when he goes from walking onto the floor to actually dancing. It is unlocatable.

Once he takes his place on the floor with his new friends, he starts whirling like a dervish. And then he is dancing the jig, and he is moon-walking a bit, and he is doing the watusi quite a lot. Slowly the crowd turns to watch Prospect. Kitty and Trevor do their best to keep up. Even the giant hyper-holograms are giving the floor over to him. And, man, sweat is pouring off him in sheets really. He is making it rain.

His two companions instigate a chant that the crowd joins in on, "Go, Prospect. Go, Pre-born. It's your birthday. It's your birthday." And it feels just like that to Prospect. Like it is his birthday. The day of his birth. And that's how it goes for this magic time. After a while, he loses track. Has he been dancing for a few minutes or a few hours? When he finally leaves the floor, it's not because he is tired or doesn't want to dance. It's because his throat is so very dry.

Trevor orders him a tonic and lime, which has quickly become his favorite bar beverage. Kitty's mouth just hangs open. "Meow! Where'd you learn to dance like that, Prospect? Not bad for a beginner." He just smiles and shrugs and drinks his drink.

The music has shifted to a slow song, and he can actually hear Trevor again. "Double woof. Those moves of yours were hot, Big Guy. You were turning *me* on. You were turning the whole club on. Did you feel it?"

"I don't know what I feel right now, Trevor. Except that I just had the time of my life." He takes a long gulp of his refreshing, sparkly drink.

His Referral raises his glass in a toast. "A toast…to whatever the hell you feel like toasting," says Trevor. And they clink their glasses in a gesture of solidarity. And though they've had a great time and are united in this feeling—it occurs to Prospect that they may be all toasting different things, hoping for different outcomes. Trevor and Kitty hoping to persuade him to leave the Pre-born Project, and Prospect hoping to arrive at a birth decision.

25. LOVE UNDER GLASS

After their great night at Hallucination, the three of them come back to Trevor's drenched in sweat, smoke, and alcohol. "Kitty and I are gonna jump in the shower upstairs. We'll see you in a few." Trevor and Kitty climb the spiral staircase up to his room. Prospect is instantly drawn to the sunken living room with its three huge plasma TV screens. On one screen is an infomercial showing identical twins wearing identical dresses. On the next screen there is a blindfolded prisoner begging for his life.

But it is the third screen that fascinates Prospect the most. For it is on this screen that he witnesses the delicate growth of a human fetus. And then the baby is born and her body ripens into a healthy teenager with the hopeful beginnings of breasts. A cell phone floats down gently into her hand like a new appendage. Through the miracle of time-lapse photography, he now sees her body wrinkling, her brunette hair going undeniably gray, her spine curling into a question mark. And then she is dead. A thousand rose petals rain down upon her. It is so sad, Prospect has to turn all the TVs off just to stop thinking about it.

And now he knows why this feels so familiar, like a hundred movies pinwheeling in his head. It reminds Prospect of his CyberSavant. Of his days in his mother's womb. He feels positively homesick.

෧

Prospect remembers what Trevor had told him in the car as they drove away from the nightclub. The notion of scientists again playing God, allowing an embryo to decide its own destiny. "Prospect, my man, I'd like you to seriously consider quitting the Pre-born Project," he said. "Man does not have the right to control the destiny of future generations. Translation: Stop fucking with God's perfect plan."

"I'm not trying to—do anything to anyone's plan," he told his Referral. "I'm just trying to do the right thing."

Trevor laughed at him. "God has already *done* the right thing…by inviting you into this world. Who are you to turn down His invitation? Just tell Trish you want out of the project. That you don't want to make the choice to be born or not."

"Trevor, what would you do if I told you that I'd already made up my mind? That I plan to continue with the project?"

Trevor smiled a smile that made him look both happy and not happy at the same time. "Then…my Pre-born friend…I'd have to kill you."

෧

Upstairs, Prospect can hear the shower running in Trevor's room. He quickly hops into the shower on the first floor. When he is done, he turns the faucets off. "Prospect, aren't you coming to bed?" shouts Trevor from upstairs. "Kitty and I want to tuck you in." There is giggling from upstairs.

The Pre-born carefully climbs the steps of the spiral staircase, unsure of what awaits him at the top. He pauses for a moment on the stairs. "Well don't stop now, Prospect, your public awaits you," says Trevor. "Tomorrow, we'll talk about politics and art and where society is headed. But tonight—well, there's a lotta love in the room tonight."

There's that word again. Love. "I don't feel anything," he replies to Trevor.

As he climbs the last stair, Prospect suddenly finds himself in the middle of a huge bedroom which is perfectly cylindrical in shape. But what strikes him most is the glass dome ceiling that comes down over the bedroom like a cake dome over a cake. At the exact center of Trevor's room is a large circular bed. Prospect is invited to lie back on the bed by one very naked Trevor Grueling. He almost doesn't notice that on the other side of the bed is one very naked Kitty.

With his clothes on, Trevor seems fit enough. A clean-shaven guy with a cleft chin, he could be a Canadian Mountie. But without his clothes he is outstanding: his barrel chest has swirls of black hair on it, and his washboard stomach has deep ridges upon which one could easily do one's laundry. That boyish Mountie face of his makes his manly body all the more surprising. His penis, even when soft, is a presence to be reckoned with. Through a man's penis, wars are waged…contracts

145

are signed…babies are started. For a man, everything begins and ends with his penis.

Kitty suddenly seems bashful now that she is unclothed. Her breasts rise up like two beautiful waves in a stormy ocean. Atop her breasts are brown nipples which rise and fall with her breathing. Her gentle hourglass figure concludes with a lovely posterior. A small scar along her stomach marks her definitely human.

∽

Trish flips on the Preb-Cam. She'll be leaving the hospital shortly and just wants to do a check-in to see how the current Referral is going. As the screen powers up, she is struck by what she sees: a naked woman and two men on a big round bed. She realizes Prospect is having sex! A three-way to be exact. She's glad that Karl is not present to see this.

∽

The Pre-born has never seen people naked before. Not in person. Though he did see the naked giants, but they weren't really people. They were hyper-holograms. Without even thinking, he touches the bodies of Trevor and Kitty. Her breasts are as soft as his chest is hard. Another difference he discovers is that *he* has a penis where *she* simply has an opening. The opening to a woman is an exalted place, and only special guests are permitted entry. In that opening, love is made…promises are made…babies are made. It is a special place. As special to the woman as the penis is to the man.

Meanwhile, Kitty and Trevor are admiring the Pre-born. "He's adorable, Trevor," she coos. "I could just eat him up."

"Oh, don't worry. *We will.*"

They lay him on his back in the middle of the circular bed, tie a black silk blindfold over his eyes. The first thing Prospect feels are hands moving through his hair, smoothing it. Then, he feels hands cradling his head for a few minutes. Something warm on his earlobes: lips, tongues. Each thing that she does to one side of his body is matched by his actions.

They unbutton Prospect's batik shirt, sending the tropical birds printed on its fabric flying into the dark. Their mouths begin to kiss his chest. At some point, Prospect loses track of which hands, whose mouth. It doesn't matter. He removes his blindfold. He counts to ten to try to catch his breath. Prospect reaches out and places one hand on a luscious breast and the other on a hard pectoral muscle. It doesn't matter. He kisses him, he kisses her, he kisses them. This must be what pleasure is. "But is this also what love is?" he wonders to himself.

Now there is a hand pulling at Prospect's manhood, a hand massaging his stomach, a tongue moving along his inner thighs…it is *oh,* it is *ahh—*

And now he feels the coming orgasm, that mysterious thing he has learned about through his CyberSavant—that fabulous frenzied shooting out of you, the unstoppable ejaculation.

And then the chlorine smell of DNA.

Double helixes.

Letters to the future.

His first orgasm is so intense he feels like he has broken something inside his body…when actually something has been fixed. Prospect imagines the sight of the three of them from overhead, from somewhere in the night, as they make love on this round bed. To someone looking down through the cake dome ceiling they must look like cannibals, creatures devouring each other to stay alive. Or lifeguards performing mouth-to-mouth, trying to drag each other back to the land of the living. In fact, they are neither.

The three lie together on their backs, breathing, looking up at the stars. For a while, no one speaks. Prospect thinks how amazing this glass ceiling must look during a rainstorm. Finally, Trevor says something. "You could love someone your whole life...and never fuck them," he sighs with a knowledge that comes from years of living.

"You could fuck someone your whole life...and never *love* them," Kitty says with a knowledge that comes from years of trying to make a life—and failing miserably.

But it is Trevor who tells the hardest truth, "And once in a great while when the planets align—you can make love to someone you actually love. But it won't last, Prospect. Just believe me when I tell you...it won't last."

"We hold these truths to be self-evident," says Kitty, taking a sip from her martini glass. Prospect finds himself getting tired, wanting to drift off to the deepest of sleeps. But first he has a burning question.

"So did we find love tonight? Did we love each other?" Prospect asks.

"Is he the sweetest man you've ever met, or what? Not at all like you, Mr. Grueling," she says.

He takes a puff on a cigarette. "We made love tonight, Prospect. That doesn't mean we *found* it."

But but but.

Trevor blows out little rings of smoke that rise up toward the glass dome. "Prospect, this whole love thing…it's so over-rated. It's unreliable. It's not even something in your control. You can't purchase it over the counter with cold, hard cash… so how valuable can it really be? Sex on the other hand is dependable. Sex is unambivalent. It's a tangible commodity. You either cum—or you don't. You either connect—or you fail to. It's just one of many good reasons to be born. But don't be born for love. Don't be a sucker."

"I love it when you talk about sex as a commodity," says Kitty. "It gets me so hot. But tell the kid what you recommend he should do about the bio-experiment, Trev."

"Right. Prospect, buddy, you've got to tell Trish you want out of the Pre-born Project. Plain and simple."

The Pre-born's eyes drift up to the glass dome above. "And why is it that I'd want to quit the project?"

"Prospect, at some level, you've got to understand that in any experiment—there's got to be a guinea pig. Some poor soul who either gets the placebo or who gets the untested miracle cure. You, my friend, are that guinea pig." Kitty wordlessly descends the spiral staircase. Being bare-foot, she makes only the gentlest slapping sound on the chrome steps. "What guarantee do you have that there won't be some technical failure in this artificial birthing process? Let's say you make your big choice. What guarantee do you have that Trish will honor your wishes to be born or returned to the gene pool?" Downstairs, Kitty putters in the kitchen. She is mixing drinks at the bar, plunking cubes of ice into glass tumblers.

Prospect looks up through the dome at the stars scattered there. He wonders what Lito is doing right now. He thinks about his own parents Rebecca and Roberto. Are they missing him right now? He hopes that Trish is sleeping soundly in bed surrounded by a menagerie of stuffed animals instead of working late at the office. Now there is the pitter-patter of Kitty's feet winding their way up the spiral staircase. She emerges from the opening in the floor bearing gifts: drinks for everyone. A green melon liqueur that is sweet and strong and refreshing too.

"Trevor, you've given me pause. You've presented compelling reasons to withdraw from the Pre-born Project. But I've decided I'm going to continue. I want to see this thing through. I'm sorry." Prospect studies Trevor's face, but his face tells him exactly nothing.

He shakes his head slowly in disgust as if Prospect is the biggest living mistake he's ever laid eyes on.

"That's my decision, and there's nothing you can say to persuade me."

"I'm sorry to hear that," he says. And they drink their melon liqueur in silence. A silence punctuated only by the clinking of ice in their tumblers. Then Trevor turns off the bedroom light and the three of them lie in the dark. They watch a plane streak across the sky.

Prospect must have fallen asleep at some point. When he sits up in bed, he sees that Kitty and Trevor are gone. Through the domed glass ceiling, it is a beautiful summer morning. There are birds flying in the distance. He can hear TV voices floating up from downstairs. Slowly Prospect descends the spiral staircase to find Kitty watching *Oprah* on all three screens. "Morning, sweetie," says Kitty.

"Where's Trevor?"

"Seattle. Business trip. He said he was real sorry he couldn't say good-bye."

Prospect is trying to digest what she has just told him. "But he can't go. We're in the middle of our Referral."

"You know Trevor. He goes where the money is." Kitty climbs out of the sunken living room to meet Prospect on the steps. "Speaking of money, he said that you were gonna... settle up with me."

"Settle up with you?"

She seems embarrassed. "You know, pay my fee...for last night. It's one thousand five hundred dollars for groups, plus my overnight fee of five hundred. That's pretty standard."

"Oh, sure. He didn't tell me..." He reaches into his wallet. Prospect had no idea she was an escort. He's just glad he has a credit card.

"I'm kidding, Prospect! You shoulda seen the look on your face," she says. "Me and Trev, we do like our little practical jokes, I must say." She laughs a girlish laugh.

"So you're not an escort?"

"No, I'm just a woman with way too much time on her hands. Can't you tell? I'm still trying to find myself at forty-three."

He puts his wallet away. "My friend Trish says adults spend one third of their lives trying to find themselves."

"So true."

"Hey, Kitty—you and Trevor call yourselves conservatives, but you're kind of swingers, aren't you? How does that work exactly?"

"We're conservatives in the *head*—but not in the *bed!*"
she laughs. "Take care, Prospect. You're a honey." She blows
him a kiss and pulls the door closed.

Now what is he supposed to do? Prospect looks at
Oprah's face on all three screens. She just shakes her head
sympathetically (as only Oprah can). "We'll be right back,"
says Ms. Winfrey. He checks his date book and decides to
move on to his next Referral…Irene Iwanski, the greeting
card lady. Prospect turns all the TVs off one by one. He rinses
out his coffee mug and places it in the rack to dry. This is
how he leaves this place. He climbs up the spiral staircase
one last time—this double helix of chrome and glass—all the
way up, then all the way down. Just as he reaches the bottom
step, the phone rings and the machine switches on: "Trevor,
this is Bobby. I'm at the Space Needle in Seattle. I'm in the
gift shop like I said I'd be. You didn't answer your Blackberry,
so I'm calling you at home. Two questions: One, where the
hell are you? Two, what'd you finally do with the kid? Did
you drown him in the gene pool?" Bobby laughs at his own
joke, then hangs up.

26. OUR LADY OF THE GREETING CARDS

He takes a cab to the home of his next Referral, though Prospect's mind is still on Trevor Grueling. Where did he disappear to, and what did that phone message mean?

Speaking of Trish, what is he to make of her? There are times she's snippy. There are times when she's perfectly nice. And what does she do when she's not being a scientist? Does she have a family of her own? Or is she so in love with her work that wanting any other kind of love would seem greedy? Does she volunteer at animal shelters...talking down cats who've climbed too high into the trees? Does Trish ever feel *she's* climbed too high into the trees? And if so, who is there to coax her out of the beautiful branches? Just then his phone rings.

"What are you doing?" It's Lito.

"Hi, Lito. I was just thinking about you. I'm riding in a cab on my way to my next Referral."

"I'm sorry," he says.

"About what?"

"How I disappeared on you like that. I don't like good-byes. Hey, there's gonna be a memorial for Luz. The girl from the pool. Could you come and say something? Something nice?"

"Do you want me to?" he asks.

"Yeah. It's tomorrow at the YMCA chapel at 1:00 p.m."

"I'll have to check with my current Referral, Irene."

"I understand if you can't make it. Is it okay that I called you? I mean, I know I'm not your Referral anymore. But... you're cool. I kind of miss hanging out with you. Know what I mean?"

"I feel exactly the same way, Lito."

There is a pause. "Maybe after this is all over...we could be friends or something," he says. "Cancel that. That was stupid! I mean, you don't even know if you're gonna be born. God, that was stupid."

"Oh, Lito. The cab is getting close. I gotta go. I'm gonna try to make it to the memorial. It'd be fun to see you again." And now all Prospect hears is the dead silence of a departing cell phone. "Lito?" He's gone again. He wasn't kidding when he said he didn't like saying good-byes. Looking out of the cab window, he sees the streets signs. They tell him he's getting close to Irene's. He pulls out the letter which tells him her story.

Dear Prospect,

Irene Iwanski, 71, is a divorcee, Polish-American. She is uniracial. A woman who, in her day, created greeting cards for Wish U Were Here—she is now retired. For nine

years, she was married to a kindly veterinarian. Though
they never had children, they did raise their share of strays.
Irene and Paulie Iwanski have been divorced now for as
many years as they were married.

Trish

"Trish." That's how she signed it. This is the first time his
Facilitator has simply signed her first name instead of "Dr.
Trish Mesmer." They are getting to know each other. Like an
onion, layer by layer, one skin at a time. Why do people cry
when they peel an onion?

He hears Irene Iwanski before he ever sees her. It is the
thud of her metal cane, its rubber tip striking the ground, that
announces her arrival. Prospect stands at the front door to
Irene's small home. Sheer pink curtains flutter from the open
windows of the living room. They move like jellyfish in the
summer breeze.

She leads him inside. There are greeting cards as
far as the eye can see. They are hung on the walls of her
house like works of art. Some are framed, some are color-
xeroxed and blown up to poster size. Some are attached
to a clothesline like laundry hung out to dry. There are
even card racks that turn like the ones at the gift shop at
Infinity. Each slot is labeled with the greeting card occasion that it was designed for. This is a woman who lives in
a house of cards.

Irene spins a rack with her yellow cane and says, "Pick
a card…any card." As he reaches for one she snaps, "No,
not that one." She points to one in an envelope covered in

silver glitter. He pulls the card from the rack and reads it aloud:

I am standing in a train station, surrounded
by commuters making their arrivals and departures.
I have pondered the prospect of your arrival
as I have considered the necessity of my departure.
One day we will trade places, you and I,
I and you.
And then what will you do? And then
what will you do?

Remember me, Prospect. Forget me. But do not ignore me.
Irene

"You wrote that for me?" he asks. Irene nods.

"I've written so many condolence cards lately—it was a relief to write a happy one. But the truth is, more than the happy cards, a person should always stock up on sympathy cards. Boxes of them. Because there's so much to be sorry about!" she laughs. "Sorry for your loss. Sorry about your weight gain. Sorry you were laid off. Sorry the cancer is spreading. Sorry you're still single. Sorry you're still married. Sorry your family is so messed up. Sorry you have no family. Sorry the Tooth Fairy is so toothless, and that there is no god to light your way. Sorry it rained on your parade. Sorry about your wife leaving you. Sorry about the horrible miscarriage of justice in this country. Sorry about your miscarriage." Irene sighs for a moment, lost in a private thought.

"Better luck next time," she continues, her right hand moving gracefully through the air as if signing a greeting card floating before her. "Better luck to all of us. At least you're still alive. At least you're still here. Here we are."

Irene is a horrible listener, but a terrific speaker. She is old. Older, he means to say. She is remembering as fast as she can.

"I know what you mean about sympathy cards," Prospect says. "I know this girl who died recently. I don't know if there is a greeting card that can say how sorry I feel." He tells Irene about how he met Luz, about the dream in the ocean, about the starfish, how she said more words in the dream than she ever said to him in life.

"I knew a girl who drowned in a rain puddle. Barely two inches of water. It was a tragedy that shouldn't have happened," she says. At first her story sounds funny, like the beginning to a joke. But when she finishes her story, neither of them are laughing. It is the story of how Irene Iwanski lost her first and only child through miscarriage. How her unborn baby Lily Anne died—not in a rain puddle—but in the fluids of her own body. And though it was no one's fault, the loss was such a shock to Irene that she couldn't bear to try again. Prospect tells her he's sorry about her loss. It seems that every story he tells her from his short life…only reminds her of a story from her long one.

"Irene, I have a favor to ask," he says. "There's going to be a small memorial for this girl I met. My Referral, Lito, wanted me to come…"

"If you're going to ask me if I'd accompany you, I'd be honored."

"That's great. It's tomorrow at 1:00 p.m."

"I have the perfect dress."

As night arrives, his hostess brings out sheets for the sofa where he will sleep, a pillow for his head. She tells him to make himself at home. Whatever he needs—he should feel free to get it. No need to ask permission. Prospect thinks about his first day with Irene. Overall, it has been a lazy day. For forty-five minutes, he watched her do a crossword puzzle. He offered to help, but she said that would be cheating. So he just peered over her shoulder at the words that she scribbled into black and white squares. He looked up the words in her dictionary to make himself useful. She liked when he read the definitions to her. Then for a few hours, Prospect helped her organize her kitchen cabinets. They grouped cereal boxes together, throwing out things that looked like they had gone bad. They ended the day by preparing a meal together which took almost two and a half hours to prepare and less than twenty minutes to eat.

Now all the lights in the house are out. He can see the streetlights through the jellyfish curtains. It is enough light to help him see, in case he needs to get up in the middle of the night. Prospect can hear Irene breathing softly in the next room. He hopes she is having a nice dream. Sleeping in new places takes some getting used to. He climbs out of bed and spins the card rack. He chooses a card at random and opens it. Inside, it says:

Decisions made in an instant can last a lifetime.

27. IN MEMORIAM

Early the next morning, Prospect hears Irene making a pot of
tea in the kitchen, and she is baking something. The whole
kitchen smells wonderful. She tells him she's baking almond
cookies. Irene's "perfect dress" for the service takes him a bit
by surprise. It's called a muumuu. The muumuu is a vision of
tropical exuberance, depicting the sea and its many creatures:
schools of fish darting from side to side, an octopus here, a
sea turtle there, blue-green coral reefs. It makes him miss the
Shedd Aquarium, which in turn makes him miss his mother.
Around Irene's neck, she wears a circle of fresh flowers. And
pinned as a brooch to her dress is a starfish. She has fashioned
an outfit out of pieces of his story!

"I'm not the kind of person who wears black to a
memorial," she says, not bothering to say good morning.
"People are sad—why make your clothes sad too? Besides,
the dead like color." He takes his place at her kitchen table
as she serves him tea and cookies. He is tempted to ask her

if she's ever been dead before, but it seems too smart-alecky. Even for him.

"How do I know the dead like color, you're wondering," Irene says. "I've been doing research on the dead. The afterlife. Reincarnation. Heaven. We're all going to die. Might as well study up for it. We study for everything else." She stands before a mirror on the inside of her closet door and brushes out her white hair, flipping the ends up a bit for style. Somehow the image of Irene chatting with the dead about fashion preferences strikes Prospect as funny. And though he knows he shouldn't laugh—he does.

"So you can talk to the dead?" he asks, smiling.

"Yes. They're a surprisingly lively group."

Prospect half laughs.

"Did I say something funny?" she asks with a most serious look on her face.

"No, ma'am."

She puts her brush down on the tabletop. "Listen, Prospect, I know I'm a silly old lady, but I'm the best silly old lady I know how to be." The words are starting to catch in her throat, "So I'd appreciate it if you showed some respect for my beliefs." She brings her dishes to the sink and rinses them.

Prospect feels terrible. She has made these cookies for him, and he has ruined their meal. "Absolutely, Irene. I'm sorry if I…I mean it wasn't my intention to—"

Irene picks up her handbag and slings it over her shoulder. "Lock the door behind you, please," she says. She drives to the memorial in her beat-up station wagon. They ride in utter silence, which is very uncomfortable. And Irene does not seem like the silent type.

When they walk into the chapel, there is a small group of people. Prospect is surprised and delighted to see Lito, and he's wearing a suit and tie! How handsome he is. There are a few people hovering around a table filled with snacks and sodas and coffee. At the front of the chapel on a small table is a sad little cigar box. Lito has asked that people bring some small things to put into the box, which he will later bury in the ground. Lito sits in a pew by himself, busily jotting notes in a pad.

The Pre-born sneaks a sideways glance at Irene. He wonders if she is still mad at him He can't really tell. As she looks at the small crowd of mourners with sympathy card in hand, he can see she doesn't know whom to give it to. Perhaps there is no family present. What to do? Here is a woman whose whole life is about knowing her way around a greeting card, about knowing just the right moment to present it. Suddenly Irene is handing the card to Prospect. He opens it carefully and reads it to himself:

I never knew Luz Ramizez.
But I know a boy who knew her
only for a few minutes in a dream.
And he can't stop thinking about her.
She must've been something.

"Irene…" he says. "I'm sorry I upset you."

"Nonsense. I was just being over-sensitive. My family has never taken my belief in alternative spirituality seriously, you see. It really wasn't about you at all, Prospect."

Irene's forgiveness and the words of her greeting card inspire him to want to say something at the memorial.

After Lito makes some remarks about how he knew Luz, he opens the floor for others to speak. He gives Prospect a look. Shyly, Prospect walks up to the podium. He looks into the faces of the people before him. "I never met Luz Ramirez when she was alive. When I lifted her body out of the pool, she was dead already. But later I had a dream where she thanked me for pulling her out of the pool and trying to save her. In the dream, Luz told me she lived in the ocean now, and that she liked it…because starfish glowed at night like perfect night-lights…and that she was never afraid or lonely anymore." Lito is beaming at him, his eyes widening with interest. "That's all she said really. She wanted me to tell you…so you'd know."

As Prospect sits back down in a pew, Lito locks an arm around his neck. "You are so awesome, dude," he says.

Afterwards, people walk up to look at a photo display of Luz's life. Just some dog-earred polaroids taped to poster-board. Prospect sees Irene remove her starfish brooch and place it in the cigar box. And the box doesn't seem so sad now that it is filling with trinkets. When it is his turn, he searches his pockets for something to give Luz. All that he comes up with are two quarters and a melted chocolate turtle. It's better than nothing. Still, it's not a starfish brooch. Not by a long shot.

28. BAD GUYS

"It's so not like him," Kitty exclaims on the phone. She's talking so fast it's hard to understand her. Trevor never made it to his business meeting in Seattle. He has been missing now almost two days. "He's not answering his cell phone, not retrieving messages from his home answering machine, not returning emails or instant messages. That's just not like Trevor."

"Maybe he needed to escape for a while," Prospect says. "Everyone needs a break now and then."

"Trevor hates to relax. He's only happy when he's multi-tasking," she says. "I thought I should tell you because…until he's found, well, Trevor's a missing person. You and I were the last to see him. I had to give the cops your number."

Prospect tries to picture where Trevor might be. Different scenarios float through his head. He sees him tied up, helpless, in a chair as a kidnap victim with bamboo shoots under his fingernails. In another scenario, he sees him drinking beer with some strange men as they all laugh hilariously. In another, he sees him lying in a hospital somewhere with a sign above him scrawled with the words AMNESIA VICTIM.

What Prospect doesn't know and what Kitty hasn't told him is that Trevor is not missing at all. He is actually embarking on the first stage of a plot to discredit the Pre-born Project, and to persuade Prospect to end his involvement. By disappearing, Trevor hopes to raise questions with the press about the safety of the Referrals. He plans to consult his Referral contact list and enlist the help of another Referral in this plot. Trevor's background in moving forward agendas in the business world transfers well to the world of mass media and social networking. An email here, a Twitter there, can do wonders to stoke the fire. Not bad for a man who's wonder-challenged.

∽

The next morning, Prospect is awoken by the ringing of his cell phone. It's the police.

They'd like him to come down to the Belmont Police Station to answer a few questions. "Ask for Detective Dunleavy," the voice says. Prospect apologizes to Irene for the interruption of their Referral, promises he'll be back as soon as he can. He heads for the station.

In a plain room at a large wooden table without even a pitcher of iced tea, the world's favorite Pre-born sits. Not a lemon wedge in sight. There is a just a beat-up coffee station and a long glass mirror on the wall, which surely is a two-way mirror. Maybe there are people standing on the other side, watching his every move. Maybe there is no one at all—just sheets of paper waiting silently inside manila folders, particles of dust rising and falling in a high-intensity lamp's beam of light.

It's not so strange that he finds himself as the subject of an interrogation. It's a natural thing to ask questions, to be curious. Prospect is the most curious person he knows. Hasn't he interrogated his Referrals in much the same way?

"You're not a suspect," Detective Dunleavy assures him right off the bat. "But your testimony could help us locate Mr. Grueling. Hopefully it's nothing. But he *is* a wealthy man. We told his parents we'd look into it. They're big donors to our annual policeman's charity drive." Detective Dunleavy says that Kitty told him that the three of them were out for the night. And bartenders at Hallucination confirmed that they saw Trevor with someone who fit Prospect's description.

"So let's start at the beginning. How do you know Trevor Grueling?"

"We're…co-workers."

"What kind of co-workers?" asks the detective.

೦ᨏ

About five miles north of the Belmont Police Station, in Evanston, Trevor Grueling's stomach rumbles in a local coffee house. The walls are beige, the coffee is brown, and there are no paintings whatsoever to disturb the beige/brown continuum. It is called the Nondescript Café. Trevor orders an egg salad sandwich with a bowl of chili. He looks out the window at the view of a brick wall and dials a number carefully on his cell. It rings. Someone answers. "Hello," says the voice.

"Victor, it was nice to meet you and the others at the Referral meeting last week."

"And who might this be?" With his free hand, Victor Pastelle dabs a bit of red onto the canvas.

"I'm sorry. This is Trevor Grueling. I'm one of the Referrals in the Pre-born Project. What did you make of Karl and Trish? They're odd ducks, aren't they?"

"Yes, but that's not necessarily a bad thing. I'm a bit odd myself."

"Listen, Victor, I looked up your work online. Your paintings are remarkable."

"Thank you. But I'm sure you didn't call me up just to blow smoke up my easel." They both laugh. Then Victor puts Trevor on speakerphone and sets the phone on an end table. Victor's cat paws at the cell phone like it's a mouse. The cat bats at the phone, and it spins a little on the table.

"Quite right. I have a proposition for you, but I'd rather talk to you in person. Do you think we could meet for lunch?"

"No can do. I'm in the middle of a painting."

"What if I told you I might be able to set up a meeting with you and the art buyer for Big Farm?"

Victor stops dabbing. His cat hisses at the phone.

"Should I take that as a no?" says Trevor.

"Sorry, that was just my cat being judgmental."

"Tell me where you live and I'll pick you up. Lunch is on me."

"Ah, you've found my weakness. A starving artist can only turn down so many free lunches."

Victor's cat scampers off to the kitchen.

∽

"Detective Dunleavy, could I bother you for some coffee?" says Prospect, stalling a little for time. The detective pours; Prospect adds cream and sugar. He is aware that his co-worker answer sounds evasive and that's not a good thing. "Trevor and I were participating in a bio-experiment based at Infinity Medical Center."

The detective scratches a few notes on a pad of paper. "And what was the purpose of the experiment?"

Prospect rubs his chin for a moment. "Basically, Trevor and I were scheduled to meet for two or three days. It has to do with the future. And babies. Being here by choice rather than by chance. Evolution," he says. "But suddenly he had to fly to Seattle for an important business meeting. That's all I really know."

"Everybody's doing bio-experiments these days. To be honest, science was never my strong suit," he says. "Fighting crime, capturing the bad guys—that turns me on. That gives me a woodie. Know what I mean?"

Prospect nods.

"You better not turn out to be a bad guy, Prospect. That's all I'm gonna say."

"No, sir."

"You know what happens to bad guys?"

"They get small punishments?"

"You got that right. And sometimes they get big punishments."

The detective gives Prospect his card and asks him to call him if he hears from Trevor. And he urges Prospect not to leave town if he can help it.

No matter what the detective says—Prospect knows that until the case is solved, until Trevor Grueling is present and accounted for—he is definitely a suspect.

Imagine that: a suspect *and* a prospect!

29. A LOVELY RIDE

Prospect is happy to leave the station and head back to Irene's. When he returns, he finds Irene has already planned an outing for them. A "day trip" is what she calls it because it will take a whole day to go there and come back. They'll have to take a few interstates and countless highways to get there. They are going to a place called Strawberry Fields. She has heard from friends that it is a charming destination with countless roadside fruit stands and a shocking assortment of products made from strawberries—their big local crop. Everything from homemade strawberry pies and preserves… to shampoos and beauty cosmetics made from fresh strawberries. When they're done sightseeing, they'll have a picnic. This is the last day of his Referral with Irene.

Once they are on the road, Prospect starts to lose track of where they are. One road leads into another; one interstate flows into a different one. Outside the car, the trees and hillsides and billboards fly past them like they are in a cartoon.

"Trish thought it would be good for you to meet someone who was completely different from you. As different as night and day," says Irene, keeping her eyes on the road. "Well, here I am. Different. I've wanted to tell you what makes me different from you for some time, Prospect."

He turns to look at her. She has his full attention.

"I'm dying," she says. Her hands remain steady on the wheel. She turns to look at him briefly to make sure he has heard her. To make sure the breeze whipping through the car has not whipped her words away also. Then her eyes return to the road. "Do you know what that means?"

He thinks for a moment. "Cessation of life. Your heart stops beating. Irene, I'm so sorry." He's not sure what to say.

She pulls down the visor because now the sun is almost directly in her face. "I've been lucky. My cancer has been in remission for years. But now it's back with a vengeance, and this time I'm afraid it will have its way with me." As the car makes a slow turn, the sunlight flares to the side of her. She becomes a silhouette, and Prospect doesn't like this. He can't see her face. It is erasing her, and there's nothing he can do about it. "We're fundamentally different, you and I," she explains, "because you are moving *toward* life…and I am moving *away* from it."

"I don't want you to go away."

Now another turn of the vehicle restores her face. "I want you to know, my friend, that it's been a lovely ride. The view has been breathtaking, the passengers delightful, and the food delicious. And I'm not talking about our day trip either. Dear Prospect—I recommend you take the ride…in spite of all its flaws and failings, of which there are many. There's nothing else like it. That's all I really wanted to tell you."

They have pulled up to a strawberry stand along the road. Irene grabs a basket and together they begin dropping the most delicious-looking strawberries into it. As the basket fills, they continue their conversation.

"How long, Irene? How long do you have to live?"

"It could be months; it could be weeks. Death doesn't keep a calendar."

"Isn't there something that doctors can do? There are breakthroughs every day—"

"Science doesn't have all the answers," says the retired greeting card writer. "Science has never discovered why some people's hearts are closed and some are open. And it has never explained to my satisfaction why I have to die." She places a pound cake swirled with strawberry syrup into their basket. It looks too beautiful to eat. "I have throat cancer. That means there will come a time over the next several months when I will have to be fed through a tube. It's the end of food as I know it, the end of deliciousness. And I'm afraid it's also the end of singing, which I love almost as much as I love food."

"But, Irene, really I don't see what the big deal is. So you can't taste your food, or sing some silly old songs. You can still make your greetings cards. You can still get up in the morning and enjoy life." He bites into a strawberry.

"*What's the big deal?* You talk about life like you're an expert on the subject after two weeks. Let's be honest, Prospect: you're just a tourist here. You're slumming." She laughs a deep laugh. The basket is full so she sets it down on the counter. "You're tasting a little of this dish and a little of that one. Life is a feast, but everything *costs* something."

"I'm still new here, Irene," the Pre-born says. "You've been here your whole life. Maybe you could help me by telling me the right answers sometimes—even if I'm not smart enough to ask the right questions."

Irene does not answer his cheeky question. She just gives him a half smile. The cashier starts ringing up their purchases. They get back in the car and pull off. Irene drives them to a pretty spot in the middle of what appears to be a field. They spread a large blue and white blanket on the grass.

"Please slice the pound cake and surround our slices with strawberries...and pour us some seltzer water," she says. He does so, cutting thick slices of cake for both of them.

"We need some plastic forks and spoons too." Her wish is his command, for now he knows that his friend is not only elderly, but dying too. Irene unwraps some of the Cornish hens she brought for their consumption. Before long, they have laid out a fine meal for themselves.

"Irene, please tell me about what matters to you in your life. Something that you think is important for me to know."

She pauses with a tiny drumstick in one hand and a strawberry in the other. She takes a bite of each. "One thing you should know is that some decisions in life, many of them, are irreversible. You can make a decision in a matter of seconds that you'll have to live with for the rest of your life. I'll give you an example. After I decided to divorce my husband Paulie, I never remarried. It wasn't that I thought I should only marry once in my life. It was because having Paulie Iwanski for nine years—loving him, being loved by him, hating him a little, forgiving him—that was enough for me. That was a lot for a simple girl from the cornfields of Iowa."

He is not sure he is getting her point. "But you were talking about *making irreversible decisions,* weren't you?"

Irene laughs. "So I was. Well, last week I asked Paulie if he'd marry me again. I got down on one knee and everything. He just laughed. 'We're great friends today, Irene,' he said. 'Why mess up a good thing?' And that was that. I couldn't undo my decision to divorce him. Did I make the right decision to get a divorce? I think so. Oh, Prospect…I'm old. I'm the opposite of you."

The Pre-born is learning something about Irene. Her conversations are self-propelled. Like she could just as easily tell her stories to the trees or a passing cloud.

"Before we head back to the city, I thought we might take a visit to the Strawberry Dipper swimming pool," she says. "It's quite the attraction. But I wasn't sure if you were…up to it."

"Why not?" he says.

"You're not afraid?"

"Of what?"

She chooses her words carefully. "Of going into a swimming pool? The last time you were in a pool…that poor girl drowned."

"Oh, that's true," he says. "But I don't blame the swimming pool for what happened."

Irene smiles. "I'm glad." The two of them spend the afternoon floating on inner tubes, studying the clouds above them. It's such a simple thing but it gives both of them so much pleasure. "This is lovely, Prospect. If summer comes and I don't spend at least one day lying flat on my back studying cloud formations – I feel I haven't had a summer." Prospect looks at a cloud and wonders how high up it is. And what does he look like down on the ground from the cloud's point over view? He gets dizzy just thinking about it.

Finally it's time to go.

"Oh, Prospect…" she coos. "We've had a good time today, haven't we?"

"Yes, ma'am." They change into dry clothes and make their way to the car.

"I have a big favor to ask you, and you're welcome to say no," she says. "The cancer is killing me very slowly—and I want to die faster."

"I don't understand."

"I'm planning on taking an overdose of pills today, but I don't want to do it alone. Would you sit with me and keep me company in my final hours?"

"But, Irene, maybe science will find a cure for you," Prospect says. "Trish says they're discovering things every day!"

"Dear boy, I lost faith in science years ago. And I lost faith in a higher power years before that. Now it's just me."

They drive in silence back to her house. But this silence is different than the angry silence. It's a talk-to-the-clouds kind of silence.

His phone rings. "Hello?"

"Is this Prospect?"

"Yes."

"It's Kitty. I'm sorry to bother you."

"It's no bother, Kitty. Have you heard from Trevor?"

There is a pause. "Trevor's a good friend of mine. But I like you too. And it's because I like you that I decided to call you. There's something I want to tell you."

"What is it, Kitty? You can tell me anything."

"There are two things you should know about Trevor by now. One, he hates bio-experiments. And two, he likes practical jokes."

"Yes. I've noticed."

"What if I told you he isn't missing but he's hiding? That he's just trying to get you in trouble with the cops?"

"Is that what's going on? That makes perfect sense. Thanks for telling me, Kitty."

"I just thought you should know. But this conversation between us, it never happened. Know what I mean? If the cops ask me, I'll just deny it. Trevor's got some issues, but he's my buddy too. That's all." And then there's just silence. He hangs up his phone.

"Everything all right?" asks Irene.

"No. But it's better than it was," he says. They drive on in silence.

⌒

Victor and Trevor sit together at the Nondescript Café, eating lunch. Trevor is very much in his element. Years of corporate warfare, mergers, and acquisitions have trained him in negotiations. He can easily identify what Victor desires. He knows what bait to set before him and, most importantly, he knows exactly what he wants from Victor in return.

"Pardon my cynicism," says Victor taking a bite of his cheeseburger, "but what do you get out of all this?"

Trevor drinks his iced coffee swirled with three packets of Equal. "Ah, in return I'd need you to create a series of paintings that will disturb Prospect so deeply that he will want to end his participation. You're an empath. If anyone has a shot at accomplishing that, it's you."

Victor dips a french fry in ketchup. "Is my getting the art commission dependent on Prospect's quitting the project?"

"Afraid so. But worst case scenario, you lose a week of painting time and some canvases. Best case scenario, you earn enough money to live on and paint with for the next five years! How sweet is that?"

"Tell me more about the art buyer. How do you know this person?"

"His name is Manny Dominguez. I've told him about your work. He likes the portraits on your website. He owes me a favor big time."

"I don't have to mention all of the conflicts of interest coming up for me right now. Can I have some time to think about this?"

"Afraid not," says Trevor. "Everything's moving along at warp speed right now. If you can't do the work, I'll find someone else. But since you are internal to the Pre-born Project..."

Victor extends his hand. "You have a deal."

Trevor shakes his hand. "Great. Here's a written letter of agreement that spells out the terms of the transaction. I just need your countersignature. Oh, one more important detail. Big Farm must *never* know about my involvement in this."

"Why?"

"The reason doesn't matter. What matters is your discretion. Can you be discrete?"

"I can. And I will," says Victor. He signs the contract.

"This is great. Prospect is currently meeting with his Referral Irene Iwanski," says Trevor. "Then next up will be you. His final Referral. Trish has saved the best for last. A Referral with a twist."

❧

Irene pulls her car into the driveway. She and Prospect enter Irene's homey house of cards. Then Prospect speaks. "How will I know? When you're really gone?"

She takes his fingers and puts them on her wrist. "Feel this little vein in my arm? See how it beats? When you can no longer feel my pulse, that's how you'll know."

Irene wants him so badly to do her this favor…and he doesn't want to disappoint her, or to let her die alone. He must trust whatever his Referrals want to share with him. He reluctantly agrees to do the favor.

"I love this house. I fell in love with Paulie here. And fell out of love with him too, the bastard. All my happiest memories are here." She straightens a picture on the wall. "Now if anyone asks what happened—tell them I chose to end my life because the cancer was too painful. Suicide became legal a few years back, but murder still is a crime. So it's important that they understand this was *my* choice."

"I understand, Irene."

"Tell them we both lay down for a nap after a light meal, and one of us never woke up. Call the police and tell them you can't wake your friend and you're worried. Ask them to come to the house."

"I will," Prospect says. Irene sits in her easy chair, but there is nothing easy about what she is about to do. She empties a bottle of pills into a bowl and crushes them to powder with a tea cup. Then she pours the powder into a glass of iced tea. She looks at him for a moment. Her hand shakes. He steadies it.

"Thank you, Prospect. I do so hope you choose to be born. You'd be a lovely addition to the human race." She drinks the iced tea in a couple of large gulps.

ço

Trish Mesmer and Karl Bangor watch the Preb-Cam. They are spell-bound, dabbing at their eyes with tissues.

Karl speaks first. "Finally a Referral that comes out unequivocally to encourage Prospect to be born! We could have used five more just like her."

"Irene is a terrific Referral. I knew she'd make a good case for being born."

"I didn't expect this Referral to be so...sad," Karl says, blowing his nose. Trish turns off the Preb-Cam. She shakes her head.

Karl looks at her. "Did you know?"

"What?"

"That she wanted to end her life?" he says.

"I knew she had health issues. But she downplayed them," she said. "I had no idea they were so severe."

"That could have backfired on us. You really need to screen these Referrals more carefully. You know that, don't you?" says Karl.

"Duly noted," she says. The two colleagues move toward the door. Then Karl stops and faces her.

"I have to be honest with you, Trish. Corporate thinks your management of the project is getting sloppy. They think you're getting too chummy with the Referrals and with the Pre-born. In short, unless there is a marked improvement in your handling of things, frankly, you're fired."

"Thanks for the heads-up, Karl. I'll see what I can do." She turns off the lights, pulls the door closed, and locks it. Inside her office, it is dark and quiet. Only the blue light on the TV monitor blinks, telling the time…along with the words: "Preb-Cam recording."

৶৹

In Irene's living room, she and her Pre-born friend sit on the sofa. "Would you like to watch TV for a while?"

"What would you like to do, Irene?"

She thinks for a moment. "I'd like to order a large deep dish pizza with anchovies and pineapple."

"What if it doesn't come in time?"

"Then you'll have leftovers, won't you?" She laughs. She calls in her order and proceeds to tell Prospect about her life. Luckily the pizza arrives quickly; Irene relishes each bite. He can't eat much. He notices her speech is getting slower, her eyelids seem more heavy. As she tells him how she met her ex-husband…she lets out a long sigh.

"Irene? Are you okay?" She is silent. Her chest is still. Prospect gets up to gently shake her shoulder, but there is no response. He feels for her pulse, but there is no pulse to be found. This is how he knows that Irene has left for parts unknown.

And suddenly the room is so very still. But there is nothing stiller than Prospect himself. For he has just witnessed the death of a friend. He touches his face, and it's wet. It's so wet. Like the time he was at the amusing park and it was raining. Only it's not raining, and he's not at the park. He's here.

He reaches for the phone and dials the police. "Hello? I need someone to come to the house right away. My friend and I lay down for a little nap, but one of us never woke up…"

30. PROSPECT'S BLOG

I think I'm in trouble.

When the police arrived, it wasn't as simple as Irene had predicted. They weren't convinced her death was a suicide. Because I was the last person to see her alive, you see. They said I was what they call "a person of interest." This was different than saying I was an interesting person. They asked why would a woman who devoted her whole life to writing greeting cards… why would such a woman not leave a suicide note of some kind? One final greeting card to the world? It was a great question, but I didn't have a great answer. They took me down to the Belmont Police Station, home of Detective Dunleavy. When I entered the meeting room, he was waiting for me. He was just finishing off a crossword puzzle. He didn't look up.

"What's a thirteen-letter word for a mandatory interview?"

"Excuse me?" I said.

"Work with me. A thirteen-letter word…for a mandatory interview."

I shook my head. I had no idea.

"By jove, I think I got it! INTERROGATION." *He put his pencil down. He looked at me." I thought I told you to keep your nose clean, Prospect."*

"I don't want any trouble, Detective," I said.

"Too late for that. People have a habit of disappearing around you. First Trevor. Now Irene. What am I supposed to make of that?"

I imagined I was on one of those TV shows where the innocent person looks terribly guilty no matter what they say, and the guilty person goes off to a tropical resort and drinks drinks with umbrellas in them. "Um. Maybe I'm not a people person?"

"Well, that's an interesting theory. Because I find that you're quite good with people. You're polite. Charming. Respectful. What's not to like?"

"Well... Trish thinks I call her too often with too many questions. So she doesn't like that. And Trevor—he thinks I have too much faith in science and not enough in God. So he didn't like that."

He jotted scribbly little notes on a notepad. "What didn't Irene like about you?" he asked. His eyes were focused like a laser beam on mine.

"She said that I acted like a know-it-all when in fact I didn't know very much at all because I'm like a tourist here."

The detective's eyes widened like saucers. "And that was a source of tension between you two?"

"Tension? No! There was no tension."

"There's no need to get defensive."

"I'm not getting defensive. She just thought I was...self-centered."

"And that's why you killed her?"

"I didn't kill her! She took her life because of the throat cancer."

The detective stood for a moment. He moved to the water cooler to get himself a drink. Crushed the cup and shot it into the waste can.

"So what was the nature of your relationship to Ms. Iwanski?" the cop asked.

"We were friends. Am I in trouble?"

"What kind of friends were you?"

"Are there different kinds?" I asked, but the detective's expression told me he didn't like my question. "She was teaching me…how to write greeting cards." I found myself getting nervous.

"Do you understand why you're here?"

"Here at the police station, or here on earth?"

"Are you being smart with me, son?"

It went on and on like that. Our conversation went in little circles that went nowhere. Nowhere that Detective Dunleavy found satisfying anyway. Everything I said seemed to annoy him. He kept coming back to the question of why she wouldn't have left a suicide note. And that's when I remembered what I remembered. That odd little greeting card Irene had given me the first day I met her. I still had it in my bag:

I have pondered the prospect of your arrival
as I have considered the necessity of my departure.
One day we will trade places, you and I,
I and you.
And then what will you do? And then
what will you do?

I think she knew she was going to take her life the day I met her. She had it all planned out. When she said "One day we will trade places" I think she was saying that she would die, and I would be born to take her place. I think she gave me her suicide note before she took her own life. I explained this all to the detective. I showed him the card.

He said that it just proved his theory—that a suicidal greeting card writer could not resist leaving a note. He said he'd have the lab analyze it. Compare it with other samples of Irene's handwriting. If I didn't hear back from him tomorrow—the handwriting checked out. But he also said he'd be keeping an eye on me. His last words were, "You're off the hook for now for the death of Irene Iwanski. But your pal Trevor Grueling has been missing since last week. So you remain a person of interest to me. I'm keeping my eye on you, my friend." He said it in a way that almost seemed friendly.

Almost, but not quite. He said I was free to go.

I don't like all this pressure. Being a human is stressful. I'm starting to think I may not want to be born after all. I haven't told Trish yet, but I'm writing this down and telling myself. Because I have to tell someone. So I'm telling my blog.

DISCLAIMER: I wrote the above from memory. The interrogation went on for a while. These are the parts I remember best. If I didn't say exactly these things, I probably meant to. I wrote this as a kind of a record of how the police mistreated me. Detective Dunleavy was just doing his job, I know. But he was trying to trick me into saying that I killed my dear friend Irene Iwanski. And that's not what happened. I have a pretty good memory, and I don't like people tricking me. In this way, a policeman and a reporter are similar. Their job is to get to the bottom of things and discover the truth, and to make that truth known to everyone. Their job is NOT to make up their own truths, and that is why I wrote this all down.

I did what Irene asked me to. She said her life was coming to an end and asked me to keep her company. She asked me to order pizza because that was her favorite food. We ate together. When she stopped breathing, I felt for her pulse, but she had no pulse. I called the police, and the police came. I was helping my friend. Why was the detective trying to say I had hurt my friend?

I wish Irene was still alive. She could explain everything. Where do people go when they're not here anymore? If Irene was still alive, she could sing a Gregorian chant and make people behave themselves.

I miss you, Irene, wherever you are.

31. THE SHOUTING MAN

Prospect takes his seat on the train. He closes his eyes once again. And he sees her alive: Irene Iwanski. Our Lady of the Greeting Cards. He is sitting on the train thinking about Irene and the strawberries when suddenly he hears a man onboard announce to the other passengers, *"I'm calling about my phone bill. It isn't right!"* And suddenly Prospect knows who is speaking. He turns around and sees The Shouting Man.

"It isn't right how you gouge people. You've added services I never wanted added. You've taken away services that I thought I would die with." By the time he has finished his call, the phone company agrees to give him last month's phone service for free and Prospect has missed his stop. He doesn't care. He wants to talk to this man. Prospect walks up to him as he is calmly putting his cell phone back in his pocket.

"Excuse me," Prospect says. "You were on the train last week. I don't mean to intrude. But your wife. She was sad." At first the man looks puzzled. Then he adds, "I wanted to know

how your wife is doing. I wanted to know how *you* are doing."
The man's face is unreadable. He is just looking and looking at the Pre-born.

Finally the man says, "You heard the conversation about my wife?"

"Yes, I didn't mean to listen, but I couldn't help it. You were talking loudly."

The man says, "And you want to know how we're doing?"

"If you want to tell me," Prospect says, very respectfully. He is studying his face for signs of emotion. Prospect can't tell if the man is glad he came up to talk to him or if he was about to punch him in the face. "If you don't want to talk about it, I understand. I know it's a difficult time."

It occurs to Prospect that The Shouting Man might start shouting all over again. Instead he says, "Can I buy you a cup of coffee, young man?"

"I would be honored."

They get off at the next stop and walk to a diner on the corner. The man, whose name is Gunther, buys them both coffee and toasted pecan rolls. "So, tell me about yourself. I want to know everything about you."

"There isn't much to tell really."

"Don't be humble. Why don't you start by telling me where were you born? It's so rare to find a kind person. I thought maybe you were from another country."

"Oh, that's an excellent question," Prospect says. "The short answer, I guess, is I'm from Chicago."

Gunther pours cream into his coffee and passes the creamer to his new friend. "I can tell you're a very compassionate person. May I ask what type of work you do?"

It would be easy for Prospect to tell Gunther who he is. That he is a Pre-born and that he doesn't really have a past. That his body was manufactured by Big Farm Technologies, and that the only reason he can speak to him at all is because of his CyberSavant. But Prospect doesn't really want to *go there*, as they say. It will only get in the way of their getting to know each other.

"Work? I'm…well…between things right now. If you know what I mean," Prospect says, continuing with the charade.

"Of course. No shame in that. So many are underemployed these days. What is your general field of endeavor? Your area of expertise?"

This question makes him chuckle. "Ah, I'm an expert at nothing, Gunther. Actually, I'm pretty new here."

"I bet you are in social work of some kind."

"Yes, I suppose I am."

For a moment Prospect is exhausted from so many questions and is glad for a pause. "I wouldn't worry about your wife," Prospect says. "I think she'll be fine."

"You do?"

"I think she just has to…find her own way. Ya know?" Prospect just smiles and take a bite of his pecan roll.

"So why do you think I don't have to worry about my wife?" he says.

Prospect dunks his pecan roll in his coffee because he saw someone do that on a TV show. "Because that's what we all have to do, Gunther. We all have to find our own way. You too. Don't you think?" Gunther's face is full of amazement. Like he has given him some unbelievable gift.

"You have a unique way of looking at things. How old are you?"

"I'm a lot younger than I look," Prospect says and gives him a big wink.

Gunther leans forward. "Have you ever been in love?"

"I don't think I've ever…loved anyone before." Gunther looks at him like he's from another planet. "Is that bad?" he asks.

"In your whole life? Surely you've loved someone a little?" he says.

"No. I don't think so." Gunther is looking at him like he's not from his tribe at all. "Well, I should be going now, Gunther. Thank you for the coffee and pecan roll. I'm glad I finally got to meet you."

"Me too. And don't worry," he says. "You have plenty of time to find the right person. You have your whole life ahead of you."

"Maybe," Prospect says. And this confuses Gunther.

They walk back up the stairs toward the train. But he must go north, and Prospect must go south. He waits with the Pre-born on his side of the platform for a while.

"I don't have plenty of time, Gunther," Prospect says. The roar of an approaching train is now heard in the distance. "There is a small window of opportunity…before I make my big decision." The train comes to a screeching halt as it pulls into the station.

"And what decision would that be?" Gunther asks as Prospect steps onto the train.

The Pre-born turns to face him. "If I want to be born." There is a look on Gunther's face like a light bulb has just been turned on. The doors close between them. He can hear Gunther shouting something outside the train, but he can't quite hear him. The train slowly starts to move and the man runs alongside it. Prospect looks closely at his lips to try to make out the shape of his words and then he understands. *"Pre-born?"*

Prospect looks back at him and nods slowly and clearly. Gunther smiles because now he knows who his new friend really is. Gunther stops running because he has come to the end of the platform. He waves good-bye. Such a nice man. Prospect knew he liked him…even before he met him.

32. THE SECRETS OF SCIENTISTS

Back at the hospital, in Trish's office, the debriefing is under-way. Trish pours herself something from a green bottle she keeps in a drawer. She doesn't offer Prospect any, which is unlike her not to share. "Did you know Irene had cancer?" he asks.

"Yes," says Trish. "But I still can't believe she would end her life like that...and not tell me. And to make you watch. That's awful." But it was Irene's life after all. It was not like she owed anything to Trish, he thinks to himself. But he does not say this out loud.

"Did you know that Trevor had been the subject of a bio-experiment? That he opposed the Pre-born Project?" Prospect asks. "Did you know that Trevor is missing?"

But before she'll even answer his questions, she has something to say. She takes a sip of her drink "I need to tell you something, Prospect, before you hear it through the rumor mill." She whispers into his ear, "Nothing is certain…but there is a chance I may be replaced as your Facilitator." Trish voice is thick with emotion. Prospect can't believe he's hearing what he's hearing.

"But why, Trish?" he asks.

"Actually, for many of the reasons your questions allude to. As you know, I report to a man named Karl Bangor. He heads up new product development for Big Farm. He in turn reports to Corporate," Trish says. "There is a feeling that I am not managing the Pre-born Project efficiently. That I seem distracted and am making errors in judgment. They're concerned, as am I, about the death of one Referral and the disappearance of another. I've been warned that if one more mishap occurs on my watch—Karl will replace me."

"What do you say to that?"

"I like bio-experiments to be organic, spontaneous. But I do need to keep a firmer grasp on the Referral process. I didn't want to micro-manage, but I may have to." She takes out a cigarette and lights it. He has never seen Trish smoke before. Ever.

"But this is *your* project. No one can do it—or should do it—but you."

"Believe me, I have every intention of seeing this project through." She takes a puff on her cigarette and the burning end turns bright orange. "There's something else I want to tell you, Prospect. Please have a seat." They sit down on the couch.

"The Pre-born Project, in many ways, was inspired by my grief over a child," she says. It's a complicated story and the details don't really matter now. Though they mattered a great deal at the time. Long story short, some years ago I had a son and gave him up for adoption. And at the moment I was handing him to the social worker, I wondered if this was a decision that I was entitled to make. Wouldn't it be better if the baby could choose what would happen to him? Where was his voice in all this? Missing. And as I began to devise the parameters of the Pre-born Project—I saw a chance, an opportunity—to bring my child back to me, if only for a while. And let him choose for himself."

"I'm not following you," Prospect says. "How could the Pre-born Project bring back your child?"

"Don't you know, Prospect?" She looks at him meaningfully. Puts out her cigarette in an old soda can on her desk. Prospect ponders the riddle she has put before him. And then she says one word with an enormous smile on her face: "Lito."

"What does Lito have to do with -- "

"Lito is my son," she says.

Prospect is speechless.

"Lito doesn't know he's my son," she says, "but *I* have to be the one to tell him, if I decide to tell him at all."

"Wow," is all the Pre-born can manage to say. He can see how this can be a good thing and a bad thing in Lito's eyes. It's complicated. "Are you hungry, Trish? Would you like to go get something to eat?"

"Oh, I need to manage our time together a bit more wisely," she says. "Debriefing like this is fine, but I think it's better if we don't have meals together."

He just gives her a blank stare. "What do you mean?"

"As your Facilitator, it's not required that you and I bond." Prospect narrows his eyes a bit on that remark. "That's what your Referrals are for. I'm more your conduit to the outside world."

"*Conduit?* Is that all you are to me, Trish?" Prospect is angry. "You know *everything* about me! You choose my friends for me, you monitor what I'm feeling, and why I'm feeling it, and in the end you'll know probably whether I want to be born or not—even before I do. I don't think my wanting to have dinner with you is unreasonable. And if you do…then we probably have less to talk about than I thought."

There is a long pause. She is deep in thought. Finally she smiles and whispers, "Let's talk about this at our next debriefing." Prospect can't believe her answer. She stands to walk him to the door. "You have just one more Referral. And then it's the big press conference where you'll announce your birth decision on live television. We're almost there, Prospect. Please…have a little faith. The project is going very well. I'm very proud of you." The Pre-born looks at Trish like he doesn't even know who this woman is.

This new and improved Trish.

As they walk out into the corridor, Trish says, "Oh my God! I almost forgot! There's someone here to see you. She's been waiting for some time in the lobby for you. I'll bring her up to your room."

Prospect goes to his room and waits for his mystery visitor to appear. And then there is a knock at the door. He opens the door to a young woman with bright pink hair, the color of cotton candy. A large backpack trails behind her like a turtle's shell.

"Hi," the young woman says. "You're the one they call Prospect, aren't you?"

"I am. Do I know you?" he says.

She offers a dazzling smile. "Not yet. I'm Joyce Boulanget."

TUNNEL OF LOVE

33. AN UNEXPECTED VISITOR

Prospect stands in the doorway filled with feelings. He is one part stunned, one part elated. "Omigod. Is it really you? The Disappearing Daughter...Joyce Boulanget! I dreamed one day I would meet you. Would it be okay to hug you?" he asks.

She opens her arms. They hug. There should be a photograph for such a hug. He doesn't know why she is suddenly so important to him. This new ally, this missing branch from the family tree. But he feels less alone with her beside him.

"I heard you were looking for me. A little bird told me," she says. "I think it was your private investigator. Lito something?"

"Lito Sanchez? Did you meet him?"

"It was pretty hard not to meet him. He practically stalked me on campus. Not to mention, he sent me like fifty-plus messages: Facebook invites, twitters, Skype invitations, phone messages, and text messages."

"I'm so glad to hear that. I owe him the rest of his fee," he says.

"And I heard the Pre-born Project was launching, and that Mom was involved again. When I was a Pre-born, I would've killed to talk to another Pre-born. I figured I owed it to you."

"Is it true what I heard? That you were the first Pre-born?"

"Guilty as charged." He leads her to the couch in his room. They sit down.

"You chose to be born. And you were born. But instead of being a happier person, you—"

"I was a fuck-up. It's true," she says. "But it wasn't the project's fault, or that the thesis was flawed. I could have been happy; I just chose not to be. It's the rebel in me that preferred a more difficult path through the forest. I was actually happy in my own twisted kind of way, but Big Farm Technologies couldn't see that. So they gave me an exit strategy."

Prospect studies his sister's face. "What do you think I should do, Joyce? What do you recommend?"

"Boy, you are talking to the wrong person. I stopped giving advice years ago," she says. "No, I'm afraid you're on your own with this decision. But good luck with that."

"Can I get you some coffee, water, soda?"

"I'm good."

"So you've been gone from the family for a long time. Where do you live now? How are you doing? Will you see Mom and Dad?"

She looks around her brother's white, white room. The single orange tulip in a clear glass vase makes the room so beautiful. "You deserve to have some answers," she begins. "I live in Minneapolis. I just started college. I'm studying bio-engineering. But then, who isn't these days? I guess you could say I'm on a journey." She laughs at this.

Prospect picks up the tulip from the vase and presents it to his sister. "Don't say I never gave you anything." She hesitates at first. Then she takes it. Twirls it between her fingers.

"I just wanted you to know that if you decide to be born...I guess I'll be your big sister, if you want one," says Joyce. He suspects she has given this some advance thought. "I chose to be born and look where it got me. Estranged from my family, exiled from Chicago. Life ain't awful, but it sure ain't like the glossy photos in all the brochures."

"Nothing like the brochures," he says. "I'll remember that, Joyce. I know your life has not been easy."

She laughs. "Who wants an easy life? That's like playing tennis without a net."

"I want you to talk to Mother. Let her know...you're okay," he says.

"I can't. You do that for me, if you like."

He reaches for his cell phone. "Let me take a picture of you at least." But Joyce flips his phone closed.

"No contact means no contact."

"It would really mean a lot to her. In case."

"In case?" she asks.

"In case I choose not to be born. I think it would mean a lot to her that you're alive."

A sadness crosses Joyce's face. "Not as much as you might think. Well...I've got to go now. Minneapolis is calling to me. And I have finals coming up."

"Joyce?"

"What."

"Thank you." He asks her if they can trade cell numbers. They do. But she makes him promise not to give it to their parents.

"It was very nice to meet you, Prospect Boulanget," she says.

"I have a last name! No one ever told me I had a last name."

"Don't say I never gave you nothin', squirt."

"Joyce. Do you think I'll ever see you again?"

She thinks for a second. "To be totally honest…probably not. Just know that whatever happens, your big sister will be rooting for you." As Joyce starts to walk away, Prospect notices her backpack. Her *Hello Kitty* backpack. Then she stops and turns around. "Oh, one last thing," she shouts. "If you ever happen to get into a fight with that asshole Karl Bangor from Big Farm, you should know he's got a glass jaw. Don't ask me how I know that. Old Karl deserves a good punch or two. Tell him it's from Joyce Boulanget."

Prospect gives her a thumbs up. And off she walks, her mind already focused on finals week.

◦◦

Prospect is exhausted. There's so much new information, and not all of it good. As much as he doesn't agree with the new changes, he also doesn't think it's fair that Trish be replaced by some joker from Corporate.

He calls Lito to ask him to meet at seven in the morning at the hospital. He tells Lito he finally met his sister, and that he owes him five hundred dollars. Also that he has another project to talk to him about. And that he shouldn't be late. Prospect has to start making some clear plans for the future. Before the future becomes the past and he's out of time.

34. ALPHABET SOUP

There is a knock on Prospect's door. Lito enters, chewing on a cherry Twizzler.

Prospect and Lito embrace. Then they kiss on the lips, because they liked it so much the last time. Lito's mouth tastes like cherry Twizzlers, which makes his kiss even more delicious.

"Mmm. You taste good," says the Pre-born. Lito smiles. "Hey, thank you so much for bringing Joyce to me. That was awesome. You are awesome."

"Stop," Lito says. He has never learned to take a compliment.

Prospect hands him a check for the balance of his project fee. Lito slides it into his billfold. "I think I could get used to this holding-down-a-job thing."

"We don't have much time. You have to focus like you've never focused before." Prospect sits him down in the chair and pulls his chair up close to him. "I just wanted you to know that I'm going to talk to my parents about you. About looking after you, if you know what I mean. And if it doesn't work out with them—there's always my sister Joyce to turn to. But this has got to be our secret, understand? "

"That's cool. Do you have room service here? I haven't had breakfast yet."

"Focus, dammit! This is important," Prospect says. "I don't know if I'm going to choose to be born or not, but either way I want to make sure you're taken care of, okay?"

"Okay, what are you so stressed about?" Lito asks.

"Life isn't all random. It's not just a paper fire that starts all of a sudden in a trash can. It's also a flower sprouting in a coffee can that someone planted and planned for," the Pre-born explains. "If you lose interest in it, stop paying attention for one moment—it can die on you. Fortune tellers find patterns in tea leaves at the bottom of a cup. That's what you've got to learn to do. See the connections, connect the dots. Don't piss your life away and blame it on your ADD or your parents who abandoned you.

"Now *if* I am born—there's gonna be a time lag. When I'm born, Lito, you'll be eighteen. A man. I won't remember anything from my Pre-born life. They're gonna wipe my memory banks clean. So at some point, you're gonna have to start reminding me…how we first met, and how you came to live in our house. If I choose *not* to be born—you've always got the Boulanget family to fall back on. Does this make sense?"

Lito is trying to understand. "So if you're born and your folks kind of adopt me, we'll be brothers, sort of?"

"Right, but a lot of this is gonna depend on you. Do you follow?"

"Well…"

"What did I just tell you, Lito?"

"You said…" he starts.

Prospect looks at his watch. He thinks of the Referral he still has to meet, his morning debriefing with Trish. "What? What did I say?"

"It's too much," Lito says. "It's too hard."

"Try."

He rubs his index finger against his lip. "You said…it's not like pages on fire."

"That's good," Prospect says.

"It's like…"

"What is it like?"

"…like flowers all in a row. There is a pattern, and I must find it. It's my job."

"That's right." Prospect feels a flicker of hope for him. He gets up from his chair and starts to get ready to show Lito the door when Lito's voice stops him.

"When you're born, I'll be a man," he says. Prospect turns and looks at this teenager's shining face. "When you're ten, I'll be twenty-eight, and I'll have to start reminding *you*…" says Lito.

Prospect laughs out loud, and Lito joins in. "That's right! Remind me of what, Lito?" There is a knock at the door. Prospect ignores it.

"Of who I am and how I came to live with you. Of boys who sleep on bus benches at night and girls who sleep in swimming pools. Of ADD and DCFS and HIV and the whole fucked up alphabet we come from—"

The door opens wide. It's Trish. She's early, and they were supposed to meet in *her* office. Suddenly there is tension in the room.

"Lito! I didn't expect to see you today," she says. She is holding a newspaper in her hand.

"Hey, Trish…and a good morning to you," he says.

She smiles. "Well, Prospect and I have our check-in meeting this morning. Pretty soon he's going to appear at a big press conference that's all about him and his decision."

"Keep this Pre-born out of trouble, will ya?" he says to Trish. "Well, I'll catch you later, P-man."

"Have a great day, Lito," says Trish. Just as the door swings closed, she says, "What was Lito doing here? You finished your Referral with him a while ago."

"I'm just trying to help with his ADD. Coach Dinwiddie said Lito needed a goal in life. Or at least some projects to help him focus."

"That's very good of you." Trish throws the newspaper onto his bed. "Read this. Read it and weep."

On page three, she has highlighted a story. The headline reads: "Bio-Experiment Volunteers Vanish." Trish notes that it is the first negative story in the media about the Pre-born Project. The article talks about Trevor's disappearance and Irene's suicide and goes on to raise questions: How well-drawn are the guidelines of the Pre-born Project? Are Referrals being placed in jeopardy? What really happened to Irene Iwanski and Trevor Grueling? Big Farm is not happy."

Prospect reads the article. "This is terrible. Your boss must be upset."

"I think we should postpone your last Referral till the media interest dies down," she says.

"Trish, I don't think Trevor is missing. I think he's hiding," he says. "Don't you see? He figured out he can do the most damage to the project by disappearing. I'd bet serious money that he's alive and well and having a good laugh at our expense."

"That's an interesting theory. If I didn't know you better, I'd say you're becoming cynical. Is that possible?"

"I think I trust people too easily. That's what Lito told me anyway."

"Well, whether Trevor is hiding or missing—he's a problem until we can find him. I just talked with Corporate. They're asking me to step down from the project."

Prospect does not want to hear this news. "What are you going to do, Trish? You've got to fight for what you believe in, don't you?" She nods but is not convinced. "Do you want to know what I think we should do? I think I should stay in my room for a few days till the media attention blows over. While I'm here, I'm gonna go online and do my damndest to track down Trevor Grueling. You tell Big Farm there's just one more Referral to go, and there's no sense in changing Facilitators now. That I insist on continuity and I *refuse* to work with anyone else."

"Would you really say that to Corporate in a face-to-face meeting?"

"I would love to have that chance. I mean, what are they going to do, Trish? Fire me?"

She laughs. He continues, "Bring on that Karl Bangor person. He's not just fucking with you now. He's fucking with me. And I will *not* be fucked with. I am unfuckable! Because I am Prospect Boulanget, and I can shut down this experiment any time I want."

"Your language, Prospect!" Trish has never seen this side of him. It is a little disconcerting, a little troubling. But also quite thrilling, if she does say so herself.

"Just tell me the time and the place and I'll be there. And I won't just be speaking on your behalf. I'll be speaking on my behalf too." Trish likes this new side of Prospect. It's as if he is evolving…right before her eyes. Like a piece of black coal transformed by tons of pressure and the passage of time into a diamond. A diamond that cuts glass.

◌

Now that Prospect has agreed to meet with Corporate, she's a little more hopeful. But she needs to step up her game. Time to play a little hardball with the big boys. She logs into her tablet and shoots off an email missile to Karl Bangor. She blind copies Karl's boss.

Karl,

I need to call an emergency meeting with you and your supervisor from Corporate. We need to meet ASAP. Preferably yesterday. (A little joke there.) In the next few hours will be fine. It's about the future of the Pre-born Project. Please get back to me. I can make myself available any time today. If you can meet right now, even better.

Dr. Trish Mesmer

Lead Scientist and Creator of the Pre-born Project

She sketches out her strategy. She goes to Prospect's room to strategize with him.

Rule one of corporate hardball: Schedule meetings but don't reveal to your adversary the full agenda for the meeting. She has told Karl Bangor it's an emergency meeting on the Pre-born Project. But does not reveal the full nature of the meeting. If called or emailed, she will evade his questions and assure him that all will be explained at the meeting, and not a moment before.

Rule two. Bring unexpected guests to the meeting. This is one of the best ways to throw said adversary off balance. Trish will bring her secret weapon—Prospect himself. Karl and Corporate have never met him in person. Prospect's rising public profile will likely make them fawn over him a bit as he is gradually emerging as a kind of bio-celebrity. They will not likely want to misbehave or argue in front of him. Especially knowing that Prospect will have the microphone all to himself at the final press conference.

Rule three. Know the precise outcome you desire for the meeting and stop at nothing till you achieve it. She analyzes the dynamics of the situation to understand where her position is strong and where it is weak. She considers exactly what she is willing to give up and what she is not willing to give up. The meeting is over when Trish gets what she came for. She wants to retain her position as Facilitator of the project.

They take turns role-playing possible objections from Corporate. Prospect is nervous that he is not very experienced in matters like this, but Trish assures him she will do the heavy lifting. It will be like singing a duet. As long as they are in harmony, their song will be compelling. But if they mess up, if they contradict each other, that will only help make Karl's case. Trish gets nervous as they role-play when she sees Prospect losing his focus. For this meeting to be a true success, Trish and Prospect be a well-oiled killing machine.

35. A MEETING OF MINDS

It's early afternoon when Prospect and Trish arrive at Big Farm Technologies. The lobby is very sleek. A waterfall from the second floor flows down into a pool of water in the lobby below. The pool shimmers with orange carp that dart through the water. A mini-forest of tropical plants transports the lobby visitor to a place of exotic luxury.

On the walls are paintings of farm life: cows being milked at dawn, chickens pacing in a yard, fields of grain as far as the eye can see. The paintings are not horrible, but they seem to have no connection to the tropical waterfall. The lobby décor appears to be the result of an argument in which there was no clear winner. Welcome to Big Farm. Once they check in at the security desk, they ascend in a clear glass elevator.

Prospect has scribbled a few notes in ink on the palm of his hand, just in case. He notices that he is sweating more than usual, and he has a bit of a stomachache. Butterflies too.

The doors slide open, and the admin assistant escorts Trish and Prospect down a long hallway to the conference room. They find Karl Bangor and his boss, Julianne Hasegawa from Corporate, seated at the table, whispering. There is a glass pitcher of water and glasses on the table. The hosts rise to greet their guests. "Trish Mesmer...this is Julianne Hasegawa, Senior VP. Oh and...I don't believe I've had the pleasure."

Trish smiles. "Yes, I'm thrilled to introduce to you... Prospect. He is, of course, the Pre-born of the Pre-born Project fame." Julianne's jaw gapes open and closed. She looks like one of the carp in the lobby pool. Poor woman.

"Oh," she says. "I, I...well, this really is an honor, isn't it?"

"Trish, you didn't mention you were bringing a guest," says Karl.

"Oh, for heaven's sake," says Trish. "Prospect isn't a guest. At Big Farm, he's practically family."

Trish's strategy works perfectly. Julianne's role in the meeting is to be the attack dog for Karl, but Julianne is so starstruck by meeting Prospect in person, she seems to have forgotten why she's there. And while Karl thinks this meeting is to discuss the turnover of the project to him—it will soon becomes another meeting entirely. It will be a bit more awkward to have this meeting with Prospect present. The four of them take their seats.

"Trish, you did see the article I emailed you, the one slamming the Pre-born Project, right?" Karl says. "And I told you in plain terms that Corporate demanded you be replaced. This is a meeting to discuss the turnover of the project."

"Maybe you didn't read my email closely, Karl. I said this meeting was to discuss the future of the project. Nothing more. And as I called the meeting, I believe my agenda is the correct one." Trish smiles benevolently.

Now Prospect leans forward over the conference table. He carefully opens the palm of his right hand. In smudged black ink are the words: KEEP FACILITATOR. "Julianne, I think changing Facilitators this late in the project is a very bad idea. Trish and I are a team. To replace her at this time, well, I think…it's dangerous." Prospect glances to Trish. She nods.

"He's right, Julianne," Trish says. "Continuity is everything. To have the data of a bio-experiment captured and interpreted by two different Facilitators, well, that's a recipe for disaster. Historically, such changes in project management end badly."

Karl rolls his eyes. "Since when are they a team?" he mutters under his breath.

"Did you say something, Karl?" Julianne asks.

"Nothing," he says.

Again, Prospect consults the palm of his hand to see the words: TREVOR, IRENE. He continues. "Now I know you're worried about Trevor and Irene. Trevor told me the day I met him that he would do everything he could to mess up the Pre-born Project. I'm sure he's in hiding. In fact a friend of his basically told me that." He rises and pours glasses of water for both himself and Trish.

"We need a credible name, a phone number, a way to verify this," Karl says, jotting a note to himself.

Prospect looks to Trish. "I'm sure we can provide that to you."

Karl passes his cell to Prospect. "Why not call the person now? So we can start the vetting process?"

Trish looks to Julianne. "Is that really necessary?"

"Karl has a point," she says. "We can't just take your word on it. Or even the word of a stranger on the phone. But it will start the vetting process." Trish looks back at Prospect.

The person he would call is Kitty. But whether she'll cooperate and betray her friend Trevor is another question. "How about this? I will try to reach Kitty and put her on speakerphone. I don't think she'll want to get Trevor into trouble, but maybe I could get her to talk about him and what's he's up to."

"That's a great idea, Prospect," says Trish. Karl and Julianne have no objections. Karl pushes a few buttons to activate the speakerphone. Prospect looks up Kitty's number in his phone book and dials. It rings. Someone picks up. "Hello?"

"Hi, is this Kitty?"

"Yes, who's this?"

"Hi, Kitty. This is Prospect. How are you?"

"I'm fine."

"Have you heard any more from Trevor? I mean, how long does he plan to stay missing?"

Kitty says nothing. "Am I on speakerphone?"

"No. This is just a big room. It kind of echoes—"

"I told you everything I know, Prospect. I have to go now. Good-bye."

Julianne jots a note down. "She didn't deny that Trevor was planning something. Karl, can you follow up on this without making her suspicious?" He nods, jots another note. They write in little leather-bound pads.

Prospect looks at his hand again to keep himself on track. "Now as for my good friend Irene…" He falters, trying to remember his next point.

Trish aborts a sip of water and sets down her glass with a jerk. "As for Irene, we know that Prospect had become very close friends with her," Trish interjects. "The police have interviewed him, and they're confident that her death was just a tragic suicide. A suicide note was recovered."

"That's right. They found a note." Prospect looks to see if his answer satisfies Corporate.

"Karl, were you aware of these breaking developments?" Julianne asks.

Karl knows if he says he was aware of them, then he has failed to keep his boss updated. If he says he was unaware of them, he is incompetent. So he drinks long and slow from his water glass.

Prospect opens the palm of his hand to find an inky blur. Between his sweating and his handling of the water glass, the letters of the words have smeared together. It seems to say: GET AIDS. His eyebrows furrow. Get AIDS? This makes no sense to him. He tries to sound it out under his breath. "Get ads…get laid…Gettysburg Address…" Julianne is puzzled by his muttering. Trish looks worried. Then Prospect figures it out. "I'm sorry. What I wanted to say is…Karl has always said how important it is that the project wraps up as quickly as possible. I believe his exact words were: 'The sooner the project finishes— the sooner everyone *gets paid*.'" Julianne shoots a look at Karl. "Trish and I would like to get back to work as soon as possible."

Julianne Hasegawa is beaming. "Prospect, I *like* the way you think. In fact, I'd like to have you on my team one day.

You are just the breath of fresh air I've been telling Karl we need around here. It's a shame you aren't born yet! Please, hurry up and be born." And she laughs wildly. "What do you have to say, Karl?"

Karl finally sets down his empty glass on the conference room table. "Actually, I think a change of leadership is crucial at this point. And I'd hardly call the death of a volunteer and the disappearance of another…good teamwork." Julianne listens patiently. "And until Trevor Grueling appears in the flesh, I assure you he's still considered a missing person in the eyes of the media. That's a liability for the project."

"Trish, your response?"

She looks into Karl's eyes with kindness and grace. "Experiments, by their very nature, are unpredictable. That's why they're called experiments. But I've decided I am going to keep the Referrals on a shorter leash, just to be safe." Julianne jots this down in her notebook.

"Could I remind everyone that the initial concern from Corporate began with the newspaper story about the vanishing volunteers?" Karl says. "I offer up my services to prevent further damage to the credibility of this project. Trish cannot provide that—as she is perceived by the media as the cause of that damage." Julianne is starting to drift over to Karl's side.

"Excuse me, but as the subject of the Pre-born Project— could I put in my two and a half cents?" says Prospect. Everyone stops and looks at him.

"Of course," Julianne says.

The Pre-born pauses to gather his thoughts for a moment. He glances out the big conference room window to an office building across from him. A PowerPoint demonstration is in progress; he's grateful he doesn't have to sit through it. "My view is very simple," he announces. "If Trish does *not* continue with the project—I will *not* continue either." He catches Trish's eye, and she is beaming.

"Do you mean that if Trish is replaced—you would prematurely choose not to be born?" Karl asks. "Because I don't think we'd have a problem with that."

"No, Karl," says his boss. "You're not listening. What Prospect said was he would choose *not* to choose."

"That's right," he says. "I would not appear at the press conference to announce my birth decision. And I would not be Big Farm's spokesman for the project."

Julianne clicks her pen and shuts her notebook. "I do believe Prospect's vote trumps everyone else's. I'm returning the control of the project to Trish. Now if you'll excuse me, I have another meeting." She stands up, as do all the others. She extends her hand to the Pre-born. "It was a pleasure."

As Julianne and Karl leave the room, she says, "I asked your opinion to be polite, but so help me, Karl, if you give me grief every time…I'm gonna stop asking." Trish and Prospect wait for them to exit. Once the Big Farm staff are gone, they raise their water glasses in a toast.

"Nicely played," Trish says. They clink their glasses. Prospect looks once more at the palm of his hand.

The words on the Pre-born's hand have melted into an inky blur.

36. PROSPECT'S BLOG

*L*ito and I are standing before no less than eight vending machines in the basement of Infinity. There's a soda machine and an ice cream machine and a chip machine and a sandwich machine and a coffee machine and a few candy machines. A person could live a whole life down here I think. It must be the middle of the night because there is not a soul around. The cafeteria across the way is pitch dark and quite closed. From time to time, I see gurneys moving through the hallway, but no one is aboard them, and no one is pushing them! They are ghost gurneys. They scare me a little, but they amuse me too.

"Hey, Lito, do you want to go somewhere really cool?" I say. "I'll show you my special place if you're interested."

"Sure. Show me the cool stuff," says Lito.

"Follow me," I say. We take the elevator to the highest floor of Infinity. So high up that our ears pop, and I think there are parts of us that we leave on the floors below. When we get off, we walk up a secret stairway two more flights. I open the heavy metal door.

We stand on the rooftop, and the view is what I came for, one reason I brought Lito here. The view, as they say, is breathtaking. It's such a crystal clear evening, I feel like I could reach out and touch the buildings, the cars on Lake Shore Drive, the stars over Argyle Street. Like I could guide a car back into its proper lane, or push a falling star back into the sky—with the gentle nudge of my finger.

My friend walks to the edge of the roof. I join him there. "This is majorly cool. I'm impressed."

"Hey," I say. "Have you ever done something you didn't think in a million years you could do?"

"Like what?"

"Have you ever flown before?"

"I've never been on a plane."

"Who said anything about a plane?" And I look at him with a special look until I think he really understands my meaning. I put my arm around his shoulder and together we lean over and look straight down at the tangle of traffic and city lights below.

I make a sudden move like I'm about to push him over the edge, to scare him I guess. But I keep a good hold of him.

"Jesus Christ! What'd you do that for?" he shouts.

"I believe all humans can fly, don't you? It's in our nature. It's just our doubt that keeps us stuck here on earth."

"Prospect, my man. What have you been smoking?"

And with my arm wrapped tightly around his neck—I don't know how else to say this—we step off the roof and fly. We don't fall. We hover. We hold our air space. It's the weirdest feeling in the world.

And we're okay. Everything is okay. We're going to be okay.

DISCLAIMER: The event above is actually from a dream I had.

37. TWILIGHT

Prospect is back at the Kopi Cafe. He sees that two more goddesses with hand mirrors are dangling from the ceiling. He makes a mental note to himself. Then he takes out his last Referral letter and reads it. His favorite waitress with the chandelier earrings keeps his coffee cup filled to the brim. His vegetarian sandwich was quite good. "How's your day going today, Bob?" she says.

"It's going pretty darned good actually," he replies. "How about yours, Sally?" The waitress looks at him like she's about to say something. Then she shakes her head and laughs. Maybe she doesn't like her new name Sally. Maybe she likes it a lot. She doesn't say, and he doesn't ask. But he feels closer to her somehow. This Sally. "Oh, I wanted to purchase one of the goddesses with the hand mirror. Could you add that to my bill?"

Sally beams at him. "I don't do this for everyone, Bob, but I'll do it for you!"

Dear Prospect,

Your last Referral is Victor Pastelle (Pastelle is his art-
ist name, by the way. His real name is Victor Ansari.)
He is 49, Middle Eastern. A resident of Evanston, Illi-
nois—he considers himself happily divorced. Victor is a
semi-successful, mid-career painter with a small but loyal
following in certain suburban circles. He is what is called
an empath—one who can feel the feelings of others on a
profound and mystical level. He then turns those feelings
into paintings. I look forward to debriefing with you after
your stay with Victor.

Of course when you return in a few days, there is the
press conference August 26th in the main auditorium of
Infinity. The twenty-first floor. They will be broadcasting
live at 8 p.m. sharp, so we'll want to go over some talking
points in preparation for it. YOU MUST RETURN TO
THE HOSPITAL NO LATER THAN 4 P.M. You will
surely be the focus of everyone's attention and curiosity. It
is there that you will reveal your ultimate birth decision.
I want to thank you now, before the media frenzy begins,
for your openness to the Pre-born Project in general...and
to me in particular. No matter what you decide—I will
never forget you.

Trish

Sally now approaches his table with a nice turquoise
plastic shopping bag. At the bottom of the bag under gauzy

blankets of white tissue sleeps his Indonesian flying goddess. She also leaves the check in a little plastic dish. Prospect pays and goes on his way. He will give it to Trish Mesmer as a thank you gift. And as a reminder to have more fun in life.

๛

Evanston is one of the prettier suburbs of Chicago. It is a place filled with college students from Northwestern University and baby-boomer intellectuals who know good art when they see it. It's twilight. When Prospect's taxi pulls up in front of the building, he thinks there must be a mistake. It looks abandoned or, at best, it looks unloved. He gives the cabbie a ten-dollar tip if he'll wait till he is sure it is the right place. As he studies the names on the buzzer, the cab pulls away with great speed. That's when Prospect sees a note taped to the door telling guests to enter by the back stairway. When he makes it to the third floor where the artist lives, he looks in through the screen door and is startled to see a man staring back at him. For a moment they just look at each other. Finally the man laughs and says, "We could do this Referral thing through the screen door—but I thought it might be easier if you came *inside*." He opens the screen door wide for him as Prospect enters his home.

"Oh, hi, sorry. You must be Victor Pastelle."

"That would be me," he says, squinting at him as if he were looking into the sun. Though Victor is in his late forties, he is a big strong man with a ruddy complexion. He has jet-black hair. He keeps it spiky with gel. He has a gold stud on his left ear lobe.

"Please, come in," he says. He guides him down a long hallway to what he says is his painting studio. In this room there are several large paintings on easels, covered by white sheets. Prospect stares at them with great curiosity.

Victor notices his fascination and says, "It's a new project. It isn't finished yet. When our time together is done, I will do an unveiling of them all. But you must give me your word that you will never peek at my veiled canvases. Only the artist should unveil his or her work to you. Do you understand?"

"Yes, Victor. I promise."

Victor smiles. "The final painting will be of you."

"Me?"

"I hope you will be a willing subject."

"I'll do my best," he says.

Victor leads him to the living room where they sit on a bright red sofa shaped like the lips of a beautiful woman. "Victor, thank you for agreeing to be one of my Referrals. I know some basic facts about you, but why don't you tell me in your own words."

Victor reaches for a cigar box on the piano. "I don't smoke," Prospect says.

Victor flips open the box's lid. "Neither do I. They're chocolate!" he explains. Prospect watches Victor unwrap the tin foil, and he does likewise. Then he bites into the sweet velvety candy. Delightful.

"If there's only one thing you remember about me, Prospect, it would be that I am an artist," he says. "Nothing else matters. Not my ethnicity, not my faith, not my sexual orientation, not my politics, not whether I am single or partnered. An artist, by definition, is a freak. I think that's why Trish chose me to be your last Referral," says the painter. "Do you know what artists do?"

"Um, well, an artist makes things…that weren't there before? I never really thought about it."

"Ah, so you think a baby is a work of art then? Since two parents join forces to create a baby which didn't exist prior to that moment?"

"I suppose so," Prospect says, "but I think when people talk about art, they're talking about music or motion pictures or poetry. I think the paintings you paint are art."

"I'm so glad to hear it!" Victor says a little too enthusiastically. "I've been telling my friends for years that I'm an artist." He bites deeper into his chocolate cigar. "Would you like to hear my definition of an artist?"

"Very much."

"An artist creates art. And art is the beautiful and terrible debris that is left after life has been truly lived. It is the place where our most passionate dreams and our most horrible nightmares commingle, fornicate, and give birth to some unthinkable offspring."

"I kind of like your definition better than mine." Just then, a cat brushes up against the Pre-born's leg.

"Oh, that's Chase. He just wants to say hello." The cat jumps up onto Prospect's chair and his tail goes straight up into the air. He pets Chase and rubs under his chin. The cat starts purring. Victor squints at them. Prospect can't tell if he's squinting because he's smiling or because he needs glasses. Chase curls into a ball and falls asleep in Prospect's lap.

"Artists must do anything and everything possible to make room in the world for their art. Because when artists stop fighting for that, stop making art…they cease to exist. They become ghosts. So it's important that those who are not artists forgive artists for their trespasses, their transgressions. For whatever compromises they must make. Do you understand what I'm saying, Prospect?"

Prospect rubs his chin, as if that will help him think. "I think I follow you." But he's not sure he does.

Victor stands up. "Well, I'm going to start our lunch." He moves to the kitchen where he turns up the gas burner under a large cast-iron skillet, filling it with strips of bacon. "Do you eat bacon?" he asks. Prospect nods. Soon he is slicing up avocados, using a huge, shiny knife that seems far too large for such little vegetables. Next he carves up slices of turkey breast and places them inside big chunks of bread. "Lunch is served," he announces.

They sit having lunch in Victor's dining room, enjoying their meal. Through the window, the Pre-born notices it's dark outside and his host has not turned on any lamps. "Tell me about your friends," Prospect says.

"They're mostly artists and social outcasts like me." Victor must sense his discomfort, for he gets up to turn on a floor lamp by the sofa. Still, a single lamp in an apartment of this size only draws attention to the shadows it casts. It's the light of dreams and nightmares. Prospect's host walks over to the front window and studies his neighbors chatting on the sidewalk below.

"Tomorrow, I'd like to paint you if that's okay with you. Have you ever been *rendered* before?" he says. "Would you be my subject for a sitting?"

"I'd be honored, Mr. Pastelle."

"Call me Victor."

"Okay, Victor."

When finally it is time for Prospect to go to sleep, Victor brings out some sheets and a pillow and lays them on the sofa. He turns off the lamp. Prospect has gotten used to sleeping in strange places by now. Chase climbs up onto the sofa and lies down in a ball at his feet. It is fairly quiet in this neighborhood. He can even hear the refrigerator hum in the kitchen, and it keeps him awake for a while. But at some point, he falls asleep. When he next opens his eyes—it is morning.

38. THE SITTING

They spend most of the next day in Victor's studio. Prospect sits in a chair shaped like a large human hand. There's something comical about it. Victor studies him. "When I meet an interesting subject, I just have to drink him in," the painter says. Prospect spends this time reflecting on the people he's met, the feelings he's felt.

Has it really been almost three weeks since the Project began? He wonders if he has lost some of his innocence. The magic world of science has lost some of its luster, now that he's peeked behind the curtain a bit. Prospect has noticed how humans are drawn to science fiction movies with their foreboding glimpses into the future, but it's not the future Prospect is afraid of. It's the present that scares him the most.

"Whatever you are thinking right now, I love it," says Victor. "It gives your face such gravitas, such sad beauty."

Victor opens a box filled with an array of charcoal pieces that he will use to sketch with. "I don't just paint what I see.

I paint what I don't see as well. I don't know what the image means. I sleep on it. Literally. And in my dream state, the text comes to me, the images, the meaning is gradually revealed."

Prospect pictures Victor in bed as words float across the ceiling of his bedroom like lonely search lights.

Victor asks him to take an odd pose. He has Prospect stand and raise his arms in front of him. The painter does a lightning-fast sketch. "I have a talented new apprentice who helps me on larger projects like this. Would you like to meet him?" Prospect nods. And then, he hears the footsteps of a man approach from another room.

When he looks up, he is surprised to see Trevor Grueling.

"Prospect, we have to stop meeting like this," he says.

"What are you doing here? And where have you been?"

"It's not against the rules for Referrals to meet Referrals," Trevor says.

"You wouldn't be trying to sabotage the Pre-born Project, would you?" says Prospect.

"I will neither confirm nor deny."

"Do you know Trish has been looking for you?"

"That's touching. But as you can see...I'm immersed in the world of art. When they removed my sense of wonder, they also removed my chance of being a real painter in my own right. But I'm pretty good at painting by numbers." Trevor produces a palette of different colored paints and begins dabbing at the canvas as they talk. "After meeting Victor at one of the Referral orientations, we talked a bit about painting. I used to like to paint before my bio-experiment. So I asked Victor if there might be some way we could...*collaborate.*"

Victor adds, "Trevor has some natural talent. It saddens me to think what kind of painter he might've become if he hadn't been part of that car crash of a bio-experiment." The painter stands before the canvas that Trevor had been working on. He begins painting in the smaller details of the image. "When they removed Trevor's sense of wonder, several other qualities were gutted as well. His ability to imagine, to hope. Trevor Grueling today is a passable human being. But he is a shadow of his former self."

Trevor walks back toward them. "Victor doesn't mince words, does he?" he laughs. "He's trying to teach me to wonder again…through art. No scientist has ever offered to do that."

"Where are you staying these days?" Prospect asks.

Trevor rolls his eyes upward. "I'm just above you, in the attic. It's a bit more humble than my penthouse, but it's amazing what you can get used to when you're on a mission. And I am on a mission."

Victor considers the canvas from many angles. He covers one eye with the palm of his hand and studies the painting. He turns his back to the canvas and then turns quickly to shoot a glance back at it, as if to catch the painting unawares. "We've done some good work today, men. Trevor, will you take the canvas to my room please?"

And on this night, while Chase purrs on the sofa, and Trevor tosses and turns in the attic above him—Prospect is fully awake. Because this is his last Referral, and everything is rapidly coming to an end. And because he is dying to see the painting Victor has done of him. How has he rendered the Pre-born?

Prospect's curiosity gets the best of him and he tiptoes toward his room. He hears Victor muttering to himself, but he can't make anything out. He carefully puts his hand on the doorknob to his room and it twists open. He quietly walks a few steps into the room and sees Victor sleeping in bed. The new painting waits on an easel at the foot of his bed.

"Prospect, what are you doing in my room?" says Victor with complete clarity.

Prospect jumps. "I'm sorry, Victor. I thought you were having a nightmare."

"And what if I was having a nightmare?" He gets out of bed and puts on a robe. "What would you have done then?"

"Well, I'd try to wake you, I suppose."

"And why would you do that? I told you my best breakthroughs come in the dream state," he says. "If you intrude again—I'll have to ask you to leave. Now please shut the door after you."

"I'm sorry, Victor."

But Victor isn't listening anymore. He is in some kind of communion with the painting. "The boy is new," he whispers to the painting. "He doesn't know any better. Now where were we—" This is the last thing Prospect hears Victor say as he pulls the door closed.

The Pre-born lies down on the sofa, thinking about the big press conference tomorrow night. And soon he is snoring.

∿

At some point in the night, someone can be heard climbing the wooden stairs. Two men talk in whispers, but Prospect is sound asleep.

"Do you think my paintings will persuade our young friend?"

"Your paintings are amazing. I believe your paintings could have a deep effect on him."

"And if they don't—is there a Plan B?"

"We could always just kill him," says Trevor as casually as if he had just announced that they could take him bowling. Just as casual as that. "After all, he hasn't been born yet. So it wouldn't be murder exactly, would it? It's a gray area."

Victor laughs. "Yes, a gray area. I love gray areas. I think I have a summer home in the gray area." A man descends the stairs, enters his room, and gently closes a door.

◌

During the night, Prospect has a dream that involves blood, betrayal, and flowers. At the end of the dream, he wakes with a start. He wonders what he has gotten himself into, and how he will get himself out.

Chase licks Prospect's face. The cat looks deep into Prospect's eyes as if they've known each other longer than they have, as if Chase wants to know what's keeping his new friend awake tonight. But Prospect doesn't know how to explain it, not in a way a cat would understand. Prospect's life is so much more complicated than a cat's life. But that's not Chase's fault, and it's not really Prospect's fault either.

39. THE UNVEILING

He awakens to daylight. Prospect walks from room to room, calling out to his host. He passes by the sofa shaped like a pair of lips in the living room and it makes him giggle. He can hear Trevor walking around in the attic above. Victor's bedroom door is ajar. Through the crack in the door, he doesn't see the painting on the easel, nor any trace of Victor.

"Victor?" he calls out. There is no sound. He enters the room. He gently tugs at the sheet that covers the first painting and it falls to the floor.

He sees the figure of his mother in a forest at night. He recognizes the dress and her body language. She is planting a garden of some kind. But what is sprouting just below her feet is surprising: an ear of corn, a cucumber, and the upper torso of a Barbie doll. There is text painted onto the canvas below this image:

SHE BURIED HER TRUTHS IN THE BACKYARD, NEXT TO THE CUCUMBERS AND THE CORN.

The painting troubles him. The spooky nighttime forest. The doll buried in the dirt. It evokes his mother's feeling that she murdered her daughter. But how would Victor know anything about this? All in a day's work for an empath. He pulls down the sheet to reveal the second painting.

In this painting, he sees the figure of Trish Mesmer. She is perched in the branches of an apple tree. Her legs dangle over a tree limb. Directly below her, it appears that Lito has fallen to the ground. Red apples dot the grass around him. But has he fallen accidentally or been pushed? Perhaps he has been pushed out of the nest. The text is short and sweet:

THE FRUIT NEVER FALLS FAR FROM THE TREE.

This picture seems cruel. Like a bad joke. A joke at Lito's expense.

Just then he hears footsteps climbing up the back stairway. He can't tell if it's Victor or not, but he doesn't want to take any chances.

He quickly throws the sheets back over the first two paintings. The footsteps continue their steady climb up to the landing. There is the jangle of keys at the back door. Prospect sits on a human hand chair, pretending to be reading a book.

"I bought some groceries. You're probably starving. Please help yourself," he calls out. He pauses to put the groceries away. Finally he enters the living room.

"Hi, Victor," Prospect says as casually as he can. "How did my painting turn out last night?"

"Patience, my young friend. All will be revealed this afternoon."

Victor says he must get more paint brushes from the art supply store. He will pick them up soon. He trusts his guest will find a way to entertain himself. As the door closes behind him, the Pre-born listens to his footsteps descend the back stairs. And then he hears nothing.

Prospect whips out his cell phone. As the phone rings, he pulls the sheets again from the first two paintings. "Trish—this is Prospect. What can you tell me about Victor Pastelle?"

"Well, he's a painter. He lives in Evanston—"

"I mean what have you told him, Trish? He seems to know a whole lot that he shouldn't know."

Trish laughs. "He's an empath. It's his job to know more than he should."

"Well, I should warn you that one of the paintings is of you and Lito."

"Really?"

"And get this, Trish. The painting suggests a family connection between you two."

"Make sure that no one sees these paintings. They can never leave his house."

Prospect hears Trevor walking upstairs. "I can't believe I forgot to mention the best part. You'll never guess who lives upstairs here. Trevor Grueling!"

"Prospect, you're not making any sense. Why would Trevor—"

"He's Pastelle's apprentice. He's been faking his disappearance, just like I suspected. Can you send Detective Dunleavy over here?"

"I don't see why the police need to be involved. No crime has been committed, has it?" Prospect looks closer at the detail of Trish Mesmer, perched in her tree. It is a spitting image of her.

"But if Dunleavy sees Trevor is okay, he'll know I'm not a person of interest anymore."

"I'm sorry, but *Scientific American* magazine will be here any minute at my place for a photo shoot. If I don't get back to you shortly—I'll see you at the hospital at four o'clock."

"It's always about you, isn't it, Trish?"

"What are you talking about? Really, Prospect. I don't have time for this conversation."

"No, you don't. You've made that clear."

There is a moment of tension between them unlike any they've felt before. It scares them. To have come this far and maybe to see it all fall apart. Trish tries to regroup. To find words that will ease the tension. But she also needs to stand up for herself.

"Prospect, this is a stressful time for both of us. You're getting close to making your decision. And for me, the press conference—it's a very big thing."

"I know that."

"But this is what you're not getting. You've been the center of attention all along. As it should be. But somebody dreamed up the Pre-born Project. Somebody busted their butt trying to get funding, trying to be taken seriously. That somebody was me." From her window, Trish sees the journalist and photographer approaching her place.

"Trish, do you think you're telling me anything I don't—"

She turns away from her guests for a moment. She speaks now in a low voice with great intensity. "So goddammit, Prospect, it's not just about you anymore! It's a little about me too. This is my moment too. I don't want to blow it, but if I'm not careful…the moment will slip forever from my fingers. If you do choose to be born one day, you're going to realize that being alive is not just about you either—it's about your parents, your boss, your friends, your colleagues, your lover, the whole goddam world—and each of them will want something from you, and they'll want it yesterday. So I'm sorry if I'm not very present for you right now, but we're going to get through this. Everything is going to turn out all right."

Prospect sees Trevor entering the painting studio. "I have to go, Trish." He hangs up. Trevor can't help notice that two of the paintings are now unveiled. He smirks. "Curiosity killed the cat."

Prospect is startled. "Oh, I wasn't trying to—"

"Of course not. You weren't the least bit curious about the other paintings, were you?" Trevor walks over to a still veiled painting. He unveils it.

"What are you doing?" he asks.

"You might as well see the rest of the collection. Then Victor can do the honors and unveil the last portrait." Prospect is eager to see more.

In the third painting, the central image is of Irene Iwanski. She is lying in bed. Huge, over-sized greeting cards create a kind of blanket over her. Prospect kneels on one side of the bed with his palms joined in prayer. The text below the image says:

SHE WANTED TO LIVE TO BE ONE HUNDRED,
BUT IT WASN'T IN THE CARDS.

This painting is harsh. It does not render Irene as our lady of the greeting cards, as the near-saint he remembers. It renders Irene as a fool, a court jester. It doesn't help that he misses her. Still, her face remains radiant. And then something amazing happens. Irene turns her head in bed and winks at him! How can that be? Is it a trick of light? Is it from lack of sleep last night? He looks at Irene again. Again, she winks at him.

"Did you see what I just saw?" he asks Trevor.

"What did you see?"

"Okay, in this painting here you've featured my Referral Irene," he says. "I could swear she just winked at me."

Trevor smiles. "Victor's paintings have been known to have a life of their own. I've heard stories."

Prospect looks back at the painting. The painted image of Prospect now lifts his head up from prayer and gives his breathing self a thumbs-up. Prospect blinks and looks again. The painted image has become still .

"Let's look at the fourth one," Trevor says. The cloth falls to the floor revealing a painting of Trevor himself. Judging by his expression, it is one that he is seeing for the first time.

In the next painting, a huge microscope dominates the painting. Trevor lies upon a big glass slide under the gaze of the device...his arms and legs extend beyond the edges of the slide. A giant pair of tweezers hover over him. The text says:

THEY REMOVED HIS SENSE OF WONDER—BUT THEY COULDN'T REMOVE HIS SENSE THAT HE'D BEEN BETRAYED.

Trevor steps back to take in the painting. Shakes his head slowly. "This is why I don't want you to participate, Prospect. Because so many things can go wrong in a bio-experiment. But maybe you'll have to learn the hard way. Like I did."

Just then a key turns in the back door and Victor Pastelle is home. He walks into the living room carrying a bottle and some glasses.

"Well, I see you've started the unveiling without me."

Prospect speaks first. "I'm so sorry, Victor. I couldn't wait. Your work—it's beautiful. But scary too. I know I should have waited—"

"You promised to wait. The unveiling is no one's prerogative but the artist's."

"I know. I'm sorry."

Victor looks annoyed. Then he notices Trevor. "And why are you crying, Trevor?"

"You've turned my predicament into art."

Victor pats him on the back. He opens a bottle of champagne and the cork goes flying. He fills glasses with bubbly. "Have some champagne, boys. I propose a toast. To empathy. And the imagination." The three of them drink the bubbly drink. It tickles Prospect's throat.

"Prospect, you've clearly saved the best for last." Victor reveals the final painting. The one that is of him. The white sheet floats to the floor like a ghost.

In the final painting, Prospect Boulanget wears a baseball cap with the word "Evolve" stitched on it. He is standing high on a platform in a big-top circus tent. The rim of the yellow tent encircles him. Far below is a tiny little wooden bucket filled with water. This is the bucket he is to dive into. Prospect stands on the platform at a dizzying height. The painted caption reads:

BEING BORN REQUIRED A LEAP OF FAITH
FOR WHICH HE HAD NEVER BEEN PREPARED.

In spite of the beauty of the image, what Prospect feels more than anything is absolute dread. Dread of making decisions. A ferocious fear of heights, rivaled only by his fear of the future. When Prospect looks at the painting, he somehow sees everything from the point of view of his painted self. Sky high. The image makes him dizzy. This painting makes his birth decision seem fraught with peril…terrifying…inconceivable. "Wow," is all he says at first. He reads the text again: "Being born required a leap of faith…for which he had never been prepared." *Is that true?* he wonders. Has Trish Mesmer given him an impossible task? Has Science betrayed him too?

The yellow circus tent stretches skyward above him. He stands on the tiny platform, higher even than Trevor's penthouse on the fifty-sixth floor. Prospect's heart beats faster and faster. He hears the audience below scream for him to jump. Mostly he is aware how he longs to be down on the ground where it's safe and boring and predictable. This is a dream from which he can't wake up. And there is only one way to get down from this high place. He has to jump.

But Prospect feels sick. He feels nauseous and feverish, so he runs to the bathroom and throws up. It feels like something is turning his body inside out. What comes pouring out of him surprises him:

A chocolate turtle.
A condom.
Pecan pie from Bakers Square.
Something that looks like a stone but isn't a stone.
And a tiny, living starfish.

The small stone-like object is actually a piece of paper. He unfolds it again and again until finally he can read the message. It says: FIND SOMETHING I CAN LOVE.

Prospect must have passed out at some point because when he wakes up, he is lying on the sofa in Victor's living room. He doesn't remember how he got there. He opens his eyes slowly to see Victor and Trevor hovering over him.

Trevor waves his hand slowly in front of the Pre-born's face. "You were talking in your sleep. Something about wanting to leave the project."

The Pre-born sits up. "How long have I been asleep?"

"About two hours," Victor says. "I've seen a range of reactions to my work, but never one quite like that." And now Prospect senses himself returning to the present moment in Victor's studio. He is not high in a circus tent anymore.

"So before you pass out again, please tell us what you thought about my paintings," Victor Pastelle insists.

"Can I be honest?"

"Please." Both Victor and Trevor lean forward to hear his answer. They are hoping this is the turning point, the moment they've been hoping for.

"Your paintings make me sick," Prospect says. For a moment neither man knows what to make of this ambiguous, near-laughable statement. "Oh, I don't just mean they made me throw up, which they did," he says. "No, they sickened me in a much deeper way."

Victor's spine stiffens with this remark. "Really?"

"Well, the paintings definitely have some power. Don't get me wrong. But the images are kind of depressing and… corny too, right?"

"How so? Please illuminate me," says Victor.

"Please don't take this the wrong way. I'm no expert." Prospect walks over to the painting of Trevor. "But take this one. Trevor under the microscope. It's not what you could call beautiful. Maybe that's your point. Is that your point, Victor?"

Trevor speaks. "I like it very much. A work of art speaks to different people in different ways. One person's Monet…is another person's velvet Elvis."

Victor steps in front of the painting as if to shield it from further criticism. "This series of paintings emerged directly from what I sensed as an empath from the depths of your own heart and soul, Prospect. Whether or not they make for great art is not the question. I wanted to hold up a mirror to you so that you could see the future you are facing. And the truth you are avoiding."

Prospect looks at the paintings again in this new light. It is the painting of himself that he finds hardest to dismiss.

Trevor speaks. "You have gotten to see these five extraordinary paintings inspired by the Pre-born Project. It all comes down to this: *Do you want to be born—or not?*" Trevor and Victor's eyes focus expectantly on their young guest. Chase walks into the room and looks up at Prospect. Even the cat wants to know his decision.

Prospect looks at the painting of himself. The platform is impossibly high. It reminds him of that view from Trevor's penthouse where he looked out at the twinkling lights of the city and tried to imagine his place in the world. On that given night, he could picture it. It called to him. But today— with each passing day, each new disappointment, each new betrayal—the twinkling lights have grown dimmer.

Just then there is a loud banging at the back door. "It's the police! Open up!" Prospect freezes in place, uncertain what to do. The banging continues. Trevor opens the door, letting two cops enter Victor's home. The first one in says, "A lady called to report a missing person was in fact hiding at this location. Do you know anything about that?"

"Umm...Well..." Prospect begins.

"Prospect, you're not obligated to say anything," says Victor.

The lead cop puts down his pen and just looks at Prospect with utter surprise. His eyes narrow. "You're that kid from the bio-experiment, aren't you?" he says. Could it be Prospect's photo has been leaked to the press? "My daughter's a big fan of yours. If you could just autograph my notepad, she'd be thrilled." Prospect looks at the cop's nametag. His name is Kyle.

"I've never given an autograph before."

"You better get used to it," he says.

Trevor steps forward and presents himself to Kyle. "I think you're probably looking for me," he says. "But I didn't break any laws. I was just kind of taking…a sabbatical, ya know?"

"The courts will make that decision. If you faked your disappearance and manpower was devoted to searching for you—you wasted taxpayer money. Bobby, while we're here—take some pictures of the place, in case we need documentation."

"Will do." The cop photographer starts taking pictures of the house, Trevor, Victor and Prospect. When they start taking pictures of the paintings, Prospect steps in front of them.

"You can't do that. These paintings are part of a private collection."

The cop gives him a look and says, "They ain't art anymore, bud. They're evidence."

40. THE PROSPECT OF
MY ARRIVAL

*"In the end, we have to ask ourselves what will qualify
as a successful outcome of the Pre-born Project. I would
like to think that science and humanity will benefit either
way—whether the Pre-born chooses to be born, or chooses
to return to the gene pool. For either choice will tell us
how inhabitable our world appears to a passing visitor.
And hopefully we will discover how to make happier
babies along the way."*

— Dr. Trish Mesmer, Scientist

Big Science Magazine

Prospect accompanies Trevor to the police station. At first
Trevor claims he was just taking a little vacation. But under
questioning, he finally admits to Officer Kyle that he staged

his disappearance. He agrees to do one hundred hours of community service. Prospect tries to reach Trish to see if she wants to speak to Trevor, but she's too busy preparing for the press conference, just hours away.

"Prospect. I have you on speakerphone," says Trish. "I'm sorry I yelled at you last time. The media attention we're getting is insane. *Nightline* is interviewing me via satellite in a few minutes. But what really matters is you. Are you okay?" In the background, he hears the television blaring.

"Yes, I'm fine." He hears his own voice and it sounds flat, toneless. The music is gone. "I know this is your moment too, but I really think you have to step in and take some control of this experiment!"

"That's great. Stay where you are. I can send a driver to come get you. There are talking points we have to go over—"

"Trish!" he yells.

"What, Prospect? What's wrong?" There is the sound of sudden laughter from the TV.

"I don't care anymore!" Prospect shouts. Through the telephone, he hears a round of applause.

"What do you mean? Of course you care. You're a caring person. That's how I *raised* you."

"You didn't raise me, and you're not my mother," he says. "Listen to me for a minute! Now I may see you tonight, or I may not. Either way, I don't want you to be mad at me. Just make up some excuse why I'm not there. You're good at that."

"What are you talking about? You've got to be at this press conference! It won't make any sense without you." She sounds scared and sad and bossy all at the same time. Outside some squad cars speed off into the night, their sirens wailing.

"It's what we've worked for. We have to be there. It's for the sake of human evolution.

"I'm gone. I don't know where I'm going, but I'm not staying here. This has all gotten too stressful for me," he says. "Look, you were supposed to...take care of me. I need to talk to you but you don't have time, and I don't care anymore. I'm quitting. I'm quitting the Pre-born Project." Trevor was right all along.

"You can't quit," she pleads. "Without you, I'll be a laughing stock. You can't do this to me, after everything I've done for you--"

"Good luck, Trish. And good-bye." He flips his cell phone closed.

When Prospect looks up, Kyle and the other officers are staring at him. "Is everything okay, Prospect?" says Kyle. "My shift is over. I can drive you anywhere you need to go." Such a nice man.

"I'm fine." He looks at Trevor who looks like he could use a Happy Meal right about now. "Trevor, do you want to hang out with me for a while? We can watch the press conference on TV somewhere if you like. But I want to go where no one will find me."

Kyle pulls Prospect to the side for a moment for a private chat. "Do you really think this is a good idea to go with this guy?" he whispers.

"I think he's harmless. I want him to know that I don't hold a grudge against him. That's all."

"I don't trust him."

"You don't have to trust him. Trust me. And my judgement."

"Just be careful," says Kyle.

Prospect and Trevor grab a cab and take it to O'Hare Airport. For a while, the Pre-born just wants to be at a place where airplanes are arriving and departing from all over the world. He likes to think of people boarding planes, going on new adventures. It makes him think of his own adventure. And the prospect of his arrival.

They book a room at the Hyatt. Prospect decides to order up some room service and talk about what has happened and drown their sorrows in sushi and pasta. They turn on the TV as the press conference is about to start. Trevor has discovered a little refrigerator in the room. Inside it, there are bottles of soda and packages of cheese and crackers. They help themselves.

Prospect thinks back to Officer Kyle's generous offer to give him a ride to anywhere he wanted to go. He is kind and compassionate and gentle.

All the things Prospect used to be.

"I have a godson named Luke. Smart kid," says Trevor. "He's curious about you. Do you want to know why?"

"Please tell me." He drinks some ginger ale.

Trevor puts cheese on a cracker. "Because he thinks about his short life—he's only five, you see. He thinks of all the good things that have happened to him, and all the bad things. And he tries to imagine if he knew then what he knows now... would he have chosen to be born? What would he do if he were in your *zapatos*? And you know what? He can't answer. The question is too big; it gives him a headache." Prospect laughs.

The Pre-born looks back at the TV and sees Trish Mesmer at the podium. He turns up the volume. "Look—it's Trish! She looks nervous." She is trying to smile, but not succeeding. Trevor and Prospect sit on the bed and study the screen. The host, an older man, asks her a question. "Ms. Mesmer, you've talked a lot about the progress of the Pre-born Project—and it sounds like an amazing project—but I thought we were going to be able to meet the Pre-born himself today."

She forces another smile. "Well, that was what we'd hoped for. But Prospect is currently finishing up with his last Referral. It's taking a little longer than expected."

A woman asks, "Is it possible they might finish up while we're still on the air? We do have deadlines."

Trish looks to someone off-screen. Probably to Karl Bangor. "That's a hard call. But if it can be done—it will definitely happen. Prospect has a great story to tell. By the way, you'll see in your press packets, the names and faces of the different Referrals whom Prospect had the privilege of encountering. It's quite a diverse cross-section. I can take a few questions if you folks would like."

She looks out at the crowd. They all talk at once, but the question that is heard most clearly is this one: "Is there any truth to the rumor that Prospect is *not* with a Referral, but that he is in fact *missing*?" It comes from a tall man wearing a bow tie.

Trish pauses, then slowly speaks. "We have no evidence to support that rumor. The well-being of the Pre-born is of great importance to us, as you can imagine."

"Then you have no evidence to assure us that he *isn't* missing either?" says the same reporter. But Prospect can't watch any more. He asks Trevor if he wants to go with him to Infinity. But his Referral has no interest in that.

"Look, Trevor, I understand your not wanting to go to the press conference with me. I can jump in a cab—"

Trevor places his body between Prospect and the door. "What if I told you the door is locked from the outside...and that you couldn't leave this room if you wanted to?"

～

Back at Trish's office, her new assistant is watching the Preb-Cam for her. Her assistant is none other than Lito Fulton Sanchez. This is just one more way that Trish Mesmer has devised to get closer to her son. To become involved in his life without arousing suspicion. She has given Lito the task of keeping tabs on Prospect. Where is he hiding, who is he with, is he stationary or in transit? Lito sips his mocha latte and adjusts the reception on the TV screen. On the monitor, Lito sees Trevor Grueling having an argument with Prospect. It looks like they are in a hotel room somewhere. Lito hopes that the Pre-Cam will reveal the name of the hotel or a likely location.

～

Prospect pauses a moment to study the expression on Trevor's face, which is suddenly very serious. "You wouldn't," Prospect says.

"Wouldn't I?"

He pushes his Referral to the side and reaches for the doorknob. It's locked. Trevor moves purposefully toward the television. He raises the volume very loud. Trevor pulls a gun from his bag. It's shiny and black. Light bounces off the barrel. On one wall is a sign: "Thank you for choosing Hyatt O'Hare." Lito makes note of it. He's been there before.

"Trevor, what's that for?" Prospect says. He lets out a nervous laugh.

෨

Lito panics when he sees the gun. "Holy shit!" he says. He dials Trish's cell, but it goes to voicemail. He could call the cops, but that would be bad press for the project. He decides to hop into his car and drives as fast as he can. Even at top speed, he won't make it to the Hyatt for a good twenty minutes.

It won't be soon enough.

෨

In this perfectly ordinary Chicago hotel room, something extraordinary is about to happen. Trevor points the gun straight at Prospect. "I tried to persuade you to leave the project," he says. "I asked you nicely, but you refused. So here we are. In this awkward situation."

"Oh, I get it! This is another one of your practical jokes. What's the gun made out of? Rubber?" Prospect laughs a carefree laugh.

Trevor aims the gun at the TV and shoots out the screen. It shatters into several pieces.

"Then again, maybe not. Trevor, you don't want to do this," he says.

"I had an epiphany the other day, Prospect. I knew your press conference was coming up. How can I prevent the Pre-born Project from moving forward, and why am I such a fuck-up? And then it hit me: You were never born so in a sense you can never be killed!"

Prospect is trying to think what to say. "You're not a killer. That's not who you are. You're somebody's son for god-sake. You're a Conservative in an Increasingly Liberal World. You just want to make the world right."

"My God is a loving God—" Trevor says.

"Science has dealt you a bad hand."

"But He's also a jealous God." Trevor is not listening anymore, if he ever was. "When you make these big life-and-death decisions on your own, you diminish His power. God hates that. He really does. I hope you get the chance to meet Him one day. On His terms. Maybe today is your lucky day." He cocks the hammer of the gun.

"Put down the gun, Trevor. I've already told Trish I quit the project, Trevor."

"There's only one way you can truly quit the project." Trevor studies the gun for a moment. Again, the Pre-born notices how the light bounces off the barrel. "Have you ever thought about what a gun is, Prospect? All it does is push molecules apart. Rearranges the shape of things. And yet that simple act can cause so much...damage." Trevor's voice is eerily calm. Like a man who's made up his mind about something.

Prospect grabs the barrel of the gun. Trevor holds onto it with all his might. It's a tug of war. The Pre-born tries to pry the weapon from Trevor's hand, but his fingers are welded in place.

"Years ago, science took something away from me," Trevor says. With his other hand, he starts to choke Prospect with all his might. "Today I will take something away from science. And then we'll be even." His voice is more calm than it should be. Trevor now aims the gun squarely at Prospect's head.

"I trusted you, Trevor, and this is how you repay me?" And now Prospect has managed to turn the gun back to Trevor, to point it at him.

That's when he remembers something that Trish told him at the very beginning of the experiment. That his physical body had no fingerprints, no unique DNA. And that if he were ever to commit a crime—there'd be no way to trace the crime back to him.

It's kill or be killed.

Prospect pulls the trigger. There is a loud bang. The gun vibrates in his hand even moments later.

At first there is no blood, and Prospect wonders if he missed. But then the blood starts to seep into Trevor's blue-and-white striped Kenneth Cole shirt, a red flower blooming in the middle of it.

"Omigod," Prospect says out loud. "I killed someone. I killed Trevor."

Prospect thinks how Trevor's face looks oddly peaceful, as it never looked in life. Where did all that bitterness go? Part of Prospect feels good that he pulled the trigger. Trevor was a bad man, and he had stopped him from doing bad things. But that good feeling gives way to another feeling. Guilt? He has hurt another human in the worst way possible: he has ended a life before its time.

"I am becoming one of them," the Pre-born thinks to himself. "This is how it starts." He feels his heart growing hard and cold as a stone. He wonders if he will still get in trouble for this. Trish will never forgive him for what he's done. How could she? And what about his parents? Who would want such a person for a son?

He pictures Trish Mesmer standing in a dark, cavernous auditorium in a halo of light. He thinks of all the questions the reporters will ask that she will not be able to answer. Only Prospect's appearance in the flesh will satisfy the hungry crowd.

He decides he will do one last good thing. He will help a friend in need. In that moment, he decides he will go to the press conference after all.

But the door is still locked. Then he does something he saw in a movie his CyberSavant showed him. He shoots at the lock on the door several times. When he turns the knob, the door opens. He runs down the corridor away from the life that he has just taken. He runs from the innocent person he used to be.

He leaves the hotel, steps out onto the street, and hails a cab. "Infinity Medical Center, please," he says. "It's an emergency." And the driver floors the gas. Through the cab windows, the streetlights and cars go blurry. He thinks how Trish has a right to want her share of the spotlight. He can't blame her. She was the first person Prospect saw in the world when he first opened his eyes. They share a history.

But does he want to be born or not? That is the big question.

That's when Lito's face floats up like a balloon in front of him. It hovers in the cab inches from his face. "What about our big plans, Prospect?" says the face of Lito. "We were gonna be a team. What happened to the dream?" But before he can answer, the face floats up and away through the ceiling of the cab.

Prospect thinks hard about Lito. He thinks of all the arms that might one day reach out to embrace him, to choose him. This thought pulls him in the opposite direction. Like a magnet. But the Pre-born also remembers how people have disappointed him. Where was Lito now that Prospect needed him? He was nowhere. In his hour of need, Lito was nowhere. Goddam Lito. So much for teamwork. So much for the Tunnel of Love.

Prospect notices the thought of being born no longer makes him tingle. His tingling days are over. Instead he just feels dread, like when he looked at Victor's painting and saw himself standing high on a ledge, looking down at the tiny bucket below—that's exactly what he felt: dread. He felt anger too, for he had been duped. He imagined that somewhere people were laughing at him.

In this moment, he leans back in a speeding yellow taxi and makes up his mind: He will not be born. He refuses. He will take his chances on the gene pool. If he really thinks about it, he started making up his mind in that moment when he pulled the trigger and shot Trevor at the Hyatt Hotel. His body knew it as he unveiled the final painting of himself and threw up so violently at Victor's house.

Prospect reaches into the bag that Trish has so carefully packed for him. He opens a small plastic bottle, and a blue pill rolls into the palm of his hand. The bottle had come with Trish's note, and he had read it several times. He knows the pill is only to be taken if he chooses to return to the gene pool. It will allow his borrowed body to vanish…and his spirit, his Prospect-ness, will begin making its way to the gene pool at Big Farm Technologies. The embryo in his mother's stomach will vanish too, as if it were never there. His mother will not even remember she was even pregnant. The mountain of baby items in the extra bedroom will puzzle her for weeks.

The Pre-born holds up the small blue pill and swallows it. He takes a swig of water from the bottle in his bag. And then he waits. He waits to see if he feels any differently.

41. ARRIVAL

Prospect crisscrosses the city in a cab plastered with bumper stickers for the Pre-born Project. When the cab arrives at its destination, he pays the bill and gets out. He stands at the entrance to Infinity Medical Center. Huge Hollywood searchlights sweep the heavens over the hospital.

Inside, the media circus is in full swing. There is a juggler in the hallway tossing plastic fetuses into the air. Vendors are perched in various alcoves hawking T-shirts bearing the words "The Pre-born Tour." The back of each T-shirt announces an impressive list of sponsors. Prospect sees patients in the waiting area gathered around an enormous flatscreen TV. Trish is speaking onscreen: "The truth is I decided not to screen Prospect's Referrals," she says. "We wanted Prospect to meet people as unknown quantities, just as we all do in life." He dashes toward the elevators. Inside the elevator, he hears the broadcast of the press conference over the Muzak speakers. A man's voice says, "Do you have any regrets about your decision to forgo the background checks, in light of his disappearance?" The elevator lights track his silent ascension, floor by floor, through the building.

Another voice over the speakers says, "What does Big Farm think of your reckless actions? And what happens to the project if Prospect is never found?"

Finally he is at the twenty-first floor.

Prospect approaches the doors to the auditorium. Karl Bangor stands there. When he sees Prospect, he approaches him with great excitement. "We didn't know if you were coming," he says.

"I didn't either." Prospect watches small children holding helium balloons. The single word BORN is emblazoned on the red ones. The single word UNBORN is emblazoned on the blue ones.

"Before you go up on stage," Karl says, "I have to know that you're going to choose to be born."

"I see."

"Is that what you're going to announce?"

"No, Karl. I'm afraid it isn't."

"I know you're tired, Prospect. I can see it in your eyes." Karl circles behind the Pre-born and gives his shoulders a small massage. Prospect's shoulders are in knots. It feels good to have someone rub his shoulders.

"Listen, Prospect, I think you're going to make an awesome addition to the human race. And I think you will help us discover a whole new way to make sure we have happier babies," Karl says. "I'm not an optimist. I wouldn't know what to do with a pair of rose-colored glasses if they fell out of the sky! But I do know what science can do when it wants to. I know what a breakthrough feels like when we make one. And I think we're about to make one with you, if you'll let us.

"I have to go," Prospect says.

"Look at your Referrals. Remember what your mother said? *Be born. There will be so much more of you to experience… if you choose to be born.*" Karl even has his mother's voice and inflections down pat.

"How do you know what my mother told me?" the Pre-born asks. His brown eyes search Karl's blue eyes for an answer.

"Oh, Trish kept me in the loop on all your Referrals."

"But I never debriefed with her about my mother. Not in any detail. How did you know what my mother said?"

"She must have mentioned it to Trish," Karl says.

"My mother's a private person. She wouldn't—"

"Okay already. If you must know, we monitored your Referrals."

"You what?"

"Inside your brain, there is a tiny camera. Everything that you've seen for the last three weeks, Trish and I have seen too. It was for your own safety. It's called the Preb—"

"You were watching? All this time? My most private conversations?" All his Referrals now go flashing through his mind. "You betrayed my trust."

"Look, they're waiting for you up on that stage. The whole world is waiting. I'm not going to bullshit you anymore." Beads of sweat form on Karl's forehead. He has never seen Karl sweat before. "Okay, the world is a funny place, and sometimes we have to make funny decisions. Are there some bad apples out there? Do we have nightmares? Sure. Do good people die? Do prayers go unanswered? Constantly. But good things happen too. We humans have our moments. Sometimes we find answers. Cures. Even love. It happens. Not as often as we'd like it to. Big Farm is all about fixing what's broken in the world, in our bodies, our minds. You're a fixer too, Prospect. You just don't know it yet."

But Prospect no longer cares. "Excuse me," he says. "I have a press conference to get to." He pushes past Karl, but Karl grabs him roughly by the arms. Prospect remembers what Joyce told him about Karl's glass jaw, and how she owed him a good thrashing.

Prospect breaks free and punches Karl squarely on the jaw. It's a solid connection. The man stumbles back a few steps from the blow. He rubs his chin. "That's a love letter from my sister Joyce," say Prospect. He now walks in a straight line toward the stage. All he can focus on is the podium in a halo of light, the bouquet of microphones. And there is Trish Mesmer standing at the center of it all. Her face lights up when she sees him.

She leans with great relish into the cornucopia of microphones before her. "Ladies and gentlemen, it is my honor to introduce to you the person you've been waiting to meet…I give you Prospect."

There is thunderous applause. A standing ovation. Camera flashes go off blinding him. "For what?" he mutters to himself. "I haven't done anything yet." Finally he stands before them. The auditorium of Infinity, indeed, looks infinite. He tries to look into each person's eyes, though that's impossible.

"Hi everybody. I'm sorry I'm late. Guess I'm on Pre-born time." The audience laughs. "I heard it's always good to start with a joke. I know you're eager to hear what I've decided, but before we get to that, I wanted to thank my Facilitator and the lead scientist of the Pre-born Project, Trish Mesmer." Applause.

"Earlier, Karl Bangor of Big Farm Technologies and I were talking. I told him…I've come to the conclusion that the world is broken. Violence. Disease. Sadness. Greed. War. Why would I want to be born into such a broken world? He looked at me straight on and asked, 'Where's your sense of social responsibility, your scientific curiosity?' And I said I didn't know where those things were. But when I looked inside my bag of tricks—I didn't see them." Polite laughter from the audience.

"I don't know a lot about Big Farm, the funders of the Pre-born Project. I don't know if they're good people or bad people. But I'd keep an eye on them if I were you, members of the press. It's good they funded this experiment. But why did they fund it? There could be a lot of reasons, and maybe not all of them are noble. Maybe they don't have to be. You tell me."

He looks at Trish. She looks away.

"Ladies and gentlemen, you've been very patient. I'd like to now announce my decision if I may," he says. He looks at the sea of faces in the auditorium. The flashing cameras, the reporters' fingers hovering over laptops. "After a lot of serious consideration…I've decided *not* to be born." Reporters gasp. More flashing cameras. Reporters start shouting questions at the stage. "Prospect, what would have made you choose to be born? What would have made you stay?" shouts one man. A woman wearing a turquoise scarf shouts, "When you refer to 'the broken world'—what exactly are you referring to? Broken how?" A man with a British accent says, "Do you think the experiment was fair to you? Did you ever feel exploited by Big Farm? And what advice do you have for the human race, or are we beyond salvation?"

The Pre-born raises his hands. "Folks, folks—I won't be taking questions today. Good night, and I'm truly sorry. I wish you all the best of luck. You'll need it." He smiles and steps away from the podium. And at that moment, the children holding the blue balloons emblazoned with the word UNBORN let go of their strings, the balloons slowly ascending upward. Prospect and Trish stare at the balloons as they float to the ceiling where they bounce gently. The auditorium is oddly silent.

Finally Trish steps forward and leans against the podium for support. "I want to personally thank you, Prospect, for your candor." The TV cameras continue to roll. Trish has a written speech in front of her in case she needs it. She won't. "When I conceived the Pre-born Project three years ago, the possibility that the Pre-born would choose *not* to be born was, of course, always a possibility," she begins. "Still, rejection is always hard to take. There is much to be learned by Prospect's decision, and also from the raw video footage taken of his various Referrals. The data itself has a story to tell, and it will likely be quite a compelling story." Trish pauses. She refuses to cry; it's so girly and unprofessional. But some tears come uninvited just the same. She wipes them away. "I want you to know that there will be more Pre-borns that will follow in this one's footsteps. Please continue to support this important work. Thank you all for coming." Trish gathers her papers and leaves the podium. The sound of light applause fills the auditorium, but this is not the outcome the media were expecting, and they feel cheated. Finally the bright TV lights are snapped off.

∽

Everything now slows down, moves in dreamtime. Whether it is the effect of the pill or the moment, the Pre-born isn't sure. In this backstage world of Infinity's auditorium, everything is blue velvet curtains and EXIT signs…sawdust and glitter…a gloriously complex system of ropes and pulleys for the stage curtains. Trish and Prospect pause here, catching their breaths. For a moment Prospect is hypnotized by the glowing EXIT sign. The four letters. E. X. I. T.

He thinks about his brief time on earth. There is one thing that humans wish they knew, but really don't. That is… how to fix the broken world. So they walk through the broken streets to their broken jobs, come home tired and empty to their broken homes. They make love in their beautiful beds so they can forget how broken everything is. But what kind of life is that? Why would Prospect choose such misery? Why does anyone? People turn up their noses at those who commit suicide and call them cowards. But maybe it's the living who are the real cowards.

Surprisingly, the reporters do not come backstage looking for a story. Instead they slowly disperse to the four corners of the world they came from. They return to their registered vehicles, their deadlines, the lives they have chosen. Maybe they do not come because they sense that the true story has already been written in the hearts and minds of all who witnessed it. It is the story of how a single person—an embryo really—gave the world a failing grade, turned his back on its alleged riches, rejected the rising tide of hopelessness and hate…and simply walked away.

The Pre-born knows there are very beautiful things, amazing people, unforgettable experiences. But not enough to make him want to stay. And now it dawns on him that maybe he is not so different from his fallen colleague Trevor Grueling. That Prospect, too, has lost his sense of wonder. Not because of an experiment gone wrong, but because of his own carelessness. This makes him very sad.

One fond memory he hopes to take with him is a memory of someone he has somehow, inexplicably, come to love. In his memory he's lying in a bedroom whose ceiling is painted with glow-in-the-dark stars. A hand floats down from out of nowhere to rest gently on his shoulder, floats down from heaven like a falling star. It is Lito Sanchez's hand, though he won't remember his name. He will only remember this: that once on this blue earth, he was needed.

Prospect and Trish gather their things and prepare to leave. "I took the pill," he says. "I'm feeling very light-headed all of a sudden."

"That's how you know it's time. For your transition," she says.

He smiles at her. "I have to sit down." He sits on a chair as Trish pulls out her cell phone and dials. "This is Trish Mesmer. Please have the paramedics come to the backstage area now. It's time."

And now, from out of the shadows that define the backstage area—a familiar face. It's Lito. He looks up at Trish. "Is he okay?" Lito asks. She nods. She wants so badly to embrace Lito, but she knows she hasn't earned it yet. "I saw something bad was happening on the Preb-Cam, but I couldn't get there in time," he says to Prospect. "When I saw you were headed for Infinity, I came straight here. Nothing is working out the way we planned it, is it?"

"I'm glad you're here, Lito," Prospect says. "I wanted to...say good-bye."

Lito shakes his head. "I have to ask. When exactly were you planning on telling me that you weren't going to be born?" The orphan searches the Pre-born's face for an answer.

"Oh, sorry. Everything has been so...crazy."

Lito stares at a spot on the floor. "I thought I would have been the first person you would have told. But you told the whole world first, and I was the last to know. That's messed up." He looks up at Prospect.

"Lito, you don't know what I've been going through. I just made up my mind in the cab ride over here."

"And you had no idea what you were gonna choose before that? You had no fucking clue?" Lito notices a lonely can of Red Bull on the podium and drinks what's left of it. It's still cold. "You said we were gonna be a team. Am I right or am I right?"

"Lito, you think you understand so much, but..."

"But at least I was born, wasn't I? Which is more than I can say for you." Lito crushes the can. "Gotta hand it to you, mate. You gave a nice pep talk. Too bad you didn't give it to yourself, pringle head!"

"Lito, c'mon."

"No, you c'mon."

"I had about twenty good arguments against choosing to be born," Prospect says. "You were my one good argument *for* being born. You have to believe me." He rubs his hands against each other. They feel strange, like they are no longer his hands. And his head isn't feeling so good. "Damn, that pill is giving me a headache, Trish." She just nods sympathetically.

"Sorry I wasn't a good enough reason to be born," says Lito.

"You want to know the awful truth, Lito?" Prospect looks his friend straight in the eyes. "You *weren't* a good enough reason. But it was never really about you or anyone else. *I* wasn't a good enough reason. If I was, I might have chosen differently. If I was braver, or a whole lot drunker…" Prospect laughs.

"It's fucked up," says Lito. "That's for sure."

Trish breaks in. "In the next few minutes, Prospect will leave us. We have to head over to Big Farm. The gene pool awaits."

❧

The paramedics finally arrive. They put Prospect on a stretcher and wheel him through a back exit to a waiting ambulance outside. Lito and Trish stay with him. The paramedics continue to try to comfort him—they elevate his head, cover his body with a blanket, make sure his passageways are clear—because that is what paramedics do. But it is no longer about making the body comfortable. They slide Prospect into the ambulance. Trish holds one of his hands and Lito the other. The two ride along in the ambulance as the sirens wail. The vehicle speeds its way through these familiar Chicago streets where Prospect once walked. Once rode the bus. Once stopped and asked for directions.

"There's nothing to be afraid of, Prospect. All the hard decisions are behind you," says Trish.

"I love you, man," Lito says.

These words startle Prospect. *I love you.* (Truth is, these words startle Lito too. He's never uttered them before.) No one has ever told Prospect that they love him before. Has the Pre-born found love after all? But it's too late. He's taken the blue pill.

"You know what I think happened to you, my Pre-born brother?" Lito's impish grin is back. "When I first met you at the amusement park, you were so innocent," he says. "But in three short weeks—you got jaded." Lito laughs. The ambulance siren is loud and urgent. Prospect continues to lie on the gurney, feeling the vehicle weave in and out of traffic.

"I had a dream the other night," Prospect says. He looks at Lito. "You were in it."

"I was?" The young man is clearly flattered.

"Yes, you were."

"What happened? In the dream?"

"We were wandering through the cafeteria of Infinity in the middle of the night. It was dark and scary, so we opened a door and started climbing the stairs. The stairs went on forever but finally we got to the top. We were at a special place high above the city."

"Cool. Were there time travel machines and Cyborgs and cool shit like that?"

"No Cyborgs. We were on the rooftop of Infinity. We looked out over the sparkling city. It was beautiful. We wanted to be part of it all. And so we did what we thought we had to do: we jumped."

"Oh man. Dang. Did we splatter on the sidewalk?"

"We didn't fall. We hovered. And then we flew."

"We flew? Sweet."

This is Prospect's final gift to Lito. A story about the two of them.

It is a story about the future, with a little happiness and magic thrown in for good measure. In the broad picture of things, it's a modest gift. But it will have to do.

He looks at Lito and Trish, aware that he has reunited them for a moment. They'll have a lot to talk about after he's gone. Hopefully Trish will work up the courage one day to tell Lito he is her son. And hopefully Lito will be open enough to hear it.

But the show here truly is over, even the paramedics know it. The vital signs just aren't adding up. By the time they make it to Big Farm Technologies, Prospect will be a shadow of his former self. Trish tells the paramedics they can turn the siren off. That it's not really necessary to hurry. The minds of the paramedics move on to today's lasagna in the hospital cafeteria. Prospect thanks his lucky stars he had the chance to be alive for these few weeks. He closes his eyes. Amen. "Thank you for having me," he says to anyone who can hear him. "I had a very nice time." And now it is Trish who leans over to kiss Prospect on the cheek. There are tears running down his face. Where did they come from? It doesn't matter. They're here now.

The physical body the Pre-born has been living in will gradually dissolve, leaving him containerless. And he will wait in the gene pool for another time, another world. He hopes that by the time he passes through these parts again, the world will be better, its inhabitants more evolved, better behaved. But if he doesn't get another chance, at least he had this. A taste of the world. He found it both sweet and sour. Too sour for his taste.

When he looks at Lito leaning close to him, his friend's eyes are watery too, and it's hard for Prospect not to think he's made a terrible mistake in leaving. Lito with his buzzed, bald head and gold earrings like a pirate, and his face that lights up like Times Square. Prospect feels a pang of regret. It was foolish of him to think the world would ever be perfect. That's the job of earth's inhabitants.

He can see now how even a tiny bit of love can go a long way for earthlings, can make up for years of disappointment.

The ambulance makes its way toward its destination with its precious cargo. The shiny vehicle takes its sweet time because what's the point of rushing? Where's the fire? There is no fire. Not anymore. What is a life anyhow? Prospect asked a million people that question and they gave him a million different answers. Each and every answer was true, though he didn't know it at the time.

And now he feels himself dissolving into particles. Sparkles of light. He feels like he is swimming. Prospect finds himself entering a blinding white room.

A single orange tulip bows its head to welcome him home.

ABOUT THE AUTHOR

Born and raised in Chicago, Dwight Okita started his writing life as a poet because he was fascinated by imagery. Okita's poetry book *Crossing with the Light* was published by Tia Chucha Press. In his twenties, by a twist of fate, he appeared on the Kellogg's Corn Flakes box dressed as a chef. This threatened to eclipse his modest literary achievements! He wrote personal essays for WBEZ, the Chicago affiliate of NPR, and read his poetry on Ira Glass's popular radio show *This American Life.* In time, he went off in search of a larger canvas. In his second life, he found himself reincarnated as a playwright. Okita enjoyed the notion of making art with a group of collaborators. His produced plays include *The Rainy Season* (in *Asian American Drama* published by Applause); a darkly comic, short play called *Richard Speck,* which is one of his favorites (in *Yellow Light* published by Temple); and a collaborative play called *The Radiance of A Thousand Suns* (published by Dramatic Publishing). But in time, he missed the autonomy of being a writer speaking directly to the reader.

In his third and current incarnation, he is as surprised as anyone to find himself writing novels. The author has always had a short attention span, and the idea of reading a novel has always seemed daunting—let alone the notion of writing one. But he has found a kind of home in the world of the novel, a way in. By day, Okita works for a non-profit. He is also a website/video designer and landlord. In 2008, he appeared in the documentary "Out & Proud in Chicago." He is third generation Japanese American.

The author's poems have appeared in the *Norton Introduction to Literature*, *Unsettling America* (Penguin), and countless textbooks. His plays have been produced by American Blues Theatre, Bailiwick Repertory, and the HBO New Writers Project. The author continues to live in Chicago where he drinks way too much coffee, and is grateful for the diverse circle of friends, family, and colleagues that allow him to be part of their lives. Dwight's website is **dwightland. homestead.com**. He is working on a new novel called *The Hope Store*.

ALSO BY DWIGHT OKITA

POETRY
Crossing with the Light

PLAYS
Richard Speck
The Rainy Season

DISCUSSION QUESTIONS
FOR THE PROSPECT OF MY ARRIVAL

1. The Pre-Born Project is an experiment which gives human embryos a chance to get a taste of earth life before committing to being born. Scientist Trish Mesmer hopes that this could result in a species of people who, for the first time, were all here by choice. Do you think such an experiment could make for a better batch of humans? Discuss.

2. Let's say you are pregnant and a bio-experiment like this exists. Volunteers are encouraged to participate as they may help speed up the evolutionary process. Would you want to have your future child take part in a project like the Pre-Born Project or not?

3. Prospect is given the chance to meet a range of humanity in the form of his Referrals: from his mother to an empathic artist. Which Referrals do you think Prospect bonded with most and why?

4. If you were given an opportunity to serve as a Referral for the Pre-Born Project, what experiences would you share with the Pre-Born assigned to you?

5. In the course of the book, Prospect has the chance to experience many things: friendship, wonder, betrayal, sex, violence, fun. Do you think it was right to expose him to these things?

6. What are the reasons Prospect gives at the press conference for his ultimate birth choice? What would you have chosen in his situation? What things does Prospect not understand about life that might have made him choose differently? How does the Pre-Born change from the start of the book to the end?

7. This story might be considered literary fiction with a science fiction spin though most sci-fi tales are grounded in a dystopian view of the world. Would you consider the author's depiction of the world as dystopic or not? Do you yourself view the future with apprehension or eagerness and why?

SNEAK PREVIEW

THE HOPE STORE
by Dwight Okita

"We don't just instill hope. We install it." That's the slogan for the first store in the world that claims to sell hope over the counter.

Luke Nagano goes to sleep each night dreaming about hope and how to make more of it, ever since he lost his sister. He and his partner prepare the store for its grand opening. As media interest grows, an activist group called the Natural Hopers emerges with the mission to warn the public about the dangers of synthetically created hope. Though the store investors become rightly nervous, a steady stream of hope-enhanced customers begins to sing the store's praises.

When hopeless Jada Upshaw first hears of the Hope Store, she's outraged. She's wasted plenty of time and money on magic bullets that haven't worked. Jada sets out to expose the Hope Store for the fraud it must be -- but to do so she must have a hope installation herself. Jada's response to the installation forces her to change her plans dramatically, and to re-think the meaning of hope.

A TV station offers to present a town hall meeting about the controversial nature of enhanced hope in the new millennium, and Luke is tempted by this chance for big exposure --

but it means they'll have to face the Natural Hopers who can be loose cannons. Everything is at stake as this high-profile event could either signal the beginning or end of a global conversation on hope.

THE HOPE STORE tells a story of an unlikely friendship set in the near future, and the thorny relationships between science and faith, placebo and cure, hope and hype.

"Those who start life hopeless rarely acquire it later on. Those who are hopeful in their early years can sometimes lose hope in their later years. Can hopefulness be acquired? Can it be conjured or installed, injected or ingested, inherited or learned? Some scientists think so."

-- AlternaScience magazine

1
Slogans
(Luke)

It is a sparkling, clear October morning in the near future. I find myself waking up a few hours earlier than I usually do. Kazu is still asleep under the silver pinstriped bedspread. I am up to something. On the living room wall, I begin to hang a banner made from butcher block paper which reads:

THE HOPE STORE.
We don't just instill hope. We install it.

Once I heard a politician jabbering on the six o'clock news
and he said: "We have to install hope in young people!" He
meant to say "instill," but it was funnier the way he said it.
Creepier too. And that was the seed of my slogan. It's bloody
brilliant. I reach up and touch the paper, stroking it as if it
was alive. A much nicer version of this banner will be hung
in the store when we open our doors next week, but this is
just for fun. This is just to surprise Kazu who appears to be
deep in the REM stage. Kazu Mori is my partner. More on
that later.

    I walk into the bathroom and greet myself in the mir-
ror. There he is, that handsome devil with the classic Japanese face and salt-n-peppa goatee. I've been told I look and
act younger than my fifty-plus years and for that I must
thank my good family genes, as well as a circle of friends of
all ages. The hair brush I am holding is Kazu's. My hair is
always buzzed short; his hair is long and pirate-like. I close
the cabinet and there I am again in the mirror. Gripping the
brush tenderly, I speak into it: "I'd like to thank my late,
great parents who always told me I could grow up to be anything I wanted to be. I'm just sorry they're not here to see
this moment. I'd like to thank biotech companies all over the
planet for not being smart enough to discover the secret of
creating hope like we did. And most of all I'd like to thank
Kazu for..."

    I'm Luke Nagano and my partner in crime is Kazu
Mori. Our collective electronic footprint is not large, but

that is likely going to change shortly. In Latin, my name Luke means "bringer of light." I'm am optimistic person today, hopeful to a fault, but I wasn't always this way. Being hopeful is something that I arrived at gradually. I had my share of demons. Kazu always likes to say that people are born with certain destinies, certain levels of hope, that it's spelled out in our genetic code, for better or worse. He's a Buddhist so he also believes that our destinies are change-able, are works in progress. The idea behind the Hope Store was to level the playing field for the hope-challenged masses.

We are in the business of increasing the global hope supply which is at an all-time low -- thanks to the never-ending recession the rising murder rate, home foreclosures, and senseless wars. Those things take a toll on humanity's ability to hope. I plan to handle the marketing of the Hope Store; Kazu will be in charge of the science. Put another way, it's my job to get customers to walk in the front door; it's his job to keep them coming back. How did we create hope in the first place? That's a secret.

But I will say that three years of clinical trials have produced a compelling number of hope-enhanced people who will be happy to tell you of their breath-taking results. These hope increases are scientifically quantifiable and we're thrilled to have finally received our FDA approval.

All I can say is that over the next three months, Kazu and I have to do everything in our power to ensure that the Hope Store becomes the Next Big Thing. Simply put, we've got to be an overnight sensation, or we're pretty much toast. Our investors have made it clear that what happens in our first three months of operation will have a strong impact on our funding for the future. Do I feel under pressure? Hell yes. But I absolutely refuse to lose. Kazu and I have worked too hard on the Hope Store to watch it go up in smoke. We're too close to our dream to walk away now.

In the mirror, I see tiny red lines on the whites of my eyes. Are they bloodshot? I haven't been getting much sleep lately. I'm too hyper about the store opening. But I can't have bloodshot eyes for next week's grand opening. I reach for the Red-Out and let the medicine drops splash onto my eyeballs. Better. Now where was I? Oh, yeah. Kazu. I pick up the hair brush again. "And I'd especially like to thank Kazu Mori for...let's see...what did he do anyway? Hmm. He said I shouldn't hope for much in life or I'd just be disappointed." I grab a tissue and dab the excess moisture from my eyes. "Come to think of it -- I don't think I should thank Kazu for --"

Suddenly a projectile sails into the tiny bathroom and hits me square on the head. It is a small pillow. From the other room, he lets out a thunderous, lion-like yawn. As his eyes gradually adjusted to the sunlight filling the apartment, he notices the banner. Suddenly he starts ripping everything down. I run toward Kazu to intervene.

"What the hell are you doing?" I shout.

"You can't --" he starts to speak, then goes back to attacking my banner. I try to place myself in front of it. "You should never --" Kazu proceeds to tear the banner into smaller and smaller pieces.

"Either finish your sentences -- or stop fucking with my banner!" I say. Too late. What remains of the banner could be recycled as confetti for New Year's Eve.

"Don't you know," he begins, "it's bad luck...to post the advertising slogan for a store before the store opens?" He sits down on the edge of the bed. He seems spent.

"Kazu, that is about the dumbest thing I ever heard."

"It's the worst way to jinx a new business. The worst. I could tell you stories. About an elevator company and elevator cars plunging one hundred feet per second. It isn't pretty."

"I know you're superstitious, but this is ridiculous. Even for you."

"Even for me?" he asks.

"I didn't...you know what I mean!" I say. "You're the one that should be doing the explaining." And now a hush falls over the room. We are either pausing to reload, or considering a cease fire. "Kazu, we open next week. Do you really want to spend this weekend having a knock-down, drag-out fight?"

"You're right."

"I was trying to surprise you," I say shaking my head. "I didn't know it was bad luck. Is this one of your crazy superstitions?" I considered myself a devout agnostic, while Kazu is a card-carrying Buddhist.

"Actually, it's something I picked up from a business class at Seattle U. I took it as an elective for my PhD in biotech."

"Oh," I say out loud, but inside I'm thinking Seattle folk drink way too much coffee for their own good.

"I'm sorry I snapped at you," Kazu says "Come here." He pulls me into a gentle bear hug. "It's nerves. I just want our opening to be a smash. I take after my mother. She gets very hyper when she entertains."

"I'm nervous too," I confess. Then Kazu does the thing. It's the one thing I can't resist, an absolute power that he has over me. He uses his magic thumbs and kneads the tight muscles of my neck in a way that makes me melt. I am Japanese American; I was born in Chicago in the Hyde Park area. Kazu is Japanese Japanese; he was born in Kyoto in a prefecture. When strangers see us together on the street, they sometimes think we're brothers. If they only knew! At moments like this I believe Kazu is drawing on centuries of Japanese healing mojo and I am happy to be the beneficiary of such an inheritance. Everything wrong in the world became pretty close to right when the magic thumbs come out.

And for a moment, it's almost peaceful again in our household. If it weren't for the images flickering through my brain of elevator cars plunging through elevator shafts at the speed of light – I could almost drift back to sleep.

We sit at the kitchen table eating a festive Saturday breakfast: waffles with ripe strawberries and vanilla ice cream. Kazu checks his phone messages and I sketch out some marketing ideas. October is a month for trick-or-treaters. It's a time when people transform themselves into new creatures, when we celebrate the living and the dead. One theme idea that is starting to grow on me:

IN HONOR OF HALLOWEEN,
GET 25% OFF YOUR HOPE INSTALLATION ALL
OCTOBER.
BECAUSE A LIFE WITHOUT HOPE IS SCARY!

The science guy likes it. We both agree 25% off is enticing as it drops the regular price from $1,000 to $750. And people can also pay that in three monthly installments of $250. Until we are a known quantity in Chicago with a loyal following, we need to give people good reasons to check out our services.

Kazu and I have been together for three years now. Long enough to feel completely comfortable with each other; not long enough to take each other for granted. Still, with the launch of the Hope Store just days away, all we can do is talk shop. "You said you could tell me stories about unlucky store openings," I say. "I'm all ears."

"I don't want to scare you," he says looking at me with his soulful, black-as-coal eyes.

"Try me."

"Some stories are better left untold," Kazu says. "All I'll say is one incident involved an elevator company, their brand-new slogan, and a very tragic accident. The owner put up the logo of the company in some of his elevators before the company actually opened its doors and boom – tragedy. Very bad luck."

"Could've been a coincidence." I spear a strawberry with my fork.

"If it just happened in one elevator, maybe. But the cables snapped in all three elevators bearing the new slogan -- taking the lives of the owner and several board members," he says. "The two elevators without slogans were fine. Needless to say, the company never opened."

"Here's the weird part for me. How do you reconcile your belief in superstition and your belief in science?"

Kazu laughs. "First of all, I don't call it superstition. That's an American concept. Growing up in Japan, I learned that the world can be divided into the Knowable World and the Unknowable World. These worlds are not contradictory; they're complementary. Westerners have a hard time with that. Westerners want answers that are either black or white. Easterners accept that sometimes the answer is both black AND white."

"I love it when you get all trippy on me." I lean over and kiss Kazu on his lips which taste of vanilla ice cream. Then I lean over and kiss him again.

"Two kisses? My argument must have been very persuasive."

I take our plates and rinse them in the sink. "I'm still not convinced that my banner needed to be destroyed. Besides, does tearing it down stop the bad luck, or is the bad luck already in motion? Like an arrow shooting through time and space?"

"Time will tell," Kazu says without a hint of irony in his voice. "Let's see how the opening goes before we count our chickens."

"Please excuse Jada from school. She does not feel well. She may never feel well again."

-- from Jada Upshaw's diary

2
I Come Unarmed
(Jada)

I'm sitting near the windows at Rendezvous Cafe nursing my Plain Jane latte, spending money I don't have. Though I'm surrounded by an army of laptops, I come unarmed and in peace, unless you count these two precious children as weapons as I sometimes do. They're my sister's kids and the only way she persuaded me to take them out in public is she said she'd pay me three times my normal babysitting fee. I think she got the better end of the deal. I've never done a babysitting gig in a public place, but there's a first time for everything.

My goal today is just to enjoy my coffee on this cool fall day, write two pages in my journal, and keep the kids from trashing the place. I open my spiral notebook and pull out a pen. Out of the corner of my eye, I see Angie and Willis have decided to sit down at a table with a complete stranger. Lovely. I walk over to them. "Uh, guys, seriously. You can't just plop yourselves down at this nice man's table without asking."

The man seems more amused than annoyed. "I don't mind. Cute kids," he says and proceeds to type on his Mac.

"Yeah, they're not mine," I say and smile. I yank them gently back to my table and order caramel iced lattes for both

of them. That'll keep them busy for a while. From time to
time the man steals a sideways glance at me. I guess I look all
right. My long straightened hair (thanks to a Spoil Me Salon
birthday gift certificate) and my fairly standard-issue fea-
tures, give me a kind of black-Mary-Tyler-Moore appearance.
Though I'm not likely to ever throw my hat up into the air no
matter how, uh, you know, uh, what's the word, exuberant I
may feel. And believe me, I don't think I've ever been accused
of being exuberant. And while we're talking about my flaws, I
should mention that I stutter a little. I even stutter when I'm
thinking to myself. No big story there. I just do.

My name is Jada Upshaw. As a teenager, I was diag-
nosed with a rare condition called desina sperara which basically means "the absence of hope." Such a pretty name for
such an ugly illness. (If you say desina sperara quickly, you
can see where the word "desperate" comes from.) My condition has something to do with a breakdown in the brain's
reward system. My shrink said I have to work harder to process and to pursue rewarding experiences. Basically it means
my pleasure center is totally shot, and the act of hoping is
just not in my bag of tricks. I think a lot of people go undi-
agnosed, and others are misdiagnosed as having garden variety depression. No wonder so many of them are not helped
by meds. Here I am at the latter end of my forties and all I
can say is, "Are we there yet?"

And god knows you don't have to have DS to have a
hope deficit. You can be born hopeless, and you can become
hopeless. Some people believe you can catch hopelessness
just by sitting on a train next to a hope-challenged person.
I am totally immune to the charms of antidepressants, talk

therapy, hypnosis and homeopathic remedies, so I've pretty much been in free fall for my adult life. Doesn't help that I've been unemployed for over two years. I often fantasize about the most painless way to kill myself. In the past five years, I've tried to kill myself three times. Needless to say, I was not successful.

In Arabic the name Jada means wise, but as time marches on I think it's just shorthand for jaded, as in damn tired of living. I'm African American. In African, I suspect the name Jada doesn't mean much of anything, but what are you going to do? You can't choose your parents and you can't choose your name. So you just learn to live with them like cancer. I really would like to be happy and hopeful like other earthlings but I don't see it happening.

All I know is that January 1st is three months away, and by New Year's Eve I am determined to be "free at last." Whether that means I achieve a successful suicide, or finally figure out how to enjoy life instead of enduring it – it really doesn't matter much to me. But I refuse, I refuse, to enter the new year dragging the same old baggage behind me. I'd rather die first. And I can't bear another night of fake hopefulness, people hugging strangers and wishing them "Happy New Year." Those three words are not part of my vocabulary. Never have been, never will be. I haven't had a happy new year in half a century. Why should I wish a happy new year to anyone else?

So I'm doing this babysitting gig with my sister Sheila's two adorable brats, Willis and Angie. On this particular Saturday, their parents have snuck out to see a movie. The little monsters are opening countless packets of Splenda and sprinkling them into their iced lattes. I figure it's never too early to introduce caffeine to children. I don't hate kids. I just think all children are loud and bratty and kind of beside the point.

I haven't had a good night's sleep in thirty years. That's bound to take a toll. Do you know how tired a person feels after thirty years of insomnia? We could trade bodies for a week, but trust me, you don't want to know. When I had a dumb job as a secretary at a bank, there were some days I didn't have anything to do. I'd sit at my desk and I could feel my bones calcifying, turning to stone, then crumbling inside my body. And that was on a good day. Thank god Otis Franklin took a shine to me, though I have no idea why.

Angie, for reasons that are not apparent to me, has decided to punch her older brother in his privates. "Angie, don't hit your brother in his special place! If you do that -- he won't be able to have babies," I say. Then add, "Not that it matters much to me, but your parents probably have an opinion about that."

"About what?" Willis asks.

"About everything. That's what parents do. They have opinions. Now sit down and drink your iced lattes before they melt. Aunt Jada wants to write in her journal. Is that too much to ask?" Now where was I? Oh yeah, so I have a man in my life who loves me exactly as I am. And many of my single, middle-aged girlfriends are envious. But here's the killing part. I can't love him back! I'm numb. Loving someone, even someone as nice as Otis, it just isn't in my repertoire. I'm The Girl Who Wasn't There. Sometimes, because I can put on a good face, people mistake me for a happy person. Now that's what I call LOL funny. If you were to send a probe into the very inside of me, you'd see:

The mall is open, but nobody's shopping. Baby, baby... where did my hope go?

The kids are gradually slowing down. Willis and Angie are quietly drawing pictures on their paper placements and that's just fine with me. They must be coming down from their sugar highs. They can take a nap right here at the coffeehouse for all I care.

My eyes wander over to a huge poster that always fascinates me. It is of the Sutro Baths in San Francisco, a huge steel and glass structure from the turn of the century that was considered quite ground-breaking for its day. Large steel and glass structures, especially of this size, had not been built before. They called the structure a naturarium. The water source was actually the Pacific Ocean. Somehow the indoor water pool was connected to the ocean so folks were swimming in real saltwater.

I study the bathers, men and women, in their modest bathing suits. I wonder if I would have been happier in that era. At the Sutro Baths, if a person no longer wanted to swim, no longer wanted to be a part of this world -- all they had to do was stop paddling, stop fighting, and just let the water take them. They would sink like a stone to the bottom and never be heard from again. Their bodies would pass through a membrane and float out to sea.

When our time at Rendezvous Cafe finally comes to an end, I look down at my spiral notebook and all I see are a few stray sentences scribbled on the page. Not even close to the two pages I had hoped to fill. On the page are these words which I don't even remember writing. But who else could have written them?

Dear Angie and Willis,

I started out as a girl without dreams and grew up to be a woman without a future.

I am a walking cautionary tale. Don't grow up to be me, what ever you do. I am Desina Sperara, a comic book character with no super powers to speak of. Desina, as in absence. Sperara, as in hope or breath.

I am without the breath of hope. By the time you read this, I hope to be a distant memory.

Aunt Jada

I close my notebook and decide to stop at the ladies room before we leave. The kids say they don't have to visit the bathroom so I ask that nice man with the Mac if he'd mind terribly keeping an eye on the darlings for a hot second.

"No problem," he says. He seems kind, probably a father himself. And a Mac user to boot.

In the washroom, I notice the nice plum scented incense that wafts through the room. I wonder who makes it. Then I start to wonder: Was it dumb of me to leave the kids in the hands of a perfect stranger? He said they were 'cute kids.' I rush back to the heart of the coffee house.

All I see is my spiral notebook on the table where I left it.

The kids and the man are nowhere to be seen.

3
A Human Experiment
(Luke)

I first walked into the headquarters of the legendary LiveWell Laboratories five years ago because I wanted to be part of something bigger than myself. I was curious about clinical trials and this one for an experimental treatment for hopelessness was irresistible to me. I also suffered from bouts of hopelessness. Of course, there was no Hope Store back then. I remember meeting the handsome man spearheading the study, Kazu Mori. He offered me a cup of coffee and took me on a guided tour of the premises, showing me secret rooms and scientific equipment, introducing me to his various colleagues along the way. I remember the walls of one hallway flickered with illuminated images of brain hemispheres, functional MRI (fMRI) images showing a colorful river comprised of thoughts, regrets, facts, emotions… tracing the exuberance of brain activity, blood flow, the release of neurotransmitters, sparks of electricity. But the images were not still; the colors moved in slow motion. Each brain portrait had a title beneath it:

"This is the brain liking something."
"This is the brain wanting something."
"This is the brain while sleepwalking."
"This is the brain in pain."
"This is the brain experiencing fear."
"This is the brain in a vegetative state."
"This is the brain during sex."

"This is the brain in a creative state."
"This is the brain remembering."

I loved how every picture told a story with bursts of color here
or there. It was as if the pictures were saying: "If you really
want to understand the human story -- follow the light show."

I was intrigued as Kazu walked me past the many
conference rooms with glass windows longer than a stretch
limousine. Signs on the door read: CLINICAL TRIAL IN
PROGRESS. But through the glass, I could still make out
silhouettes moving, a facilitator pointing to a flip chart. It
was all very exciting to me somehow for soon I would be on
the other side of the door. I would be a participant in a clinical study. I remember one sign by the coffee machine read:
"Be Open To Anything... But Question Everything."

I didn't know it at the time but I was the only volunteer whom Kazu favored with such a personal tour. Later
after the study was over, he told me he gave me a tour partly
because I had arrived an hour early, yes, but also because he
wanted to. "I was extremely drawn to you for some reason,"
he confessed.

Beyond these rooms there were other rooms which also
had large glass windows. In one room, a woman was running
on a treadmill. There were three signs on the walls around
her which simply announced: PAST, PRESENT, FUTURE.
As she ran, the signs on the walls began to move, to re-
arrange themselves.

In another room, a woman was in a small theater, her
eyes fixed on a movie screen. On the screen was the same
woman: *It is her wedding day. Someone is making a toast.*

And then the image stutters, pixilates, goes dark. Another image appears on-screen. The woman is wearing a bathing suit adorned with images of red tulips. She immerses herself in a bathtub filled with water. She reaches for a hair dryer and holds it for a moment above the water. The image stutters, pixilates, goes dark.

As intriguing as these first two rooms were, I was most fascinated by the third room because I understood it the least. In this room, a man was seated while a light encircled his whole body. Then confetti began to rain down upon him, but it wasn't the regular confetti you see in parades. This confetti was shiny and fell in dream-like slow motion. What struck me was the expression on the man's face. He looked ecstatic. Like he had just learned something that would change his life forever. If that's what it looked like to have new hope installed -- I wanted to feel that feeling too. I wanted to feel it right away.